Dearest Dorothy,
Help!
I've Lost Myself!

This Large Print Book carries the
Seal of Approval of N.A.V.H.

DEAREST DOROTHY, HELP! I'VE LOST MYSELF!

CHARLENE ANN BAUMBICH

THORNDIKE PRESS

An imprint of Thomson Gale, a part of The Thomson Corporation

Detroit • New York • San Francisco • New Haven, Conn. • Waterville, Maine • London

THOMSON

★™

GALE

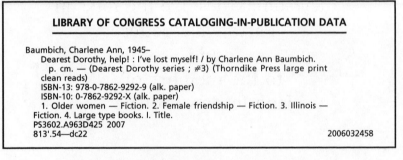

LIBRARY OF CONGRESS CATALOGING-IN-PUBLICATION DATA

Baumbich, Charlene Ann, 1945–
    Dearest Dorothy, help! : I've lost myself! / by Charlene Ann Baumbich.
       p. cm. — (Dearest Dorothy series ; #3) (Thorndike Press large print
    clean reads)
    ISBN-13: 978-0-7862-9292-9 (alk. paper)
    ISBN-10: 0-7862-9292-X (alk. paper)
    1. Older women — Fiction. 2. Female friendship — Fiction. 3. Illinois —
Fiction. 4. Large type books. I. Title.
PS3602.A963D425 2007
813'.54—dc22   2006032458

Published in 2007 by arrangement with Penguin Books,
a member of Penguin Group (USA) Inc.

Printed in the United States of America on permanent paper
10 9 8 7 6 5 4 3 2 1

Dedicated to:
all the readers who have told me they
are just *sure* I'm writing about their
town — even though they admit
they sometimes like the folks in
Partonville better,
and
to the memory of
Jane Jordan Browne

ACKNOWLEDGMENTS

Since you are reading this, let me first thank *you* because it hopefully means you're going to read the rest of the pages. Perhaps you've already read the previous books in the series. (Triple thanks if you have!) Without readers there would be no market for books about Partonville. Simple as that.

And speaking of Partonville, thank you, Linda Pozanc, for asking me about "the Partons who surely must have founded Partonville." It was a DUH! that had escaped me up until your question. Once I looked into their story, I was not disappointed.

And speaking of stories, thank you to Pastor Christine Robinson and the entire congregation of Homer United Methodist Church in Homer, Minnesota, for becoming a personal part of *my* real-life story. Not only did Pastor Christine help me understand how Pastor Delbert Junior became a UMC pastor in Partonville, but everyone

7

who attends that beautiful little church on the Homer bluff — including the puppets — have helped me to understand the grace in welcoming strangers as their own.

And speaking of strangers, up until I briefly met Matt Niemeyer, a pressman for the *Winona Post,* I knew nothing about the Harris V15A web press that keeps the *Partonville Press* in business! Thanks, Mr. Niemeyer, for being another friendly Minnesotan who took time to talk to this Land of Lincoln gal who adores hanging out (and writing) in the Land of 10,000 Lakes.

And speaking of friendly folks who are also efficient, energetic, smart, dedicated, hard working and FUN, a H-U-G-E thank you to every single person at Penguin Books who contributed to getting these books into your hands, from design, to sales and marketing (a special nod to John Fagan), to copy editors, to publicity folks (go Zaidee Rose!), to assistants, to Those Who Put Up With Me When I'm Panicked.

And speaking of Those Who Put Up With Me When I'm Panicked, Carolyn Carlson has gone above, beyond, round-and-round, sideways and extremely out of her way to direct, challenge and encourage me. She has been tender with my ego, gracious with her time and praise, entertaining when we're together, potent when she uses her Editor Voice and, most importantly, she has become my dear friend.

And speaking of dear friends, Danielle Egan-Miller has kept me from FREAKING OUT, even when I'm FREAKING OUT! A good agent is always way more than a good agent, and Danielle is definitely way more. She is a valued, respected champion. To everyone at Browne & Miller Literary Associates, CHEERS!

And speaking of CHEERS, thank you, George John Baumbich, who keeps the home fires burning, even when I'm *so* welcome in Partonville that it sometimes must feel like I'll never come home.

INTRODUCTION

*To be seventy years young is sometimes
far more cheerful and hopeful than to be
forty years old.*
— Oliver Wendell Holmes

And now, welcome to Partonville, a circle-
the-square town in the northern part of
southern Illinois, where oldsters are young,
trees have names and, for better or for
worse, the band plays on.

1

All day, Mother Nature had brewed a delicious swirl of October warmth, even for the northern part of southern Illinois. Without warning, though, nippy evening breezes blew stinging chills through Dorothy's flung-open doors and windows and right down her spine. She pulled her pink cardigan sweater tight around her chest and pinned it to her breastbone with her left hand as she hustled toward the front door to close it. "Winds of change," she'd heard her mother proclaim many times before she'd gone home to meet her Maker, and Dorothy thought of her as she repeated the phrase a couple of times with a sigh tucked in between.

Once at the doorway, mesmerized by nature's sudden onset of rowdiness, Dorothy stood shivering, watching the tree branches bob and weave, marveling at how severely tree branches — even some trees

— were bending in the testing airstreams, yet not snapping. "Yup. Winds of change," she said aloud. A gust rustled her hair and snatched the words right out of her mouth, sending them racing with the wind through all of Partonville, clear out of town and down the country roads. Dorothy's spirit quickened and her body shuddered. "Oh, Sheba! That felt prophetic! Gives me the heebie-jeebies!"

At the sound of her mistress's voice, Sheba's ears perked forward. Curled up tightly on the new white carpet, her warm cocoon suited her just fine, no matter what the winds or world were doing. In response to Dorothy's statement, Sheba opened her mouth and smacked it a few times before burying her nose further into her own doggie circle of contentment.

"I can barely stand to think yet *more* change might be coming our way . . . ," Dorothy whispered, her voice fading under the weight of possibilities. Trying to snap out of it, she straightened up and for a good twenty seconds, willed herself to stand strong against the chill, deeply inhaling the wind's crisp vigor into her eighty-seven-year-old body. "Almost as good as a splash of cold creek water to the neck," she said to her smile before closing the door. "Almost."

Not many people talk to their smiles, but Dorothy had talked to hers ever since the day her mother, who had had it with her nine-year-old's, strong-willed contrariness, had steered her by the shoulders into the bathroom and stood her before the mirror above the sink. "Dorothy Jean, take a good look at that face. What do you see, child?"

"I see a girl who does *not* want to wear her dumb blue dress to church today," Dorothy said with a humph of finality. "Look at me! I look perfectly fine in my pink sweater and dungarees," she proclaimed, her face pinched into a wad of storm.

"Child of mine, you look perfectly fine in your birthday suit, too, but you're not wearing *that* to church today either."

"Oh, yes I am. I'm *always* wearing my birthday suit. But usually nobody can see it because I'm wearing clothes over it."

Ethel tucked her lips inside her mouth, damming a torrent of sharp words ready to burst out of her. She stared at her daughter's set face, then watched her cross her gangly arms across her chest, clearly reveling in her last statement, which was, at its root, inarguable — and they both knew it. Ethel had long ago learned, however, that neither dia-tribing nor debating would move Dorothy Jean toward Ethel's intentions. No, you had to beat Dorothy at her own strengths, and that took prayer, creativity and unending patience. While Ethel engaged in mental gymnastics, she mindlessly crossed her arms against her chest as she studied her own midlife face in the mirror, as if appealing to *it* for answers. Her eyes scanned their framed reflections. Without a doubt, these two females were the shadow images of each other's stubbornness. *Lord have mercy on us both,* Ethel prayed in silence.

Just then the old Register clock in the kitchen began its ten-gong pronouncement that church would begin in thirty minutes, barely enough time for them to finish dress-ing, pack up and get to town.

"Dorothy Jean Brown, we both look pa-thetic. Just get a good gander at us. I think we should talk to our smiles and try to coax them out of their hiding places. After all, if you were the pastor, would *you* want to look at these faces while you were preaching God's word?"

Mother and daughter spent a few mo-ments moving nothing but their eyes be-tween their reflections. Pretty soon it became impossible not to giggle, which is exactly what they did.

"Look at us," Ethel said. "Don't we look like *fine* women when we smile?"

"We *do*," Dorothy said, her heart erupting with love for her mother like an explosion of happy feathers.

"Let us determine right here and now," Ethel said, resting her hands on her daughter's shoulders, "that when we find we haven't been smiling enough, we will talk to our smiles to encourage them, okay? We'll talk to our smiles until we *feel* them rumbling around inside of us. We'll talk to our smiles until they appear, so that when we look in the mirror, we can smile back at them." Ethel then leaned over and kissed the top of her daughter's fine brown hair, her warm breath melting Dorothy's remaining resistance.

Without another word Dorothy Jean Brown quickly changed into her blue dress, casting a hurried eye into her dresser mirror each time she passed it, just to make sure she was smiling back at . . . her smile.

And now, nearly eight decades later, Dorothy Jean Wetstra talked to her smile yet again, realizing it had been hiding for several days. Although she had continued to enjoy decorating her new little home on Vine Street three blocks off the Partonville square, and she truly did relish living so close to her best friend May Belle, and May Belle's dependent, forty-five-year-old son Earl, whom she loved like her own, her soul still pined for Crooked Creek Farm, the farm she had, just a few short months ago, left behind — lock, stock and crawdads. Not only that but her fierce independence had taken a severe knock when, during this same time, she'd scared herself driving and determined it was time for her to give it up, which now kept her from spur-of-the-thought visits to the miles-away farm, its land, the barn, her birthplace . . . the very home in which she had learned to talk to her smile.

Dorothy stretched her five-foot ten-inch frame and walked down the hall to her bathroom, reaching her arm around the corner to flick on the light. The cheery cobalt-blue paint that rimmed the mirror and the basketball-sized sun painted in the corner over the tub set the perfect stage for the upcoming drama.

"Come on, smile," she said out loud to her face in the mirror. "I know you're in there; I've seen you in many photos over all these decades. You know, it's band practice tonight and Nellie Ruth will be here within thirty minutes to pick us up. Do you want her or Raymond, the director, who stands *right* in front of us so I can hear him with these old ears, to have to look at *this* face while I'm trying to muster enough air to blow through my clarinet?" She put her hands to her hips, cocked her head, bugged out her eyes, and lifted her brows in a challenging gesture. "I mean, think about all the friends and happy melodies we'll be surrounded by. Think about the goodness the Lord has blessed us with by allowing me the privilege to even *have* a face — although Lord, I sometimes do wonder *what* You are thinking when letting it age into *this!*" She leaned toward the mirror and turned her head slightly to the left, then to the right, studying each crease; her ever-heightening forehead; the remains of her thin hair clinging to her pink scalp; her brown eyes, slightly hidden beneath droopier eyelids than she'd last remembered; her neck that revealed the folds of a well-seasoned, long-lived life.

Yes, that outward appearance was constantly changing. But the thing that disturbed her most was the lack of any evidence of a grateful smile for all that blessed her. "Come on, smile, I know you're in there!" *We'll talk to our smiles until we* feel *them rumbling around inside of us,* she heard her mother saying.

She closed her eyes, willing herself to examine what she *was* feeling. Sad? Lonesome? Lost? Old?

Then a subtle shift birthed in her gut. "Oh, my," she whispered, goose bumps racing up her arms. What she could *feel* was her mother's heavenly hands on her shoulders, her soft breath on the crown of her head. For a good fifteen seconds she stood motionless, receiving this gift of grace. When she opened her eyes, nearly expecting to see her mother once again standing behind her, only her own reflection appeared in the mirror. But so did her smile.

"There now. That's better. What a *fine* woman you look like when you smile," she said, wiping the joyful tears of love and remembrance from the soft wrinkles around her welcome and familiar grin. "Thank you, Lord, for the balm of sweet memories. Let the winds of change blow where they will; as long as I remember You and my smile, I believe life will go as it should."

2

Katie Durbin sat slumped on a box in the Chaos Room, as she and her son Josh had taken to calling it. Her eyes, staring at an empty wall before her, were glazed over, as was her mind. The Chaos Room was the smallest of the three upstairs rooms in the old, two-story clapboard farmhouse, and there were piles of stuff everywhere. Katie was a woman of control and order, and this . . . well, this was so out-of-order it had momentarily struck her dumb. Anything she hadn't known what to do with during the move had ended up here. What had she been thinking of when she had impulsively bought Crooked Creek Farm? Where would she put all this stuff she'd moved from their Chicago dwelling, plus all the odds and ends left from the home of her Aunt Tess, whose death had started this whole chain of events? She couldn't fit any more stuff in the other two bedrooms without self-imposing a fire-code violation, her Realtor's eye and mind — for better or for worse — never at rest.

The master bedroom was hers, although to call it "master" always seemed a joke to her since it neither had its own bathroom nor a closet big enough for half her business wardrobe, let alone her casual clothes (the rest hung on a wall-length rack in the Chaos Room); nonetheless, it was the largest of the three small rooms upstairs. The other room, the one that Dorothy used as her office, belonged to Josh. Of course, he had to have the second-biggest small room for his desk, his computer and a place for his sixteen years of accumulated guy stuff, as well as a place to sleep, which was, due to tighter quarters, now on a twin bed. Although she and Josh had moved in over a month ago, right after Dorothy's auction, there were still a few pieces of furniture in the barn that just didn't fit the way Katie had thought they would, like his old queen-sized bed, a few accent pieces and her exercise equipment.

This wasn't the first time in the last few weeks she'd stood in the doorway staring at the mess, then closed the door and decided to tackle something else, something less daunting, something more urgent, like trying to get *all* of her mail forwarded from the brownstone in Chicago, which she no longer owned, to this farmhouse in Partonville, in which she now lived — although she certainly didn't feel it was her home yet. In fact, at the moment, she felt held captive not only by this house, but by her entire life. *What on earth was I thinking when I made this decision!*

Since heat rises and the insulation in the farmhouse wasn't what it should be, the upstairs was always warm, but today it was stifling. Although there were window air conditioners in the other two rooms, the Chaos Room, previously used by Dorothy as a guest room, had only one window and one heating vent — and Katie was beginning to realize the temperature in this room would probably be chaotic too. Neither Katie nor Josh had turned on their bedroom air conditioners that day since it was, for goodness sake, *October!* In Chicago, one usually didn't need air conditioning in October. Down in the northern part of southern Illinois, apparently things were different — as different as her life had become since the move.

Beads of perspiration that had lingered on her upper lip all day now broke out on her forehead. She wondered, since it was so warm and she was forty-seven, which of these factors had created the sweat: the unseasonably muggy day or the fact that she was suddenly — and who could account for the swiftness of passing years? — a midlifer readying for the onset of menopause. Not that she really believed she was old enough for *that,* but she'd certainly been feeling and apparently acting like it lately, what with her impulsive decision to buy this place and move out of her citified comfort zone, which some people who knew her might have chalked up to rocky hormones, she supposed.

Katie stood up and shouted, "AIR! I need *air.*" She wrestled with the old wooden frame window, grunting, first trying to pull it up, then squatting lower to the floor, alternately pushing up and banging on it with the heels of her hands. *One more thing I didn't think about! One more blasted thing to replace!* Finally it let loose and opened at the same time a drip of sweat dropped from the end of her nose. She decided to open the rest of the windows upstairs in the hopes of catching a cross breeze. By the time she returned to the Chaos Room, a surprising and powerful gust of cold air was blasting through the room with enough force to lift and re-lift half of the folded-down lid on the box on which she'd been sitting. The flap appeared to be waving at her when she entered.

"AUNT TESS'S PAPERS," the side of the box said in black Magic Marker. It was then she remembered why she could never seem to stay in this room for long: her crazy Aunt Tessa Martha Walker, her mother's only sibling whom she'd hardly known, had died and started this whole chain of moving events that played like a game of musical dwellings. Aunt Tess had now moved from Vine Street to heaven, her ashes currently residing in a box; Dorothy was off the farm and in Aunt Tess's old house; Katie and Josh, lifelong "city slickers," called Crooked Creek Farm home. Dorothy had needed to sell, and Katie had recognized a prime real estate opportunity, and also sensed how disconnected she was from her son and her own soul. So she had, in an unimaginable moment, bought the farm (a metaphorical phrase that, on occasion, felt too close for comfort) and decided to move in. The only saving grace, at least at this hapless moment, was that she knew she could sell the farm in an instant and make a financial killing. Shored up by her newly remembered ability to escape if she so chose, she decided to dig in where she was — at least for now. "For Pete's sakes," she said aloud to herself, "just get through these two boxes and be done with it."

When she, being the last living heir, and Josh had had the horrible task of cleaning out Aunt Tess's house after her death — an entire house of chaos far beyond anything in this room — they had simply tossed all papers, letters and documents in boxes to be sorted at a later date in order to keep moving along. Luckily, she'd found the original trust documents, the documents that allowed her to handle Aunt Tess's estate, such that it was, inside of a JC Penney catalog envelope in the bottom of the first box she'd sifted. Having plenty else to do and no pressing immediate need to further explore these remaining boxes, she'd first hauled them from Partonville back to her Chicago home, then back again during the move. Yes, these two boxes now appeared to be the root of *all* chaos.

Again, a gust of wind lifted the box's top, this time blowing a couple letters across the floor where they landed at her feet. *Might as well start here.*

It was a terrible cacophony of sound, a sound that made Raymond Ringwald want to slam his hands over his ears. Of course he could not, having slipped the mouthpiece of his trumpet to his own lips shortly after giving Nellie Ruth the downbeat, then counting out her first few solo notes with his hand before the rest of the community band, including him, had joined in.

"*Whoa!* WHOA!" he yelped. "I think we can do better than *that,* don't you?"

"Lord have mercy on all who listen if we don't," Dorothy murmured, her fingers continuing to tap dance on the keys of her clarinet, adding, "And Lord have mercy on *us* after the Pumpkin Festival if we've forced them to listen to such a mess!" The entire group, sans T.J. Winslow, laughed. Unfortunately, T.J. had been the brunt of a few "bellowing cow" and "crying calf" comments due to his many sour clarinet notes this evening. "Sometimes my lips just don't seem to fit the mouthpiece," he'd said in defense, "and this is just one of those nights." Although T.J., the longtime pharmacist at Richardson's Rexall Drugs on the Partonville square, had taken many years of clarinet lessons as a youth, played in the high school band and then the community band for nearly all of his adult life, his playing had never improved. Nonetheless, no matter how many knocks he took, he just kept playing. Dorothy, who had conducted school bands all of her working life, could never speak against his efforts — not when she conducted him and not now when she simply played beside him — since she understood the kindred heart of one who loves the music too much to ever stop letting it flow through his veins and out into the world. "Our idea of a joyful noise is not necessarily the same as God's," she'd once said as she defended him against an onslaught of complainers. "I reckon any time we're playing *or* singing," — and she had paused here to look directly at a couple folks who were also United Methodist choir members — "especially when we're making music from our hearts, it sounds good to the Big Guy whether we're on key or not." She'd had to remember her own words of wisdom when just last week she'd wanted to suggest to T.J., who sat directly to her left during practice, "Could you please play slightly to your left, like all the way out the back door to your left?"

"Okay," Raymond said, thumping his finger on the bell of his trumpet to rally their attention, "let's begin again with Nellie Ruth's solo lead-in," a prospect that in itself caused uneasiness to zing through the group. Truth be told, Nellie Ruth's *last* lead-in solo explained some of their inability to jump in together now. Some.

Sixty-two-year-old Nellie Ruth, known around town for being sweet, conservative and a constant prayer warrior, had, with her last public solo intro at the Fourth of July band concert, stunned everyone. She was to play the first ten notes of "Summertime," the well-known song from *Porgy & Bess*. It was the very song that had knit its way deep into her sixteen-year-old heart when her mother, just before her death, had introduced Nellie Ruth to the Heyward and Gershwin masterpiece.

When, at rehearsal for the Fourth of July concert, Raymond had first announced the *Porgy & Bess* piece to the band as part of the repertoire and given Nellie Ruth the honored slot, she had been thrilled beyond measure. The melody and words had always brought on a mix of emotions: memories as soft as satin of her sweet mother; horrid things she would rather not remember about her violating, alcoholic father who had died two years after her mom. When her mother had introduced the music to her, she'd told Nellie Ruth through her tears that the lyrics "And the livin' is easy" had always been her wish for Nellie Ruth's life, rather than the sad life she'd been forced to lead. Even though Nellie Ruth had now heard the song in dozens of recordings, none sounded better to her than that of a from-the-heart saxophone player. Yes, she *loved* the measured and melodic "Summertime" — that is until Raymond, much to Nellie Ruth's mortification, set a tempo not unlike that of clomping horses trotting their way to a feed trough.

"It's just not right," she whined to Raymond, who paid her no heed. " 'Summertime' was not written to sound like an oom-pa song!"

"We're going to present strong songs set to strong beats," he told her. "After all, it is the *Fourth of July!*"

"It's just not *right*," she then whined to Dorothy on the way home from practice. "I tell you, it is just not *right*."

"I quite agree," Dorothy said after a sigh. "If I were directing, I'd do it differently. But something I learned after directing all those years is that the director *is* always right, and it's not my turn anymore."

When it came time for their performance and Raymond gave Nellie Ruth the nod for her solo lead-in, Nellie Ruth closed her eyes, took two deliberate and slow breaths and began to belt out such an unhurried, soulful and earthy rendition that instruments otherwise readied to join in froze in suspended, silent positions. No, this was not what they had practiced. Stunned faces looked on, and yet, one by one, hearts couldn't help but be softened by the intensity of Nellie Ruth's emotional outpouring. Nellie Ruth didn't open her eyes until the last note of the entire song had been held to the end of its blues-laden cry. Tears streaming down her face, she appeared to be awakening from a trance of some kind, which didn't seem very United Methodist, especially not for Nellie Ruth McGregor who was, after all, on the altar guild!

"Clearly," Acting Mayor Gladys McKern said a little too loudly during the silence that followed, before the thunderous applause rang out, "there is more to Nellie Ruth McGregor than she lets on!" (Gladys

31

went on to keep a scrutinizing eye on Nellie Ruth for the next several weeks.) Nellie Ruth's face turned as red as her hair during the standing ovation, for which everyone stood but Gladys, who wasn't about to encourage such an obvious display of self-indulgence.

"I don't know what came over me," Nellie Ruth apologetically said to Dorothy as they packed up their instruments.

"God-breath," Dorothy responded with a tear in her eye as she turned and hugged Nellie Ruth. "No doubt about it, it was unmistakable God-breath."

But that was then and this was now. Raymond, who had himself been moved to the core at Nellie Ruth's "Summertime" rendering, did, however, have the rest of the band to consider, and he wasn't going to allow room for another runaway surprise. He nodded at Nellie Ruth, then gave the downbeat and counted it out with a wave of his trumpet while Nellie Ruth played the first few notes to "Camptown Races," which, according to T.J. who saw an opportunity to finally get his own lick in about a song he detested, "can't *possibly* be played too slowly, what with all that doo-dah-DAYing that's got to go on!" When Raymond lifted the trumpet to his lips, the rest of the ten-strong Partonville Community Band (plus occasional guest musicians, including Moon Dog Miligan on guitar and Plunkin' Pete on bass) joined in, for better or for worse — and only vaguely at the same time.

"PEOPLE!" Raymond hollered. He set his trumpet down on the table next to him, reached into his back pocket and wiped his brow with his hanky, even though it wasn't at all damp. Then he wiped his eyes and his mouth and behind one ear. "People," he said in a normal tone, "we are a one-town *band,* not a three-ring catastrophe." With deliberation, he tucked his hanky back into his pocket. "Focus, please," he said in a tight and constrained voice as his eyes cast from one member to the next until he had looked directly at each of them.

They were an eclectic group of musicians. Wind instruments consisted of Dorothy on the clarinet and one beautiful flute handled like a pro by *Partonville Press* reporter Sharon Teller, the twenty-five-year-old "baby" in the group of members otherwise over sixty. Raymond and Rick Lawson, "attorney at law," rounded out the section, Rick playing an alto saxophone.

Drums were deftly handled by Loretta

Forester, auctioneer Swifty Forester's wife, who occasionally dragged her decades-old bongos out of her closet for what Arthur Landers, the band's most cantankerous member, referred to as those "head-bangin' songs not fit for a raggedy swarm of hi-eena." Loretta stored her full set of drums right there in the park district building where practices were held, not only because it was much more convenient than transporting them, but mostly since Swifty had threatened for years to sneak them into an auction. He felt their booming beat more of an intrusion into his television viewing than any kind of desirable talent.

Rounding out the rest of the percussion section — tambourine, triangle and maracas — was Wilbur, the manager of Your Store, Partonville's local grocery store, which still hand delivered phone-in orders to your door. Although Your Store delivered groceries, Wilbur often delivered a mistimed *ding* when a *ca-chuk-a-chuk* of the maracas was expected, or worse yet, vice versa.

Gertrude Hands, organist at United Methodist Church, played the electronic keyboard, often bouncing her head to the beat and swaying back and forth, something she never had a chance to do behind the organ at UMC since contemporary hymns had thus far been held at bay from her church's repertoire. Of course, that made the majority of the older folks happy, and left the rest of the parishioners — who had, via Christian radio, vacations and other church visits, been introduced to the beauty of here-and-now lyrics and melodies — eagerly waiting for progress to arrive. Those waiting would include Gertrude, although she would *never* mention such a thing to Pastor Delbert Carol, Jr.

Sam Vitner, owner of Swappin' Sam's salvage and antique store, played the only stringed instrument in the band, an ancient (or so he *says*) violin that, before he bought it, had been handed down through the decades by a royal family in France (so he says, and *says,* unfolding all the dramatic details and stories as he *says,* to anyone who inquires . . . or doesn't). Most members of the band regretted that musical talent hadn't been handed down by Sam's family, but nonetheless, he played his heart out, which was the only requirement to stay in the band. That and showing up for practice, recitals and special appearances, barring any unforeseen circumstances like "my arthritis just seemed to lock up my shoulders and fingers for a spell so I figured I might as well stay home."

To enhance the sound, or at the very least to make it an unusual one, Arthur Landers played his Honer harmonica, which he always, band practice day or not, kept in the upper center little pocket of his coveralls, ever-ready to quick-draw and shoot out a tune. Although this certainly wasn't a traditional band instrument, when Raymond had advertised in the *Partonville Press* thirty years ago that a community band was being formed and all were welcome, Arthur had arrived and said, "I reckoned ya meant all when ya said *all,* so I'm here with my *all.*" Raymond had blankly stared at Arthur, who was holding no instrument. Then Arthur flipped out his Honer and began playing "You Are My Sunshine" with such gusto that Raymond could do nothing but bust out in a smile, begin to slap his knee to keep time and welcome him into the community band.

Now here at rehearsal, Raymond looked up to the ceiling, drew in a deep breath through his nostrils, exhaled slowly through his mouth, pasted on a smile, then calmly lowered his gaze, eyeing Nellie Ruth. He repeated, "Focus, *please.* Let's pick it up from the top again." He raised his trumpet, paused for effect and gave the downbeat. Although all in all they didn't sound perfect on this attempt either, they did sound slightly better, which was likely to be as good as they would ever get.

"Saved by the ringer," Katie sighed to Jessica. Having spent most of her adult life wheeling and dealing in the fast-and-furious world of commercial real estate development, Katie had a long-honed habit of never being away from a phone. Even though not currently active in the market, she'd carried the cordless up the stairs with her, never minding she and Josh both had phones in their bedrooms. "I was just about to begin sorting through Aunt Tess's final two boxes of papers. What excellent timing you have." She tossed the two letters that had blown to her feet back into the top of the box, closed the window and then the door to the Chaos Room behind her. She headed downstairs to get herself a diet cola with a fresh lemon slice. When she and Jessica got on the phone, welcome, lively and leisurely conversations usually lasted so long that she sometimes even needed a refill.

"That sounds yucky," Jessica said. "I guess having a three-month-old is what makes the word *yucky* come to my mind." Jessica looked down at her T-shirt, which had wads of spit up, slimy drools and tiny morsels of still-damp clumps of baby cereal down the front of it. "Oh, Katie, you have no idea how yucky *I* look right now, either."

"There's no amount of anything that could make *you* look *yucky,* Jessica." Yucky was not a word Katie had ever heard roll out of her own mouth and it flicked through her mind how silly it made her feel. It also occurred to her that aside from her friendships with Jessica and Dorothy, and her sporadically growing relationship with her own son Josh, her entire life could be summed up as yucky right now — although she decided to withhold admitting it.

"You remind me of a young, light-haired Katharine Hepburn, Jessica. Yes, you are our Katharine Hepburn running the Lamp Post motel right here in Partonville!"

Jessica blushed. Compared to Tycoon Katie, as Jessica had once teasingly called her, she often felt nothing short of Podunk and putrid, not to mention currently puked on, uneducated and worn out.

"Are you there?" Katie asked. "Hel-*lo?*"

"Oh, Katie, you embarrass me."

"Why on earth would I do that? I'm just

speaking the truth." A short silence followed her statement.

"I know, how about you and I and Sarah Sue go to Hethrow and get a frozen yogurt this evening. I'll pick you up in about fifteen minutes, okay? Then if we eat them slowly enough, by the time I drop you two off and get back to the farm, it will be too late to have to go through those boxes tonight, and in the meantime, I can have a chance to snuggle Sarah Sue."

"Wish I could, Katie, but we've already had five check-ins — praise God for the income! — and we're still waiting for two more to arrive. Besides, it seems like Paul and I have hardly had time lately to touch bases with one another, let alone get some of our *own* cuddling time in, what with him at the mines all day and me cleaning rooms, tidying up fading flower gardens, not to mention bookkeeping and nursing Miss Cranky, who I think is beginning to get a tooth already. I seriously doubt you'd find her very obliging this evening anyway. How *can* you tell for sure when they're getting a tooth, Katie?"

Katie opened her mouth to answer, but suddenly Jessica blurted, "Oh! Gotta go! A car just pulled up in front of the office. Talk to you later, okay? Have a great evening. And have a few licks of yogurt for me if you go get one, okay? That way *somebody* can enjoy the calories and they won't end up on *my* new-mom hips!"

Jessica hung up before Katie could say a proper good-bye, which left her . . . alone . . . again. Staring at the phone in her hand after pushing the disconnect button, she started to dial Dorothy just to check in and see how she was doing, but then recalled it was band practice night. Josh had gone to Hethrow to shoot baskets at the YMCA with some of his new friends.

She was alone. Nobody else to call, really, to go for . . . anything, let alone yogurt. No husband. Nobody to share her evening with . . . no cuddling. *I am alone . . . and lonesome.* No rehearsals. No more city excitement or neighborhood bistros to visit. No . . . life. *So lonesome.*

But rather than allow herself to slip into a pity party (she was, after all, proudly a woman of great self control), she concluded she might as well tackle the boxes. She sighed, turned and caught the reflection of her backside in the large kitchen window. "Why did you have to mention hips, Jessica?" Since their move — since the treadmill and weights were stored in the barn until she could figure out where to put them — she'd been lax in her otherwise militant dedication to her usual rotation of workouts, including treadmill, yoga, kickboxing, Pilates, weights. . . . "Oy!" she said aloud when she studied what she perceived to be a bigger backside than she'd last noticed, even though it was still tiny for her trim five-foot five-inch stature.

"Katie Durbin, you get yourself up those stairs — and maybe you should run up and down them three times first, just to wake up your cardiovascular system — and put that chaos to rest so you can set up your workout area and office. And I mean it. Do you hear me? And you have got to stop talking to yourself out loud!" Although she only ascended the stairs once, she stomped up them — each step uttering a unique creak as she went — punching the air, alternating her right and left fists like a boxer, just to maximize the workout.

3

According to the long-established rotation schedule, it was Jessie Landers's turn to host the September meeting of the Happy Hookers, a group that eons ago had gathered monthly to hook rugs but that quite some time ago put down their hooks and started playing bunco. However, since Dorothy had not hosted a housewarming party after moving into her little house on Vine Street, she was anxious to have her new home's first official gathering — at least that's what Dorothy told Jessie when she talked her into giving her the September slot. Jessie had eagerly obliged since she wasn't fond of cleaning anyway, and this gave her an excuse to wait another good while before having to dig into the corners, what with the way Gladys loved inspecting every little nook and cranny. Actually, if whoever was to host the Hookers in November would now trade their slot with her,

Jessie figured she could shoot down two entertainment birds with only one scrub bucket since a couple of Arthur's cousins were coming from Indiana for the Thanksgiving holiday. Yes! One cleaning would knock off the Hookers and the relatives. Ba-ding-ba-dang.

Then after Jessie and Dorothy had all the dates worked out, wouldn't you know two of the members were suddenly otherwise engaged on the Hookers' usual third-week-of-the-month September time slot (how was it, they wondered, that retirement seemed to usher in more to-do things than when they'd been raising babies?). So Dorothy had, with disappointment, but nonetheless an accommodating spirit, moved the meeting back to the first Tuesday in October because the original change in dates had run smack into a few other appointments for that first Wednesday, which was the first of the month, a popular date for other doings. Whew. Although between the wheres and whens of it all the Hookers' calendars looked like scribbled messes, at last it was settled.

There was more to Dorothy's trade than met the eye, however. Yes, Dorothy was eager to have an official gathering, but it was another gathering that, because of her move, she knew she *couldn't* be hosting this year that was grieving her heart. For decades the Hookers' Christmas party, at which they didn't play bunco, but sang carols, played board games and shared pieces of their lives, had been held out at Crooked Creek Farm. Not only had Hooker members been invited, but so had spouses, families and friends. Nearly sixty people, young, old and in between, typically filled the old farmhouse with merriment and love.

But this year things would be different: not only did Dorothy no longer live on the farm, but she was, at this moment, having trouble fitting two card tables for eight bunco players into her new living room; no way would the masses be able to convene, not even throughout her entire "dollhouse of a house," as May Belle had once referred to it. As for the Christmas party, who knew what would happen this year; perhaps it was a ritual that had come to an end — although Dorothy was hoping for the right opportunity to suggest an alternative plan that wouldn't be too disruptive to the gang, and might actually mend a few ongoing gaping fences between the townsfolk and the city slickers. After all, since joining as a new Hooker member, Katie hadn't had a chance to host yet. . . .

Dorothy checked her sacred Register clock — the time-beat of her life since her childhood — and gasped. The Hookers would be gathering at her home in less than thirty minutes. "Oh, May Belle! I hope we all *fit* in this living room and don't find ourselves locked in once we get seated, that is if we can even *find* enough acrobatic ways to *get* ourselves seated," she said as May Belle helped her move, for the third time, the angle at which the card tables were set up. Sheba watched their every move with bored eyes, occasionally having to be shooed out of the way because every time they adjusted a table, she curled herself up under it — at least until they moved it again a few seconds later.

"Dorothy, I have an idea. Let's take down one of these tables and just use your kitchen table for the head table. Who's gonna care if the tables are in the same room anyway, and they'll only be a few steps apart from each other."

Dorothy stepped back to survey the situation. "May Belle, you are not only a true friend, but you are a nervous-breakdown-saver to boot. Honestly, I have been fretting over this for two days, and within five minutes of your arrival, you've saved my sanity." Immediately the two of them began folding down the card table chairs and moving them back into the guest room. May Belle noticed Dorothy huffing a bit. In order to ward off her need for a nitroglycerin tablet, but without mentioning that, she suggested Dorothy go check on things in the kitchen while she broke down the card table and tucked it away. While Dorothy was out of the room, May Belle also lifted the remaining card table and positioned it toward the front window where there was more floor space, moving it this way and that until she was satisfied with the amount of room there would be for eight ladies to navigate all the moves they'd have to make throughout the evening as new rounds started and losers and winners swapped from one chair, one table, one room, to the next.

"Okay, *now* we can set out the bridge mix, score cards and dice," May Belle said as she entered the kitchen.

"Perfect timing," Dorothy said as the last chocolate-covered raisin slid from the box into a bowl. Dorothy snatched it up and popped it into her mouth. "Better make sure they're good enough for the ladies."

She swallowed, then winking at May Belle added, "I'd say I need to check one more; you better test one too." Within a few minutes, everything was in place and Dorothy and May Belle sat down at the kitchen table to catch their chocolated breath before the evening began.

Dingdong! "Well, I do declare!" Dorothy said. "I believe my backside hitting the chair triggered my doorbell!"

"Oh, Dorothy, you tickle me!"

It was Gladys, who had arrived ten minutes early. She had been chomping at the bit to get inside this house ever since they'd discovered Tess Walker's body in it, way back in April. Each time she'd heard yet one more person talking about Dorothy's newly painted fire-engine red kitchen ceiling, she'd feared she might be the last person in all of Partonville to get a gander, not that she hadn't tried to. She'd even, immediately following an indignant moment when Arthur, who had been sitting across from her at the U counter at Harry's Grill, had asked her what *she* thought about the red ceiling — knowing full well, by the curl of his lip, that she had not seen it yet — made a misguided, uninvited attempt. She paid her bill and with determined and official mayoral steps, had walked directly to Dorothy's house, bustled up the sidewalk, stood before the door for a moment and straightened her ever-present, bronze name tag etched in black stating "Gladys McKern, Acting Mayor." She yanked down the bottom of her blazer, which had ridden up on her massive bosom, then banged — and it could be called nothing short of that — on Dorothy's door. When the door swung open, Dorothy exclaimed, "Goodness, Gladys! What on earth is it?" Surely this type of banging meant an emergency. When Gladys realized she had nothing to say that would justify her racket, she simply stood in silence, casting her eyes about, trying to see around, over and through Dorothy to at last observe the famous red ceiling.

In an instant, Dorothy had sized up Gladys's wandering eyes, gathered her mission, swallowed down a devilish grin and said, "I'd invite you in, Gladys, but I was just on my way out." She moved toward Gladys so quickly that Gladys had nearly stumbled shifting herself into reverse, out of the doorway, out of Dorothy's way. Dorothy closed the door behind her and trudged down her front sidewalk, leaving Gladys in her wake, standing on the porch with her mouth hanging open. "I won't be back for quite some time, Gladys," Dorothy said over her shoulder as she made the turn onto the curbside sidewalk, smirking, thinking she should probably feel guilty, but . . . not.

Gladys kicked her bustle into gear and breathlessly caught up with Dorothy. "I'll walk you to the square," she said. When the women arrived on Main Street, having journeyed in silence, Gladys huffing and puffing all the way, they each realized they had no destination in mind but without either of them admitting so or slowing a hitch in their get-alongs, they said their good-byes and turned in different directions. Dorothy ended up circling the block and heading straight back toward her home; Gladys, nearly plum out of breath, decided she might as well go to her mayoral office where she could take control of *something*.

Truth be known, Gladys *was* the last of the Hookers to view the red ceiling, but she figured if she got to bunco first, none of them would be the wiser. "Good evening, Dorothy," Gladys said, this time maneuvering right past her. Boldly, Gladys surveyed the living room: the massive mahogany desk from the farm that Gladys thought swallowed the room, but which Dorothy knew stood like a strong, familiar guardian and reminder of her father, whose life's business had been contained in the very same wood; the new halogen lamp that brightened the space; an ancient pocket watch displayed under a glass dome; Tess Walker's lamp with a purple fringed lampshade that sat on the end table.

Gladys finished her slow 360-degree turn, then settled her eyes on the card table next to her. "Only four players this evening?"

"Goodness me, no. All eight of us will be rolling the dice!"

May Belle appeared out of the kitchen and welcomed Gladys, making a comment about how happy she was to be playing with eight again after all their years of making do with six.

"Are we going to be playing in shifts?" Gladys asked, shuffling herself toward the hall, still in search of the famous red kitchen ceiling.

"Of course not," Dorothy responded. She didn't offer an explanation, forcing Gladys to ask the obvious.

"Well, for goodness sake, Dorothy, where on earth are the rest of the ladies going to play? On the floor? You know, I knew this house was small, but I had no earthly idea just *how* small." Without being led, Gladys rounded the corner into the kitchen, where she dropped her jaw nearly three full inches, as Dorothy would later tell Katie. "Well, I do declare! If this isn't . . . well, I have never . . ."

"Gladys McKern, even if I didn't love my red ceiling — which I do — it would have been worth the cost of paint just to see the Grand Canyon down your gullet!" Dorothy's eyes were twinkling with mischief as she glanced at May Belle who had sidled up next to her. "And just because you are the acting mayor, I'm going to let you be seated right here and right now at the head table," she said, pulling out a kitchen chair, "so you can take a load off while studying the *rest* of my kitchen. After you've had a chance to get your fill in here, I'll give you an official tour of the remainder of the place, as brief as it will undoubtedly be, what with all the *small*ness." May Belle's hand flew over her mouth. Honestly, sometimes Dorothy Jean Wetstra astounded even her, even after eighty-plus years of friendship.

Gladys yanked down the bottom of her blazer before seating herself. Since their school days, Dorothy and Gladys had engaged in a social dance all of their own. No matter what rank Gladys perceived herself to have over Dorothy — and certainly acting mayor should have been worth *something* — Dorothy continued to be the respected dear in everyone's eyes, while Gladys continued to be plagued by the memories of old schoolyard "Gladys the Gladiator" taunts. After all their years of sparring, Dorothy, being one of the few in Partonville, aside from Arthur Landers, to openly go head to head with Gladys, had, with God's help, learned to genuinely love Gladys for exactly who she was: a cantankerous, power-hungry, bossy woman, but also a Child of God, who, Dorothy had long ago determined, surely must behave the way she did to cover up some deep-rooted insecurity. "Lord," Dorothy had prayed on more than one occasion after encounters with her, "help me see You in her hard-set eyes. And if I don't, help me know it's *not* You I'm seeing because surely *You* are not that stubborn!" Even though sometimes all Dorothy seemed to see when squaring off with Gladys was a red as bright as her ceiling, it never stopped her from knowing without a doubt how much she'd miss Gladys if she were gone. Although they usually danced a bumpy tango, together they had, in spite of themselves, become used to each other.

Within a few minutes, the rest of the Happy Hookers had arrived: Jessie, who was glad to be away from Arthur for the evening; Nellie Ruth, who was feeling lucky; Maggie Malone, owner of, and sole stylist at, La Feminique Hair Salon & Day Spa, who arrived sporting Halloween pumpkin decals on her fingernails; Katie and Jessica, the two youngest and newest Happy Hooker members, whether Gladys liked it or not — and she did not — but the rest of the members had, as usual, sided with Dorothy and voted them in.

"Most buncos goes to Nellie Ruth!" Dorothy said as she handed her the wrapped prize at the end of the evening, just before dessert. They'd all gathered in the living room for the closing festivities, some remaining at the card table and the rest seating themselves on the couch and side chairs that cozily surrounded the card table.

"I just KNEW I was going to be lucky tonight!" Nellie Ruth gushed, accepting the package and ripping off the paper like a child on Christmas morning. "Oh, a CANDLE!" She opened the glass lid, put it straight to her nose and drew a big whiff. "Mmmm. Vanilla. It couldn't be more perfect! I was just thinking the other day I needed to get fragrant candles for my apartment before winter sets in. I even tried to talk Wilbur into letting us carry a few at Your Store along with the utilitarian candles we sell for emergencies. He just sighed and stared at me like I was daft rather than the assistant manager. 'Nellie Ruth McGregor,' he said, all but shaking his finger at me, 'those types of things do not belong in a grocery store.'" She tilted her head forward, pretending she was looking over the top of a pair of glasses, just the way Wilbur always did when he was making a point. "'Groceries belong in a grocery store,'" she said, dropping her voice a half octave, trying to match his intonation. She shifted her weight and cocked her other hip while planting her hand on it, another Wilbur gesture. "'Next thing I suppose you'll want me to be adding onto the store to accommodate your hankering for fancy bath oils, then just a few earrings. Next thing you know, we won't even have room for food anymore, and Nellie Ruth, may I remind you that we are a *grocery* store!'"

54

"Why, Nellie Ruth, I had no idea you were so good at impersonations!" Dorothy said as she rubbed a round, affirming circle on Nellie Ruth's back with the tips of her fingers. Everyone was roaring, aside from Gladys, who just shook her head and chalked this dramatic rendering right up there along with the past summer's saxophone incident. When the laughter died down, Nellie Ruth continued, exaggerating her own self after Dorothy's encouragement.

" 'No,' I told him. 'But it *would* be nice to offer more herbal teas and a few imported spices. That's what I'd *really* like for us to carry, Wilbur.' Well, you would have thought I suggested we carry baboons and aardvarks in aisle three, the way he looked at me." She held the candle to her nose again and continued talking between inhales and exhales, drawing the fragrance of vanilla clear down to the bottom of her lungs.

"Where did you get such a lovely candle, Dorothy?"

By this time, Jessica had ripped the paper off of her booby prize, hoping above hope that it, too, was a candle. Jessica loved fragrance and occasionally stopped in at La Feminique Hair Salon & Day Spa just to sniff Maggie's small (one short rack) but impressive offering of aromatherapy oils. They were quite out of Jessica's budget — in fact they were out of many budgets in Partonville — but Maggie mostly stocked them for herself and the shop's image as much as for sales possibilities, which were slim to none. Although Jessica's prize wasn't a candle, it was a key ring with a sparkling bauble on it. "Isn't that adorable," she said, twirling it around and around. "This might even entertain Sarah Sue, when all else fails."

Jessie received the prize for most wins: a bookmark that looked to be crocheted. She was more the practical, athletic type and not much of a reader, finding she couldn't sit still long enough to engage in lengthy strings of words, but she was grateful it wasn't a candle or sparkly bauble.

Jessica set her key ring on the table and asked if she could see Jessie's bookmark. She fingered it, counted stitches across the top row, then down the side, then turned it this way and that. "Those would sure be easy to make," she said, "and wouldn't they be beautiful with multicolored yarn? Dorothy, where on earth *did* you find such cute prizes?"

"Well, I have to admit that when I was

packing up for my move, I unearthed several gifts I'd received from students over the years, and that bookmark was among them. The candle and the key chain I picked up in a peachy little boutique the last time The Tank and I went gadding about over to Hethrow." The Tank had been the nickname of Dorothy's beloved car, designated as such because of all the battle scars on the hard-run 1976 Lincoln Continental.

The room went still. This was the first time that most of them had heard Dorothy mention The Tank since she'd quit driving and The Tank had gone out in a puff of glory at the demolition derby. They glanced at one another, wondering how or if to respond to Dorothy's ongoing loss. Dorothy felt the mood in the room begin to darken so she busted out laughing to snap it back toward festive. "Okay! I reckon we've had our appropriate, respectful silent moment for The Tank." A soft chuckle rippled through the room. "I do miss gadding about, though, that is for sure. And it's been a hard nut to swallow to learn to ask for rides here and there. But everyone has been so gracious, inviting me along when you're running errands and such. No, it's nothing like driving my own car when I want, where I want, as fast as I want, but I have never second-guessed my decision."

"Neither has anyone else in town," Gladys said. The ladies let out a riotous laugh, knowing full well this time Gladys told the truth. No doubt about it, Dorothy's lead foot and waning lack of depth perception had caused them all, including Dorothy, more than a few gasps. Dorothy still had trouble getting over the time she had pulled out in front of Katie's SUV — had not even seen her — which had caused Katie to have to veer right off the road and into the ditch. She knew God and Katie had forgiven her, but the thought of what might have happened still occasionally haunted her. She made herself recall that incident whenever she pined to drive again. In fact, it was often the topic of discussion during her Moment With the Big Guy in her bedtime prayer-chair.

"You know," Dorothy said, "it would sure add a hint of liveliness to this town if Partonville were to get its own boutique. Since I can't just head down to the creek and listen to nature or pluck a few crawdads to pass my time, I've been strolling the square when I'm at loose ends. I find we're definitely lacking imagination here. Round and round we go, passing a drug store, the grill, the bank. . . . Yes, we can still get our business done here, for the most part. But there are no places for women to lollygag shop in Partonville, especially not when you're stuck without a car. There's no reason for folks to come here who don't live here. The closest thing we have for browsing is Swappin' Sam's, and it's too far out of town for an old lady like me to walk to."

"We have Wal-Mart," Gladys said in defense of her fine town. "Wal-Mart carries candles and just about everything else. People drive from several small towns around here to go to our Wal-Mart rather than driving all the way to Hethrow. Why, you could browse for hours in there, Dorothy Jean Wetstra, and *it's* only a good healthy walk away." More than a few in the room had to bite their tongues, never having seen Gladys walk much of anywhere, since she so enjoyed driving her car with the "Partonville Mayor" decal on the sides of it, the decals she'd had made. (She had also somehow convinced Mac, otherwise knows as Sergeant Phillip McKenzie, that such a post deserved special parking privileges, which, according to chatter at Harry's Grill, ought to be stopped.) "Why on earth would we need a boutique when we have

Wal-Mart?" Gladys asked in a huff-and-puff of words.

It rose in Katie's throat to say, "Maybe all of us do not enjoy pushing a shopping cart around in a discount store to buy the exact same thing that everyone else has," but she stifled herself; after all, Dorothy was hosting and she didn't want to become unnecessarily combative in her home. That, and she was too tired and distracted to enter into verbal sparring, which she otherwise might have found entertaining. But as though Gladys had heard Katie's very thoughts, she went on to say, "Not everyone can *afford* to pay for overpriced wardrobes, gee-gaws and automobiles." She eyed Katie's silk blouse and ever-present diamond tennis bracelet, then shifted her head toward the front window through which Katie's big Lexus SUV could be seen parked at the curb. "Some folks are working and working darn hard for what little they *do* have." It was a hard-to-miss insinuation, if not a direct attack, on Katie's wealth and apparent lack of a need to work, no doubt about it. "It's nice to have a place where we can *all* afford to shop." Still, rather than respond, Katie just stared blankly at Gladys, as though she had been speaking in a foreign language. In fact, she'd remained unusually quiet all evening, preoccupied at best, and bordering on sullen at worst.

"Boy, what *I* wouldn't give to be able to buy more exotic herbal teas at Your Store or a local boutique to serve in my shop," Maggie said, "rather than having to drive to Hethrow or send away for them the way I do. What I spend for gas, time and shipping alone could be added to the price of the product and I'd be *happy* to pay. The more we all do mail order or go to Hethrow, or for that matter, pick up everything we need at Wal-Mart rather than supporting our independents with our dollars — not," she had to admit, "that they have that much to offer anymore, but isn't Wal-Mart part of the reason why? — the fewer merchants can afford to stay in business, and the less folks want to remain in this town." They all sat in silence for a moment, considering her statements.

"You know, Gladys," Maggie continued, lifting her foot and twirling it, admiring the inexpensive new brown clogs she'd purchased from Wal-Mart just that afternoon, just because they went with her burnt-orange outfit and her haystack earrings, "you're right: it is wonderful to have a big store so nearby. But Wal-Mart doesn't sell anything unique, exotic, unusual or home-made. I wonder if we did bring an upscale boutique to town if there might be some folks from surrounding towns who might even come *to* downtown Partonville to do a little shopping!" Visions of a salon expansion and high-end clientele danced in her head. Ladies who *did* want to try the latest rage in hairstyles Maggie so adored rather than the same "do's" they'd been wearing for fifty years, like the majority of ladies in this house. Maggie pondered how much she'd be worth if she had just five dollars for every bottle of Brunette Brown she'd spread through Gladys's wiry hair over the decades.

"And what about homemade goodies," Dorothy added. "Why, can you imagine how much ladies might pay for May Belle's prize-winning double chocolate brownies all wrapped up in cellophane and adorned with those clever curly ribbons she's so good at making?"

"What do you think, Katie?" Nellie Ruth asked. "You know all about development and what makes towns and commercial establishments work. What kind of boutique do you think would attract people to Partonville?" All eyes turned toward Katie, who was staring off into an upper corner of the living room. They followed her gaze, even squinted, but nothing out of the ordinary could be seen, not even by Gladys, who had immediately supposed there must be a giant cobweb dangling thereabouts — but who especially did not like others asking *Katie* what they thought about Gladys's town! It soon became clear that Katie hadn't been paying attention to their conversation. She seemed, for all purposes, lost in space.

"Katie, dear," Dorothy said rather loudly, "are you feeling okay?"

Katie turned her head and looked at Dorothy. It seemed to take a few seconds for her to bring Dorothy into focus. "Yes. I feel fine." She looked at her wristwatch and feigned a yawn. "Just tired." She pushed back, then up and out of her chair. "Time for me to head out to the farm." Jessica started to get up, since she'd ridden with Katie.

"But we haven't had dessert yet," Dorothy said. Jessica plopped herself back down; like Dorothy, she was never one to miss dessert, and she was also in no hurry to get home to the possibility of a baby still cranking her head off.

"I'm going on home," Katie said. Jessica started to get up again, then changed her mind. "You go ahead, Katie. I'll just walk back to the hotel. It's only a few blocks. My backside doesn't need dessert either, but I think my mouth does, especially since we've been talking about May Belle's brownies and I spied some in the kitchen on her beautiful Imperial candlewick cake plate in there. If I walk home the few blocks, then I won't feel so guilty."

"May Belle, would you do us the honors, please," Dorothy said more than asked. "I'm going to walk Katie to her car."

"Good night, everyone," Katie called over her shoulder as she opened the front door, Dorothy at her heels.

When they got out on the sidewalk, Dorothy looped her arm through Katie's elbow and slowed her pace. "Is everything okay, Katie? You just don't seem yourself tonight."

"Oh, I'll be fine. Please don't leave your guests."

"Don't be silly. I *want* to say good-bye to you; we simply haven't seen enough of each other here lately. They'll all be busied up ooing and aahing over the brownies for a spell anyway. And if I eat any more chocolate tonight, I won't sleep a wink. I nearly emptied one entire bowl of bridge mix all by myself.

"Tell me, dear, what's bothering you? I can see it's something important."

Katie had long ago figured out that Dorothy was highly intuitive, not to mention persistent. "I'll get over it," she said, hoping that would end the conversation, but knowing it probably wouldn't.

"Some things we need to plow through and pray over before we can *get* over them," Dorothy said. "I'm highly aware of that right now, still trying to get over leaving the farm and moving into town."

Not the prayer thing, Dorothy. Not tonight. Katie decided if she at least came clean, she could make this brief and get off the hook. "I had a somewhat lonesome moment last night, that's all. Then I started going through the first of Aunt Tess's boxes of papers we've stuffed in the Chaos Room."

"The chaos room?"

"Oh, that's the smallest room upstairs, you know, the one you used as a guest room. It's where Joshua and I have crammed everything we either didn't know what to do with or didn't have a space for, or. . . . Aunt Tess's boxes of papers ended up right in the middle. That room is making me crazy, but just the same, it kind of overwhelms me to go in there. I've used every excuse in the book to not deal with it, but it's time."

"You said you had a lonesome moment. What brought that on, dear?"

Katie started fidgeting with her keys, then pushed the *unlock* button on her remote, pressed it again, then one more time, firmly holding it down this time until the windows, programmed to do so on this command, started to automatically go down. She didn't really want to get into this topic. Not yet, anyway.

Dorothy moved to the passenger door and opened it. "Let's sit a spell and chat. The ladies are in good hands with May Belle. Better hands than me, when it comes to desserts."

Katie slumped when she watched Dorothy get into the vehicle, resigning herself to the fact she was either going to have to chat or end up taking Dorothy home with her, which on some level didn't seem like a bad idea. No, not at all, given her growing sense of isolation. Soon they were each settled into the SUV, having scooted themselves at angles to at least somewhat be facing each other. Dorothy remained still, praying in silence for wisdom, waiting for Katie to open up.

What the heck; just tell it like it is. "Dorothy, the reality of living way out in the country is hitting me hard. For my entire life, I've lived in the hum of the city. Dwelling in the fast pace of commercial real estate for so many years, I'm beginning to believe my very countenance became addicted to the adrenaline rushes. But now, now there are no sounds of the city, no important meetings to make me feel that way." *Ouch. True confessions.* "No corner deli with ethnic food, no boutiques." She gave Dorothy a lame smile, letting her know she had heard at least portions of this evening's conversation. "Aside from you and Jessica, I have no real friends here." She looked away from Dorothy and began tracing with her finger the Lexus logo in the middle of her steering wheel. "It's not that I had any real friends in Chicago, but at least I was around people who understood and accepted my financial security and competitive nature since that's the world we *all* lived in.

"I don't fit in here, Dorothy." She turned

her face toward the woman who had the mysterious ability to draw words, a deep well of words, out of her.

"Don't let Gladys's barbs speak for all of us, Katie. You'd be surprised to find out how few people agree with anything that woman *ever* says or does." Dorothy let out a couple chuckles, then she furrowed her brows. "She just seems to have a mean spirit when it comes to you, dear. I'm convinced she's just jealous, poor thing. Jealousy is a hard nut to crack. No, don't let her get to you. She's really harmless, even though she gets a little puffed up. I know for a fact nearly every other woman at bunco tonight has the potential to become your good friend, just like Jessica. And you know, since God *is* a God of constant surprises, maybe even one day Gladys and you will be good buddies!" Katie raised an eyebrow. "And land sakes, there are plenty of folks in town you haven't even met yet who you might end up having more in common with than you think. What about Josh's new friends' folks? Have you met any of them yet? Maybe even some from Hethrow?"

"He's so busy going to school, talking on the phone, signing up for this and that, running here and there, that I hardly have time to spend with *him!* Don't get me wrong; I'm happy he's making such a good adjustment. You know how I fretted about that. But now that I'm around rather than working day in and day out . . . just when I thought we'd finally have time to get to know one another again, he's got a new life, his driver's license, and he's out the door."

Dorothy tried to remember how long it had been since she'd seen or heard from Josh. He used to stop by, give her a call or at least e-mail her often, but come to think about it, he'd been pretty silent lately. She hadn't seen hide nor hair of him.

"*All* new beginnings and chapters take time, Katie. Just give it some *time.*" Dorothy wrapped her fingers around Katie's arm. "I'll move this issue right up to the top of my prayer list. You know, the Big Guy has interesting ways of giving us just what we need right when we need it. It's our job to be paying close enough attention so we don't miss it." Dorothy silently challenged herself to stay awake to God's blessings, feeling a little asleep at the spiritual wheel herself lately.

"Goodness! Here you are wishing for the noise and hustle-bustle of the city, and here I am missing the quiet beauty and familiar sounds of the country! Aren't *we* a fine pair of wishers?" A few moments of silence passed. "Sometimes, we've just got to stop wishing and activate. One step at a time. You know, once you get started going through Aunt Tess's boxes, it might be a quicker task than you think," Dorothy said with renewed vigor. "They're probably filled with junk mail anyway. I do declare, it seems like sale flyers are taking over the world!"

Katie peered around Dorothy, checking to see if the women were readying to leave yet. She didn't want to have them surrounding her vehicle and either casting a cruel eye her way or engaging her in conversation. She didn't have it left in her this evening to deal with either of those possibilities. She was also feeling selfish and guilty for keeping Dorothy from her guests this long.

But mostly, she was feeling the last thing she ever wanted to feel: needy. *Snap out of it!*

"You should probably be getting in there, Dorothy, before the women leave and you don't even get to say good-bye." Now it was Dorothy's turn to survey the situation. From what she could see through her front living room window, however, nobody was making a move for the door yet; they all still

70

looked pretty settled in.

Dorothy turned to look at Katie's face, which was once again washed over with the same look she'd had when she'd been staring into the corner of the living room. Dorothy reached out and patted Katie's cheek. "What is it, Katie? What are you not telling me?" Dorothy's warm palm, her very presence, massaged Katie's vulnerabilities.

Katie began pushing the cuticles back on her right hand with the thumbnail on her left, noting her need for a manicure. Then she traced the Lexus logo again. Then she looked out her driver's window across the street. Then she turned to face Dorothy. "Letters. I've found letters between Mom and Aunt Tess. Mom must have saved the letters from Aunt Tess, and obviously Aunt Tess saved all of her letters from Mom. How Aunt Tess ended up with *all* of them is a mystery to me, but nonetheless, she had them. Just looking at Mom's handwriting made me so lonesome for her. . . . I can't believe she's been gone over a decade now." Tears flashed in her eyes as headlights from a passing car moved by.

"Oh, honey . . ."

"It's not clear to me how long Mom had been in Chicago after leaving Partonville, but some weren't written until after she was pregnant with me. None of them I've read so far were in envelopes or had dates, other than days of the week, and I couldn't make sense out of their order.

"I had no idea Mom and Aunt Tess were so close, Dorothy. Not only did the letters make me lonesome for Mom, but they pierced me with guilt that I never bothered to get more acquainted with Aunt Tess after Mom was gone, assuming she'd *always* been kind of a nut case. But her letters are so sweet. So tender. She was clearly devastated Mom moved, and sounded desperate for her company, in fact she says just that at one point. It *crushed* me reading about her longing to see my mom. . . . So relatable . . ." Katie stopped and swallowed a couple times. "I wondered, Why didn't Aunt Tess go visit her? Why didn't she move *with* her? And why on earth didn't Mom come back *here* more often since she sure talked about Partonville enough?" Dorothy, fingers interlocked, tapped her thumbs together and shifted a bit in her seat.

"Aunt Tess talks about me all the time, often referring to me as 'that precious little bundle you're carrying,' Mom referring to the 'gift of grace I'm growing.' " Katie took a quick swipe under her eye with her knuckle. "Some of the letters, though, are confusing . . . almost unsettling."

"Unsettling? How so?"

"If it hadn't been clear Mom was pregnant with me, I might have thought they were written when the two of them were little girls. There were parts of the letters that were like in some kind of code or something."

"Code? You mean like pig Latin?" Dorothy grinned, although the conversation about letters between the sisters had begun to wash up some hard and squirmy memories.

"There were several references, by both of them, to the Core Four Covenant, and then bunches of capital letters . . ."

"Oh!" Dorothy exclaimed. Her hand flew up and covered her mouth. Simultaneously, the Hooker members spilled from her home and out onto the porch, saying their goodbyes. Dorothy quickly and privately thanked God for the perfect timing that ended this conversation. She also needed a nitroglycerin, but didn't want to worry Katie.

"I know you want to get going, Katie, so I'm going to let you get yourself home and get to bed before the ladies capture you again. We'll talk soon. Good night, dear."

With that, she bolted from the car and briskly headed toward her front door. "Good night, ladies," she said over her shoulder as she whisked through them, leaving them standing with their mouths open, poised with undelivered *Thank-you's.*

Katie started her vehicle, put it in gear and gunned it, spitting roadside gravel this way and that. When, in her rearview mirror, she noticed Jessica jogging into the road to flag her down, she didn't stop. She kept right on driving, into the night, into the country, into the black pit of her impending lifetime low.

May Belle arrived home without her candlewick cake plate and without an ounce of explanation as to why Dorothy had as much as demanded she stop cleaning up, then had shooed her out the door as though the world was on fire. For Dorothy to have acted like that, May Belle knew that surely something was heating up somewhere, and from the gravel she'd seen spitting out behind the tires of Katie's SUV, she thought she just might know from where the sparks were originating. *What* it was, however, she had not a clue.

■ ■ ■ ■

"Dear, sweet Jesus," Dorothy prayed aloud at 2:00 A.M., having tossed and turned and been unable to blame her wakefulness on the caffeine in the chocolate, "give me wisdom." Sheba stood up and moved from the end of the bed to Dorothy's face, licking her cheek a couple times. Dorothy grabbed a firm hold of her and gave her a mighty hug. "Let me know whether to speak or to remain silent, God. Guard my mouth and heart. And speaking of my heart, while You're at it, if You *do* want me to speak, keep my heart beating, Lord, until there is healing, so that precious child of Yours doesn't have to get through this alone. Oh, I know You'd be with her, but I'm the last person left who knows the whole story and can help explain it to Katie, not to mention everyone else the truth will touch.

"Now, I know You've got plenty else to do, what with everyone bending Your ear day and night. Goodness knows, I've done plenty of ear-bending myself lately during all these transitions. But You know me, God, and I do *not* bug You for signs and wonders. But this time, I need clear assurance as to Your presence in this situation. You know I'm asking on account of Katie,

Lord, not for myself. I'm trusting You for that, and I know You won't let me down, right? When You do your part, I'll be ready, okay? Because I'm trusting You to give me what I need, right? Over and out."

She nuzzled Sheba's head up under her chin. "And *please* get me to sleep or I'll be no earthly good to anyone if or when . . . Oh, there's gonna be a whopping lot of cover-ups to bust out of. Lord, You tell us the truth sets us free, well, I'm counting on it! Amen again, from Dorothy." She let go of Sheba, who all but catapulted herself back to the end of the bed as though she were running for her life. Then Dorothy pulled the covers up tightly around her chin and slammed her eyes shut, determined to release any fears. Even though she'd said an official *Amen,* before she nodded off, she whispered, "Pretty please."

At exactly 2:11 A.M., a sign and wonder arrived.

To anyone else, the sound of a cricket would have been an annoyance; to Dorothy, it was nothing short of a sign and wonder of the most magnificent, miraculous and prayer-answering kind, the kind that talked to her smile without a single word. Clearly God was letting her know that He had His eye on her, and Katie, and the entire situation, and by grace, she hadn't slept through it.

As a child, Dorothy had determined that the crickets spent their energies speaking a special language just for her, since their persistent sounds often seemed to bother everyone else. But for Dorothy, their high-spirited voices calling from the depths of the grass had always seemed to her a steady lullaby, soothing her into a sense that all was right with the world. *The earth and all of creation is alive with wonder and goodness, and God has put me here to behold it.* From childhood on, that's what she'd felt each time she'd dozed off in the country to the happy songs of the crickets.

This was the first cricket she'd heard since the move. *Glory be, if it isn't right here in the room with me!* On its seventh chirp, she erupted with riotous laughter. She laughed with relief until she cried with thanksgiving at God Almighty's powerful sign and wonder, delivered in the presence of a cricket.

Katie's body jolted and she sat upright in bed, then glanced at her digital clock. It was

2:11 A.M. Like the hazy remnants of a lingering dream, barely perceptible, she had the oddest sensation that she had been awakened by a happy peel of laughter. Although even her most valiant efforts could not produce any details about such a dream, the glorious sound still played in her head, enough so that she relaxed and fell right back to sleep.

4

"Wait up, Josh!" Shelby jogged down the school hall toward Josh's back, her blonde ponytail swaying back and forth like a metronome ticking off the cadence of her steps, backpack thumping into her shoulder blades to the rhythm. Seemed no matter how briskly she was moving toward him, he was getting farther away, and all the other chatter in the halls muffled her call. The five-minute warning bell rang and she stopped abruptly, causing Kevin Mooney to hurdle himself right into her.

"Hey," he said after he collected himself, "you oughta put out a warning signal before you brake like that! I could have lost my teeth! You okay?"

Shelby whirled around. Kevin's face held a giant grin, as though to showcase those pearly whites he proclaimed had just missed their *thwack* of peril. As far as he was concerned, she'd been worth running into, what with that sassy little figure of hers. He was six-foot tall with brown wavy hair, eyes to match, dreamy dimples, and a letter in track. He was also, without a doubt, the heartthrob of many a Hethrow High girl. The two of them stood for an awkward moment taking each other in, as though they'd never met before, rather than having known each other since grammar school.

"Sorry, Kevin. Once the bell rang, I figured I didn't have time to keep going that-a-way" — she pointed her finger toward the direction in which she'd been heading — "rather than this-a-way to my next period science class." They both looked the direction from which they'd been traveling, the direction to which her finger had now switched to pointing, as though it was a faraway land rather than the steps they'd just taken. He didn't bother to ask why she'd been rushing in one direction to go in another. *Women.*

"Gotta go, kiddo," Kevin said, giving her a friendly, yet flirty little bonk on the head with his knuckles. "I'm trying to catch up with Josh to let him know about a pickup basketball game at Sunset Park after school today."

He disappeared before Shelby could say *I*

wish you'd let him stay home one night. When am I ever going to get to see him again? After all, I'm the one who introduced him to everyone, and now he barely has time to see me! She pursed her lips and let out a disgusted "Jeepers!" as she walked toward room 215, the science lab. *Why couldn't Josh run into me some time? Maybe that way I'd have his attention, even if it knocked all of our teeth out.*

Ever since she'd first seen Joshua Matthew Kinney at his Aunt Tess's wake last April, she'd had an eye for him. After she'd spent time talking with him the next day at the funeral dinner out at Dorothy's farm, she was smitten. Some time between attending his surprise sixteenth birthday party after a Wild Musketeers game (the mostly-senior-citizens softball team for which she was the catcher), working with him at Dorothy's auction and then his move to the farm, she'd found herself hopelessly stuck on him, hook, line and tackle box. Trouble was, even though she thought they'd caught each other, it now seemed he had only favored her until he made new friends after school had started, friends she had in fact introduced him to. *What the heck was I thinking?* To make matters worse, those new friends of his, who were her growing-up old friends to begin with — most of them boys — barely had time for *her* anymore either. Tomboy such that she was, *she* used to be the one they invited to play pickup basketball games. Now, now there was Josh, *Mr. Popular.*

Even though Josh was by no stretch a jock, he was, due to his instant popularity with most of those guys, invited to sit at the jocks' lunch table in the cafeteria — and everyone was aware of anyone who sat at *that* table, especially the girls in pursuit of a major catch. Never having quite fit in anywhere at Latin School, the expensive private school his mom had forced him to attend in Chicago, Josh fed on his newfound popularity and attention, sending no less than five e-mails a week about it to Alex Gillis, his old Chicago best friend and brownstone neighbor. ("Alex, my man, Guess who's The Man with a Grand Stand Plan for the Clan of Popular Guys and Gals at Hethrow High? Josh-o, that's who!")

Since Shelby was neither a cheerleader nor one of the "popular kids," and she hadn't made the cut for the girls' softball team — which further explained her joy in catching for the Wild Musketeers — she sat at the lunch table with the "fringe kids," as they were referred to, and that was just fine with her. She found the fringers, the Wild Musketeers and her great Grannie M, who was none other than Maggie Malone, to be more fun than those full-of-themselves popular jerks anyway since all they seemed to care about was "mascara, building biceps and themselves," as she'd told Grannie M just the other day. That's also what she told herself during her entire frog dissection in the science lab, pretending all the while the frog was Josh. *How does* that *feel, Mr. Popular!*

"Nice shot!" Josh said to Kevin as he swished one in from the corner. Why Kevin didn't go out for the basketball team, nobody could figure out, other than already lettering in one sport was probably enough. "Nice pass, Josh-o," Kevin shouted back to Josh as they moved toward the other end of the court. Although Kevin was known for making baskets, Josh wasn't exactly gifted when it came to anything athletic. The fact Kevin had to reach for Josh's pass was immaterial, since they'd scored. All was well with the play, the day, the friends and the world. At least on the court. Off the court, a storm was brewing among the way-too-wildly cheering spectators of a pickup basketball game. Then again, two of them happened to be cheerleaders who were only doing what came naturally.

"Just because he hasn't invited me yet doesn't mean he's not going to," Becky said to Anita as they sat back down on the bench. "As you well know, he's stopped at our lunch table twice this week, just to talk to me."

"Gee, do you think that might be because you sit at the end of the table near the aisle that's on the way to where we have to return our lunch trays?"

"A lot of people sit at the ends of the tables in that aisle, and he doesn't stop to talk to them."

"Gee, do you think he stopped to talk to you because once you kicked your purse out in the aisle in front of him, and the other time you made a spectacle of yourself by yelling 'Wait up! I'll walk with you!'?"

"You exaggerate."

"Not."

"Do."

"Whatever."

"It's not 'whatever,' it's *when*ever are you going to give up and realize he's not interested in you, and that he's *not* going to invite you to the Pumpkin Festival dance.

Once you get that figured out, then you can prepare yourself for the fact that he's going to ask me."

"What on earth makes you think *that?*"

"Watch who he glances at when they get back down to this end of the court. Just watch." The two of them pasted their eyes on Josh, seemingly oblivious to the fact he couldn't dribble worth a hoot. In fact, it was the second time he'd had the ball stolen on account of his dexterous disabilities, which is why it was some time before his team made it back down toward the girls.

Nobody. He looked at nobody. At least not the next few trips. But he did finally turn his head their way in response to something Kevin said to him, which the girls thankfully didn't hear since it was an off-color remark about Josh's buxom fan club. Both Becky and Anita grinned and waved like goons, flipping their hair this way and that. Josh winked at Anita, then at Becky. Then the ball bounced off of his side since he was busy winking and not watching for a pass.

"See, I *told* you he was going to ask me instead of you!" Anita said.

"How do you figure that?"

"Because he winked at me first."

"That's because you're sitting closer to the direction from which he was coming," Becky responded, sounding as disgusted as all get-out.

"And that's exactly my point about your lunchroom seating situation, if you will recall."

By some miracle, just then Josh sunk a basket and both girls jumped up and cheered. His one-and-only basket arrived the same time as the end of the game. Kevin nodded his head toward the girls. "Nothing like loving them and leaving them with a 'score,' huh?" He'd used his fingers to draw quotations marks around the word "score." Josh thought it was a crude remark and winced inside, hoping the girls hadn't heard it. But he laughed loudly anyway. "Have you noticed, Josh-o," Kevin continued, "that since the Pumpkin Festival dance is closing in on us, girls just seem to be hanging around?"

"Oh, is that what it's all about? The dance?" Josh asked.

"That and the fact you're a natural chick magnet. Chicks always dig new guys, especially *worldly* ones from the big city."

"Oh, is that what they're thinking?" Josh asked with an innocent look, which Kevin thought he was feigning, although he hadn't been. Josh had never even been on a real date.

Becky and Anita were fussing with their makeup, preening while waiting. "Which one are you inviting to the dance?" Josh asked, trying not to look the girls' way again while they were talking about them.

"Neither one of those losers," Kevin said. "I've got somebody else in mind, but I haven't asked her yet."

"Who would that be? Hailey? Sondra?"

"Nope."

"Not telling?"

"Just somebody I ran into."

"Is she from our school?"

"Yup."

"Do I know her?"

"Yup." Kevin picked his backpack up off the side-court, looped his arms through the straps and jostled around until he settled it firmly on his back. "See ya tomorrow."

"So?"

"So, what?"

"So, who are you inviting?"

"I'm not telling. That way, if she shoots me down, nobody but she will be the wiser."

"Oh, like any girl would shoot *you* down!"

"This isn't just any girl."

"Okay, you're killing me here. Just tell me. If you tell me who it is and she shoots you down, my lips are sealed. If it's supposed to be obvious to me, like, you know, last year's prom queen or something, try to remember I don't know all the facts and factoids yet."

"Factoids?" Kevin looked at him like he'd suddenly grown three noses.

"Just something Alex says."

"Alex? Sounds like a loser."

Josh opened his mouth to defend his best friend from the city, but decided to shuttle the conversation back to the topic of women.

"You were talking about inviting a past prom queen?"

"No, man! Not Deborah Arnold; she's last year's news. Trust me, Josh-o. *This* girl has not been prom queen. I sincerely doubt she's ever even been kissed. But for now, I'm outta here. There are fresh lips to conquer!"

As soon as he ran off, Becky, Anita and a few other girls swarmed around Josh like flies to a picnic. In his backpack, at the other end of the court, his cell phone was ringing, ringing, ringing. . . . The late bus was also passing by the park on its way to drop off the Partonville kids. Shelby craned her neck, straining to see if that was, indeed, Josh in the middle of that flock of perfectly coiffed heads. As the bus passed along in front of them, it was clear: there he stood, talking and making google eyes at one girl after the next. Shelby replayed having earlier removed the frog's eyes from its lifeless body, but this time, in her imagination, she threw those slimy orbs to the floor and stomped on them. *That's what you get for staring, Mr. Frog, now two eyeballs short of* ever *becoming a prince.*

With her forearm, Maggie spun Gladys's chair around so that Gladys's back was toward the mirror. Then, comb in one hand and scissors in the other, Maggie leaned her own face in close to the mirror. She studied her eyebrows, first raising one, then the other. She delighted in having ambidextrous eyebrows, a rare gift, indeed. She hadn't quite gotten her brow pencil filled in evenly today, and it was distracting and annoying her every time she caught a glimpse of herself. She took the small-toothed end of the comb and rifled it through her brows a few times, then slicked the teeth ends across the top of her brow hairs, trying to get them to match the errant pencil line. "Hopeless," she said aloud.

"I *beg* your pardon," Gladys said.

"Oh, I wasn't talking about you or your hair, Gladys, I was talking about my misfit eyebrows. Some days I wish I could just be a character in Snow White and have the La Feminique Hair Salon & Day Spa mirror tell me I'm the fairest of them all, or at least fair enough, eyebrows not withstanding." Maggie saluted the mirror with each eyebrow, then winked at herself before turning to face Gladys's back to begin the haircut.

"Maggie Malone, the more you say, the more you make me nervous to be sitting here while you've got a pair of scissors in your hand. How about you just concentrate on your *paying customer* so I can get on with my day."

Signaling she was about to begin, out of habit, Maggie snapped the scissors open and closed a few times, right next to Gladys's ear, causing Gladys to whip her head toward the direction of the sound. Maggie took her pinky fingers, rested them on each side of Gladys's head, turned it forward again and tilted it downwards. "Don't worry, Gladys. You have my complete attention. In all my fifty-plus years as a stylist, I haven't lost an ear yet."

"This would be a terrible time for Partonville to have the mayor bleed to death over a beauty shop incident," Gladys said, "what with the impending . . ." Gladys stopped herself, saying just enough to hopefully get Maggie to bite, which she did.

"Impending what?"

"Impending anniversary celebration."

"Of what?"

"Of Partonville!"

"What anniversary?"

"Since I dedicate a good portion of my time reflecting on Partonville's past, it has not escaped my attention that Partonville will officially be one hundred thirty years old, come November. It occurs to me that since that is so close to the annual Pumpkin Festival, we could combine celebrations, maybe draw in more outsiders to showcase our town. You know, . . ."

"Gladys," Maggie said, jumping into the middle of her sentence, "you do not need to turn your head to the side for me to hear you. Although I have never lost an ear, if you keep wagging your head around while you talk, you're liable to walk out of here with the first chunk of bald scalp I've ever left on the back of a head — aside from T.J. Winslow's son who asked for it that way when he was about four, on account of he'd cut his own bangs down to the scalp. 'Just shave it all off,' he said. It's not what he wanted, but his mother had a stern eye on

91

him to make sure that's what he got. Up until then, that child had the most beautiful curls I'd ever seen."

Gladys slowly inhaled, then loudly exhaled. "I find I'm just very honored to be the mayor during such a momentous occasion." Maggie opened her mouth to say *Momentous? Sounds more like an* invented *occasion to me.* But she decided to just keep her trap shut. Gladys continued. "If my dear late husband Jake had survived the crash, he'd still be the mayor. In fact, he'd still be alive."

Maggie's scissors suddenly stopped snipping while she untangled that odd arrangement of words. "You must miss him very much, Gladys," she replied after a few seconds.

Gladys was quiet for a long spell, especially for Gladys. Maggie tilted Gladys's head slightly toward the left, continuing to work on her neckline. "You know," Gladys finally said in a shaky whisper, "today would have been our anniversary. Rather than having Jake to spend it with, all I've got of him is the mayoral post he left me with, that is at least until his term, *my* term, is up, in February — although I imagine I will get *officially* elected then. If I didn't have the town to run, all I'd have is . . ."

Never before had Maggie, or anyone else for that matter, seen this side of Gladys. Not even at Jake's funeral, where Gladys had been so busy bossing everyone around at church, making sure his arrangements were just so — so busy that no time was left for her to grieve. Maggie had even overheard Arthur lean over and say to his wife, Jessie, "I reckon Jake don't have his hands crossed right to suit her either, but then there ain't much he kin do about it now!" No one had ever doubted who wore the pants in the McKern household, and after Jake's death, the townsfolk decided they might as well just let her finish officiating the term, since she'd already been doing it anyway.

Gladys sniffed and Maggie froze in place, completely lost as to how to respond to an unguarded Gladys, a Gladys she'd never met before, not in all their decades of knowing each other. Sarcasm, barbs, bossiness . . . those things she expected from Gladys, knew how to put up with. But not this. She set her scissors and comb down and said she was going to go get herself something to drink. "Would you like a beverage, Gladys?"

"That would be fine," Gladys said, leaving her head hanging down long after Maggie had given her reason to keep it that way, something that didn't go unnoticed by Maggie before she backed away. In fact, she couldn't help but silently stare at this sorrowful site for quite some time. Gladys appeared to Maggie like a slain giant. For the first time, Maggie was getting a glimpse into Gladys's tender spot, which many were convinced she didn't have. Without raising her head, Gladys brushed the little hairs off her lap that had landed on the purple drape cloth, then she moved the drape to the side to reveal her handbag, something she never left unattended — what with all those "hooligans negligent parents are raising today." She unsnapped the top of her bag and retrieved a packet of tissues, then pulled one from the pack. She swiped at her nose a few times, sighed, swiped a few more times . . . then her shoulders shook, but she made not a sound. Then she blew her nose and swiped again, tucking the tissue inside her purse and snapping herself back together. And yet, she still did not raise her head. All of this Maggie saw.

An idea popped into Maggie's head and she quietly scurried to her back room, filled the hot pot with water and plugged it in. She opened the cabinet door above the towel cabinet and retrieved a box of scones she had hidden away, cellophane wrapper still in place. She went to the reception area, got two purple mugs from near the coffee pot, which of course had her new logo on them, the same logo she'd had tattooed on her ankle the year before, which had set the Happy Hookers' meeting into complete turmoil upon its discovery. According to Maggie, the logo was an open pair of upside-down scissors that supposedly created the letter A in SPA! "It's so obvious!" she'd told them. But to this day, none of them could see it. No matter; it delighted Maggie.

By the time the water was nearly to a full boil, which really took less than a minute or so in the little hot pot, she'd also opened a package of hibiscus tea bags she'd ordered. She arranged everything just so on a serving tray, setting the tea bags in a small bowl that she placed on a silver-foiled paper doily. (Purple and silver were her shop's current colors, which she changed every few years, never wanting to be bored with her working environment.) In a final burst of kindness and creativity, she went to her aromatherapy display and opened a spendy bottle of rosemary, a fragrance that was reported to give you clarity and energy, thinking this might help cheer up Gladys. She put a dollop on a nearby testing paper and set it under the doily. She gave the tray a once-over, smiled with satisfaction at how quickly she'd been able to pull together such a delightful and beautiful pick-me-up, then headed back to Gladys carrying the tray before her as though it held the queen's crown.

"Here we go," she said to Gladys, who had retrieved a magazine and was thrashing through the pages in a disgusted manner.

Gladys looked at her large-faced wrist-watch when Maggie set the tray down. "If I had known you were going to spend an hour preparing an entire banquet rather than just getting us a cup of coffee, I'd have certainly declined your offer in favor of getting on with the haircut. I have an important ap-pointment in thirty minutes with the man-aging editor of the *Partonville Press.* Let's just get on with it. I'm not thirsty anymore anyway. And what *is* that awful smell? I guess you've forgotten about my sensitive sinuses!"

Without a sip or a nibble by either one of them, Maggie picked up her scissors and comb. In sixteen minutes flat, wherein not a word was uttered by either of them, she was done with Gladys — cut, blow-dry, curling iron, comb-out and bill collection. As soon as Gladys departed, May Belle walked in.

"Welcome to the Twilight Zone," Maggie said. "You're just in time for hibiscus tea and scones. Let me reheat the water."

5

"No replays of the last few days, mister. Understand?" Katie smacked Josh's lunch money into his open palm. "You either let me know ahead of time you're staying late at school and need a ride, or get yourself on the bus. And if it's going to be the late bus, let me know that, too. What good is it for me to get you a cell phone if you don't use it? If you'll recall, by the time I got that one call, drove to Hethrow, picked you up, brought you home, made dinner, took a shower and got to bunco, I was exhausted and barely on time. Not to mention I was worried sick about you when you weren't on *either* bus — *and* didn't answer your cell phone! But I let it ride, thinking anybody can mess up one time. But now, Josh, this type of inconsiderate behavior has come to an end, hear me?"

"Mom, I'm sixteen years old. Maybe if I took the Lexus to school or had my own car, this wouldn't be such a problem."

"Excuse me?"

"It's not like you were in the middle of something, Mom. You're not even working. And it's not like important things can't just crop up. After all, that's what you told me all the nights you weren't around when we lived in Chicago."

He had pierced her with truth. But then, she'd been the sole breadwinner since her louse of a husband had left her for a younger woman — at least that's what she'd always told herself until she'd faced the truth not long before they moved to Partonville. Fact was, she'd partly kept herself busied up running from her own emotions, so much so that she hadn't even realized she'd been shutting out her son.

She was, at this moment, caught in the crosshairs of several truths. However, she quickly decided to split those hairs and exercise her parental authority. She narrowed her eyes and sucked in her cheeks. "I think there's a slight difference between feeding us and playing a pickup basketball game, Joshua Matthew Kinney. And as for you having your own car, perhaps getting a part-time job would help you be able to afford one."

"Come on, Mom. We both know you can

afford to buy me a car. Do you know how uncool it is to have to ride the bus?"

"Do you know how uncool you will be when you're grounded for a month if you continue speaking this disrespectfully to your mother?"

Josh looked at the kitchen clock as he stuffed the lunch money down into his Levis' pocket. "I gotta go. Let's just plan on this: until further notice, I'll either catch a ride home with friends, or I'll be on the late bus."

"Either way, you will be home by the time the late bus should be arriving. Clear? And if you're riding with somebody, I'd like for him or her to come into the house and introduce him- or herself. I don't like the idea that I don't even know the people who have my son's life in their hands."

"At the moment, Mom," he said as he opened the door, "it seems you're trying to keep me from *having* a life."

Katie heard the faint sounds of a bus coming down the gravel road as the door slammed behind him. Knowing their driveway was one-eighth mile long, she lurched to the door, opened it and yelled after him, "You better run your little butt off, Joshua, unless you feel like walking four miles to school today!" She, too, let the door slam behind her as she stepped back into the house. Then she tromped over to the cabinet where she kept her carafe. She filled it with the rest of the coffee, turned off the coffee maker, grabbed her mug and dedicated herself to a Chaos Room lock-in. She was sick and tired of the mess.

Three hours after Josh had left for school, the Chaos Room was officially more chaotic than it had ever been. Katie had decided to begin with the two boxes labeled "AUNT TESS'S PAPERS," getting the worst task over first. She'd briefly scanned each paper, then set it on one of the piles she'd strewn across the top of nearly everything else in the room. The biggest pile was thankfully that of "things that don't matter," which she was going to toss back into one of the now empty boxes and haul downstairs to discard. But before she did that, she found herself sitting on the floor, leaning against the wall, legs outstretched in front of her, trying to bring order and sense to the most important mound: correspondences between her mom and Aunt Tess. She had, in her sifting, discovered several more bundles of letters and an occasional orphan mixed in with either paid bills or hospital records, two other piles she'd decided she needed to study once more for family health history before pitching. But even though she'd promised herself she was just going to get all the letters in one place for now, and not dwell on them anymore until after the entire room was in shape (a matter of priorities and discipline, she'd told herself), she could not stay away from them.

No matter how many ways she'd arranged and rearranged the letters, it was simply impossible to organize them into any timeline. She'd even tried to arrange them by lines of conversation, but that didn't always work either, since references to intervening phone calls took the sisters' discussions off on different tangents. Contrary to her initial belief, she now thought no letters existed for the year between her mom's move to Chicago and the first letter in this collection. Although her mom mentioned her loneliness, she never shared any news about her dad, who had died before Katie was born. Katie had been hoping the letters would render at least a few morsels about her father, her parents' marriage. . . . She'd often grieved that she'd never even seen a photo of her dad, whose own parents had died when he was young. Her mom had been deft at deflecting personal questions about her dad, saying it hurt too much to talk about him. "So brief. So much pain" was about the most Katie ever got her to say. That and that he was very sensitive. Although Katie had inwardly grieved — and on occasion also questioned — the lack of photos *and* stories, she'd fled from the prickly feeling their voids sometimes gave her.

What remained consistent about the letters, however, were odd placements of capital letters and mentions of the Core Four Covenant. She'd all but made herself bonkers first conjecturing that like many vanity license plates, you could actually pronounce these letters if you spoke them aloud. Since they weren't always in the same order, she tried speaking them every which way. All she ended up discovering, though, was that she sounded like a donkey with a speech impediment and spoke nothing but gobbledygook. In a giant *DUH!* of enlightenment, she finally deduced that the capital letters must be *initials*. After relentless sleuthing with this new agenda in mind, she found herself feeling dumber than the speech-impaired donkey when it became evident there were only four sets of initials: CW, TW, DW and DC. Next logical deduction: they must comprise the Core Four in the covenant. But who were these people, and what was their covenant?

Hungry and suffering from a backache from sitting on the floor for so long, she looked at her watch and was shocked to discover it was 1:00 P.M. She'd *now* been in the Chaos Room for nearly five and a half hours! It was time for a break, that is if she could get her midlife body to stand up. But first, one at a time, she turned each sub-stack of letters face down, then piled one stack on top of the other so she could tuck them all into a large manila envelope she'd set aside for this purpose. It wasn't until she'd turned the last stack over that she saw the *P.S.* on the back of a letter from her mom. "Oh, how I pray that Katie's dad can one day — even from a distance, if only for the briefest of moments — at least *see* his only daughter, covenant or not! She has his beautiful and kind eyes, you know."

6

Ever since Earl had awakened, he'd been asking May Belle if it was time to mow Dearest Dorothy's yard. "No, honey," his mother had patiently repeated several times now. "It's still too early. You don't want to get folks fussing at you for waking them up with the sounds of a lawn mower, do you?" Earl shook his head back and forth. "It won't be that long now. Dorothy called last night and said she'd be over for mid-morning coffee today. When she gets here . . . *when* she gets here, Earl, you can ask *her* if it's time." May Belle smiled at Earl, her beloved forty-five-year-old son, her only child. He was determined, loyal, kind and the joy of her life. He was also retarded, which made him the worry of her life, since what would become of him when she was gone? But one thing she never wondered about him was whether or not he loved his

Dearest Dorothy, who was, next to his mother, his favorite person in his entire world, which had never, not even for a vacation, been larger than Partonville. Earl needed things kept a certain way, which was simple.

Earl walked out to the front porch and began staring down the street in the direction from which his Dearest Dorothy would, he hoped, soon be appearing. Within a couple minutes, he saw Sheba loping down the sidewalk toward him, tongue flapping into her own back draft. He knew Dorothy was on her way.

"Hel-LO, Earl!" she shouted from two houses down.

"Hello, Dearest Dorothy," Earl said quietly. He never raised his voice.

Dorothy got to the front porch where she stopped to catch her breath. "Whew. I paced myself a little too quickly this morning, Earl. And yes, it's time for my grounds-keeper to get to work!" Earl and Dorothy were very special friends. She didn't have to hear his question; she recognized it in his eyes, his stance, his readiness and ongoing love to do for her. As soon as he'd heard "it's time," he'd swiftly moved down the stairs.

"Whoa! Listen up, Earl. Don't forget your mower! You might need to get some gasoline though; you better check first. If you do need to fill her up, just tell George I'll pay him next time I'm in town. You can do that, right?" George Gustafson owned the By George gas station just a block off the square. Back in her driving days, when Dorothy wasn't on a road trip, and for all the years that George had been in business — which amounted to more than she could count — she'd purchased nary a tank of gasoline from anyone else in the vicinity. Even her late husband, Henry, swore by his gasoline. And Arthur Landers, well, he told it like he saw it, at least in his own mind: "Ya just can't trust what some fellas might try to pawn off as gas-o-line but what mighten just as likely be leftovers from too much beer, if ya git my drift. Nope, by George, I'd buy gasoline from nowheres but By George."

Earl, who was walking backwards away from Dorothy toward his task the entire time she'd been talking about gasoline, nodded his agreement to Dorothy that he understood her instructions. Dorothy hadn't even noticed when she'd walked up that he'd long ago poised the lawn mower at the very edge of the lawn, readied for his task.

He was way ahead of her. "I know you can handle that, Earl. I don't know why I even asked! You do such a fine job, honey. I imagine this'll be one of the last mowings before the snow thinks about flying though. Then I guess you can become my snow-shoveling groundskeeper, okay?"

"Okay," he said, but he was already too far away for her to hear his reply over the sounds of the lawn mower merrily thumping its way across the cracks in the sidewalk. Earl had a lawn to mow.

"Good morning, Dorothy," May Belle said, appearing on the front porch wearing one of her well-worn signature aprons. "I see you've sent Earl off and mowing. I'm surprised he slept a wink last night. You know we both love you, Dorothy, and appreciate everything you do for us. But it still makes me feel bad you pay him to mow your little bit of yard."

"Oh, pish-posh. What good are those few dollars to me? I do *not* want to hear another word about it!"

Sheba was standing right by the front door, waiting to get inside. A routine awaited her, and like Earl, she was anxious for it to get underway. May Belle pulled open the door and the ladies followed Sheba in. She darted her doggie self straight into the kitchen. Dorothy and May Belle walked through the living room, through the archway into the dining room, and then on into control central, as Dorothy often referred to it, where they caught up with the waiting Sheba. She was standing next to the counter, wagging her scruffy tail a mile a minute. Dorothy seated herself at the kitchen table where a fresh cup of coffee awaited her, along with a giant slice of apple-crumb coffee cake still warm from the oven.

May Belle reached for the tin of table scraps she'd saved from breakfast and tossed a sliver of ham to Sheba, who snatched it out of the air before it hit the green and white linoleum floor. It was a trick May Belle never got tired of watching. "I tell you, Sheba," May Belle said, "I'd give my right hand to be able to jump half that high."

"You'll try no such thing," Dorothy said, the warm gooey goodness already coating her tongue and throat. She slid the light green linen napkin out of the dark green plastic napkin ring and wiped the corners of her mouth. "I think we're past our jumping days, friend of mine."

May Belle tossed Sheba the last remaining morsel, rinsed out the tin, set it in her plastic dish rack, then sat down across from Dorothy, who had, within these few brief moments, downed her entire piece of coffee cake.

"More?" May Belle didn't wait for an answer; she arose to get the pan and a spatula.

"Just a teensy more. Teensy. Since I moved so close to you, I'm afraid I've put on five pounds. I'm glad my scale is broken; might be ten pounds."

May Belle set the pan and spatula down in front of Dorothy, then patted her own round belly. "I'm glad I've never owned a scale," May Belle said. "From what I read in the papers, folks are *fretting* themselves to death anyway, worrying about good cholesterol and bad cholesterol and carbohydrates and calories and exercise and vitamins and . . . rather than just sitting down at the table and enjoying a nice meal together. Goodness! I figure that as long as I can still get my aprons tied around me, I'll be in business. Besides, I guess since we've lived to be in our eighties, we must be doing *something* right!" A soft ripple of laughter passed between them.

Dorothy finished her snack, then picked up her plate and handed it to May Belle, who she knew couldn't stand dirty dishes sitting on a table. "Well, look at that," May Belle said, peeking through her starched and pressed, navy-and-white gingham café curtains in the kitchen window above her sink. "The sun is trying to pay us a visit!" When she pushed open the curtains, the sun's rays refracted through the crystal she'd hung from the curtain rod with a piece of twine. Dorothy had noticed May Belle eyeing the chandelier crystal at a recent rummage sale and bought it for her for a quarter. She'd wrapped it in toilet tissues, stuffed it into an empty face powder box and anonymously left it in May Belle's mailbox.

Rainbows not only cast across May Belle's face, but all the way to the table where they landed on Dorothy's linked fingers. Dorothy stared at them, smiling, sensing the promise of God's covenant. *Great timing, God!* If Katie kept poking around in those letters, Dorothy continued to feel unsettled about what she might discover, how far things might have to unfold — although maybe it was just time. . . . Yes, it was unsettling. That was the same word Katie had used to describe some of the contents of the letters: *Unsettling. And there's good reason for that,*

Dorothy had thought at the time. But she also knew God was faithful, which was, as usual, once again confirmed in such a surprising way, just like the cricket. *Thank you, Lord, for your grand style. Oh, how you talk to my smile! More dazzling than any painting I've ever seen, Jesus, and nary a penny did I pay for either one of them!*

"Now aren't we suddenly colorful!" May Belle exclaimed after she turned and saw Dorothy grinning from ear to ear, staring at her hands. She lightly touched the crystal, setting the rainbows to dancing. "Wasn't that nice of someone to leave me such a magical gift?" She walked over to Dorothy and set her hand atop Dorothy's. They watched the red, green and purplish arches sway back and forth across their fingers.

"Brings some happy life to the ugly age spots, wouldn't you say?"

May Belle patted her friend's hand while she chuckled. "Thank you, Dorothy."

"For what?"

"For the crystal."

"What makes you think it was from me?"

"The Merle Norman powder box was a dead giveaway."

"I guess there's no fooling an old fooler, huh?"

"I guess not."

Dorothy pulled her eyes away from their hands and looked at May Belle. "How about we say a few extra prayers for each other this week, since we're now bonded by rainbows?"

"You know I always pray for you, Dorothy."

"And I for you. But it never hurts to double up. And truth be told, I have a hunch I'm going to need all the extra prayers I can get. I can't talk about it, May Belle, but there's something brewing and it could be mighty big if it boils over." Dorothy bit her lower lip, her eyes revealing the depth of her concern, especially to someone who knew her so well.

"I'll pray and you just think *rainbows,* okay?" May Belle said. "God just loves giving us rainbows to remind us about His love. Yes, I'll pray, and you pray, and we'll *both* give thanks for rainbows!"

Josh stepped off the late bus scowling. He'd held his cheery fake smile as long as he could; now he was all to himself and it was time to let his wounds, confusion, anger. . . . He wasn't even sure *what* all emotions were jumbled up inside of him, but they needed breathing space, and he'd already learned that the farm was just the place to vent them. Wandering from side to side to kick a rock here and there, he rambled up the two-track gravel lane with the grass down the middle, stopping to study the sway of the trees whose fingers were laced together above him as they dropped the first fading leaves into the soft breeze. How could it be that yesterday he was on top of the world and today he felt so trampled?

He started to head straight toward the barn, a private cavern of a welcoming space, then remembered with a *Gheesh!* of disgust that he needed to report in to Sergeant Mom. He also wanted to check his e-mail. Maybe there'd be a newsy note from Alex that would cheer him up. He opened the door to the small, enclosed back porch, went up the few stairs to the interior back door, then entered the kitchen. "Joshua Matthew Kinney reporting in for lock-down!" he hollered, slamming his heavy backpack onto the kitchen counter, peeling off his jacket and tossing it across a kitchen chair, then moving straight for the fridge to see what he might pop into his mouth. Nothing. *Is she ever going to go shopping?*

He rifled through a couple cabinets and retrieved a sleeve of crackers from the only box that didn't smack of the tasteless stuff his mom always harped was more nutritious than these "fat-laden, empty carbohydrates." Turning back to the fridge, he grabbed a can of cola, then slowly went up the creaky stairs. When his left foot reached the third step from the top, several times he rocked his weight on and off again, taking small pleasure in the wooden stair he realized made the loudest, lowest-pitch groaning sound.

"I'm in the Chaos Room, Josh." The tone in Katie's voice had echoed his own voice's terseness when he'd arrived. He noticed down the hall that the door to the Chaos Room was closed. Feeling no need to open it, he went straight into his room. He set down the soda can and crackers on his desk and turned on his computer, taking a few minutes to crank up his CD player and plop on his bed until the computer had gone through its booting-up rigors. YES! He had mail!

Dear Josh-o, whoever that is. I know who Josh and the Joshmeister are. "They" are my friend. Josh-o is somebody I don't know. Guess you've just gotten too cool for me, man. Write me when you're somebody I know who might be wondering how things are with me, on occasion. Alex. (Notice that is not Alex-o.)

Josh felt punched in the gut. What was wrong with everybody? And not a single note from Dorothy, who he suddenly realized he hadn't spoken to — or e-mailed — for quite some time. He turned up the CD player another notch, hurled himself spread-eagle on his bed and stared at the ceiling. Okay, maybe he'd been a *little* full of himself lately. *But gheesh! Isn't it about time I have a turn?*

He lurched up from his bed, grabbed the soda and crackers and nearly ran down the stairs, through the house and out the back door. Rather than go around to the incline that led to the massive top barn door, he entered through the closer ground-level door and shut the world out behind him, stopping a moment to allow his eyes to adjust to the darkness while inhaling the ancient earthiness. Since moving to Crooked Creek Farm, he'd discovered a ladder in one of the old stalls that led to the top of the barn. He put the can of soda in his pocket and held the sleeve of crackers between his teeth as he ascended the old ladder rungs and arrived upstairs, the flapping sound of pigeons' wings greeting him. The top of the ladder came out right next to what had been Dorothy's favorite spot. Sliding open the small back barn door, squinting to allow his vision to embrace the light, he sat down on the wooden plank floor, legs dangling over the edge to the outside world, and opened the can. After a few hearty guzzles, he peeled back the paper to the sleeve of crackers and popped them into his mouth two at a time. A drink of soda, a few more crackers. It was a cycle he repeated until everything he'd brought with him was gone. He swung one leg up floor level and leaned back on the doorframe, letting the other leg continue to dangle. He closed his eyes and felt a few sunrays splash over his face as they darted through the swiftly moving clouds. Since he'd left his jacket in his room and the temperature had dropped somewhat, he considered how good the rays felt against his otherwise cool body.

"Cool." He wished he hadn't thought about that word again. "Too cool for me" is what Alex had accused him of being. *Well, maybe now I am too cool for you, Alex!* He stood up, closed the door, descended the ladder and walked with ever-swifter steps down past the field toward Crooked Creek, which was about a quarter-of-a-mile jaunt. The smell of fall was in the air; Landers, whose farm was right down the road, must have been burning something. By the time he was close to Weeping Willy, Woodsy and Willoway, the names Dorothy had given the largest trees near the swimmin' hole, he was running full bore. Without breaking stride, he launched himself up to the first climbing branch in Woodsy and challenged himself to get to the top faster than he'd ever made it before. Winded, he perched in the crook of the highest branches he felt assured would support his weight, and looked down on the rushing waters below. Although Dorothy told him kids throughout the ages, including herself, had jumped into the swimmin' hole carved in the hairpin turn directly below Woodsy's longest, strongest arm, he knew he was now too high and too heavy to engage in that kind of dramatics. Tempting as the idea might be, even as chilly as it was, what he imagined, were he to try it, was his body drilling right through the creek bottom clear up to his neck and him drowning in the muck, crawdads crawling into his ears and out his nose.

By the time he'd caught his breath, like the speeding waters below him, slices of the day's events hastily began to flash through his mind. Try as he might to just be in the moment, in the tree, the music of the waters, the fragrance of fall . . . all he kept hearing was Kevin's voice slamming into his ears.

"Okay, Josh-o, *now* you get to know who I've asked to the dance!"

"Oh, so mystery woman said yes, huh?"

"Not only did she say yes to going to the dance, but I'm hoping her yes trend keeps up long into the night. She's got the hottest little bod I've noticed for, well, at least two days." He winked, banged Josh on the back and began laughing like a lunatic.

As had previously happened on the basketball court, Josh was not pleased with Kevin's off-color innuendo, but like before, he smiled on the outside anyway. "So? Who is the lucky woman?" Josh asked when he finally found his tongue.

"So? So you wanna know, huh? How about I give you a few hints. Does the word blonde help?"

Josh looked to the left and right and saw at least ten blondes headed between classes in each direction. "Helps me to know she's blonde."

"What if I said baseball?"

"She plays ball for Hethrow High?"

"Nope."

"Okay, I give up."

"Let's just say I'm hoping she is *indeed* a Wild Musketeer!"

Josh stared at Kevin as his mind swiftly pulled together just *who* Kevin was talking about. His skin prickled and his chest tightened quickly enough to squeeze out a flash of resentment that catapulted straight to his mouth. "You asked Shelby? And she said yes?"

"You got it! But my man, you sound a little intense. Or are you just getting over the shock?"

"Why target Shelby? I thought you guys were friends from way back." There wasn't a hint of teasing in his voice.

"Target? Whoa!" Kevin leaned back and held up his hands in front of him, palms toward Josh. "Yes, we were friends, *are* friends — although if you haven't noticed, she doesn't look like a tomboy any more. She's all grown up, real nice." He made an hour-glass gesture with his hands, then stuffed them into his pockets. "So have you asked anybody yet, Josh-o?"

"Tell me you're going to be nice to her!"

"You haven't even told me who it is you've invited yet! How can I make that promise? Chill, dude."

"I'm talking about Shelby. Tell me you're going to be nice to Shelby!" The tone in Josh's voice was nothing short of combative.

Kevin took a giant step toward Josh, who didn't flinch. They stood nearly nose-to-nose. He studied Josh's face, leaned his head to the right and said, "I think I've struck a nerve here with Mr. Josh-o. Were you going to ask her to the dance?" After a long silence, he repeated his question. "Were you?"

Josh weighed his response, then said, "It doesn't matter if I was going to ask her or not — and frankly, I hadn't even thought about it yet. Just don't *mess* with Shelby."

Kevin wasn't used to being talked to like this by anyone. He blinked a couple times, as though clearing his vision would clarify what his ears had heard. Then he swallowed. Then he leaned in even closer to Josh's face and spoke through a clenched jaw. "I've known Shelby for a long time; you've known her for a few months. If I didn't know better, I might think you were jealous or at least really cared about her. But I haven't heard you mention her name for weeks. I haven't seen you paying any attention to her at all, in fact, and since you haven't called dibs, I consider her fair game. I will treat her the same as I treat any girl, which is to say I will treat her how she *lets* me treat her."

Josh was grinding his back teeth together, staring hard at Kevin. Kevin leaned back on his heels, relaxing his posture. "You might want to lighten up just a touch, Josh-o. Much easier to maintain friendships that way. I'll assume you're just having a bad day and that by tomorrow you'll have your testosterone under control." Before Josh could say another word, Kevin whirled on his heels and stormed down the hall. Josh's insides were so knotted up that his ears were ringing. He didn't even notice Shelby, let alone hear her "Hello, Josh!" as she zinged by him, so intent was he on burning a hole in the back of Kevin's head with his thoughts.

"I've had it with you, you stuck-up, ignoring, ignoramus." Although Shelby said it under her breath, she meant every word.

Things were hopping at Harry's Grill. Lester K. Biggs, the grill's sole owner, cook and waiter, was flipping bacon, cracking eggs, pouring coffee and ringing up customers as fast as his brain and appendages could handle them. Lester worked the griddle with his back toward the U-shaped counter, but you could be sure he neither missed a conversation nor failed to weigh in on it, no matter how many words and spatulas were airborne at the time. This morning the hot buzz among the regulars was the day's headline in the *Partonville Press* that read "Partonville to Celebrate Its Centennial Plus 30!"

To most, the entire notion seemed more odd than anything else. Acting Mayor Gladys McKern had been liberally quoted in the article (no surprise there) as she made pronouncements — and that is the exact word she used — about the "gala" and the "pride in the town's history" and the "importance of marking such momentous anniversaries." Sitting at the U this morning, Gladys had fully expected to be cheered on and congratulated for her idea. Instead, she hadn't had a bite of her eggs since she'd been spending all her time trying to *bolster* excitement while whisking away the negative banter, which, frankly, she was beginning to get sick of.

Discussions were flying this way and that about the short amount of time left to organize any kind of celebration worth its salt, what with the Pumpkin Festival and dance just around the corner. "I thought official celebrations only came in increments of twenty-fives," Lester said over his shoulder to Arthur. "You know, like one hundred, then one hundred and twenty-five, then one hundred and fifty. . . . And come to think about it, I don't recollect anyone even mentioning our one-hundred and twenty-fifth, although we did things up quite big for our centennial, even going so far as to bring in that dandy of a magician, from Champaign he was, if I do recall correctly," he said, skidding a plate heaping with three eggs, fried breakfast potatoes, three pieces of bacon and two slices of highly buttered rye bread in front of Arthur.

"Too bad that magician didn't go and make Gladys disappear before we went and made her mayor, huh?" Arthur said, winking at Lester. Of course, he said it just loudly enough for Gladys to hear him. He quickly spun his stool straight toward her, raised his coffee mug in the air as if to toast her and said, "Just kidding, Queen Lady. Just kidding."

"You know, Arthur, some days your stale humor is just disgusting." Gladys straightened her spine, pumped up her voice a couple decibels and swiveled her stool toward him. "If as many people cared as much about this town as I do," she paused and turned a quarter turn more so as to make sure those behind her could also hear, "maybe it would be booming rather than dying." She slid off her stool and stood. "I'd like to challenge some of you to get on the Centennial Plus Thirty committee and put yourselves to work as hard as you . . . ," and she stopped here a fraction of a second to look straight back at Arthur, "flap your jaws." She then raised her voice to nearly shouting level. *It's time we take a stand and declare our worth!* She seated herself, swung back toward her plate and took a bite of her cold eggs. "Figures!" was all she said before wadding up her napkin, tossing it atop her uneaten food, paying her bill and storming out the door.

Tears threatened to sprout in her eyes, but with determination, she emotionally jackhammered the negative voices from her head. *In spite of these whining inhabitants, under my able direction, this town will live — even if I have to do everything by myself!*

Back at Harry's, eyes flashed from one person to another as the truth and challenge of Gladys's statement sank in. The town *was* dying and poised to be gobbled up by Hethrow. Low murmurs now accompanied the eating, and folks found themselves at least flirting with the idea that perhaps a celebration to let the surrounding towns, especially Hethrow, know they cared about themselves *was* in order. The debates were cut short when Maggie Malone entered, waving a copy of the *Partonville Press* in the air. "Hey, everybody! Did you see my picture in today's paper?"

One of the twice-weekly *Partonville Press's* newer columns was the one Sharon Teller, the *Press's* young ace reporter, had proposed during an editorial meeting a few months earlier: "Meet Your Neighbor." She'd pointed out to Harold Crab, the editor, that it was amazing to her that she had lived in a town this small for her entire life and, if truth be told, she really didn't know that much about *any* of the residents who weren't her direct relatives. "Mr. Crab, I believe spontaneous, surprise interviews — you know, ones with just a few chatty and off-the-cuff questions along with some personal background — could help bring us closer together as a community. Maybe encourage us to reach out to folks we don't know as well. Then we'll run a head shot with each interview so people can recognize each other." Harold thought it was a fine idea, and the spot had been launched. Today's "Meet Your Neighbor" interview had taken place between the time Gladys had told Harold about the Centennial Plus 30 and today's edition, so before many in town even knew about the event.

Today's neighbor was, of course, none other than Maggie Malone, who had been the first to come out of the post office where Sharon had positioned herself. When Sharon started to explain the Centennial Plus 30 to Maggie, Sharon was astounded to learn Maggie had already heard about it, straight from the horse's mouth. (This, of course, revealed Sharon's youth since everybody knew most all news either originated at Harry's or Maggie's or the barbershop or the tavern.) When Maggie was asked what she thought about the celebration, she'd replied, "I'm *always* for celebrating *anything!* A Centennial Plus Thirty seems like a good excuse and opportunity for the ladies of Partonville to come on into La Feminique Hair Salon & Day Spa to get a new hairdo for the bash. That's La Feminique Hair Salon & Day Spa, located just a block off the square. The clock is ticking, so hurry on in. Appointments are not always necessary but good hair is!" Sharon thought it was possibly the second-worst column since "Meet Your Neighbor" had begun running, but Maggie was delighted at the opportunity to receive free advertising, since it seemed to her she'd paid plenty over the years to keep her shop's name in front of folks — never mind her clientele never grew or changed, unless one of them sadly died. Young folks traveled to Hethrow to the upscale salons with lots of buzz, aisles of stations, endless shelves of product and rock music blaring in the background.

As luck would have it, the accompanying photo was taken the same day Maggie's eyebrows had gone on all crooked, but at least the picture was blurry enough so that nobody could tell. Sharon, once again embarrassed by having her byline appear with the column, was sure, however, that no column would ever be worse than the premiere had been.

During that first editorial meeting, in order to keep the surprise element intact and to keep the column from becoming politicized, she and Harold had agreed that when she had a moment during her work day, she'd decide where her location would be: anywhere from right outside the *Press*'s doorstep, to the doughnut shop, to By George's station, to My Store or Wal-Mart or the back pew. When she arrived on location, the first person she saw would become the subject of the column, if they agreed to have their words put in print, which many would not. As luck (or bad luck) would have it, Cora Davis was the first to walk out of Richardson's Rexall Drugs after Sharon had posted herself there with excitement in her belly, a tape recorder in her hand and a camera around her neck.

Although Sharon had mixed emotions when she saw Cora — Cora being long on both gossip and wind — she at least knew she had a talker. When she held the microphone up to Cora's mouth and said she'd like to interview her for a new spot in the *Partonville Press,* Cora pushed the microphone to the little gadget aside and said, "I'd love to talk to you! *You.* I'd love to talk to Y-O-U, not a machine!" Sharon put her tape recorder in her handbag and pulled out her steno. *Whatever it takes.* (Sharon would quickly learn that the tape recorder was not her friend for Partonville interviews since the sight of it seemed to clam people up, aside from Maggie Malone, who had practically grabbed it out of her hand to get her mouth right up to it in order to make sure she got in a plug for her shop.) Sharon then asked Cora to give her a little background about herself.

Eighteen minutes later, Cora was still talking; she'd barely gotten to her high school days. So far, Sharon had only deemed a few tidbits worthy of newspaper column inches. Sharon finally interrupted and said she thought she had "quite enough" for the short column, although truth be told, she'd had quite enough of Cora. It was then Sharon realized that getting basic stats like name and years as a resident, then asking for an opinion on a current event, would probably make for more interesting reading than gathering terminally boring life stories.

When she had asked Cora what she thought about our country's peace-making efforts, Cora stopped talking. Cold turkey. She just clammed up for about a minute — which is a long time when nothing is happening — although Sharon assumed Cora was formulating her thoughtful opinion. When Cora finally spoke, all she said was, "I thought we were talking about *me*." Sharon sighed, but being quick on her feet said, "Oh, but we *are,* Cora! That's why I'm so interested to know what YOU think about our country's approach to bringing peace to Iraq." Silence for another minute, then an answer. "Oh. In that case, I think if the world would like to see peace in action, they should have been at my. . . ." Cora rambled on and on about her Uncle Duke and Aunt Pam and their stellar efforts to pull feuding factions together at the last family reunion. Sharon's eyes glazed over and her hand pretended to write shorthand on her steno, although in reality she was just scribbling endless loops of circles of every size with an occasional "blah, blah, blah" thrown in to entertain herself until Cora ran out of breath — which Sharon hoped was before sundown.

When Sharon had returned to the office looking somewhat like a deflated air mattress, Harold had asked her how it went. "Mr. Crab, let me just say two words: Cora Davis. Need I say more?" In an uncommon-yet-fatherly gesture, Harold Crab then gave Sharon Teller a quick hug, his sympathetic silence speaking volumes. Sharon would have rather skipped the debut of "Meet Your Neighbor," but since they'd agreed that there would be no bias, the premiere column went down in Sharon's personal history book as a supreme egg-on-face experience.

Your Neighbor: Cora Davis. Lifetime Partonville resident. Says, "Ladies don't tell their age." Loves living in Partonville and sharing her stories as well as learning everyone else's.

Question: What is your stand on the USA's peace-making efforts in Iraq?

Answer: She is for peace and has seen it

demonstrated in her family. She'd love to talk to you about her thoughts.

Tidbit: Cora can often be found frequenting Harry's Grill. Look for her in the front window table.

After Harold read Sharon's copy he said, "Translation: Cora Davis is an old, lifetime Partonville gossip who will talk endlessly to anyone about anything, then repeat everything she says and hears, just not always exactly the way it (a) happened or (b) she heard it. She sits in the window at Harry's so she doesn't miss a trick.

"Nice, kind, self-disciplined job, Sharon!"

In the accompanying photo, Cora's mouth was wide open.

8

Katie was breathless from dragging the clothes rack in the Chaos Room to the opposite wall. She needed to make room for the exercise equipment, or at least clear enough space to see what, if any of it, would fit. She was determined to get a mini gym set up before she became a complete slug. Although she'd toyed with the idea of getting Edward Showalter, the man who had done such a good job rehabbing her aunt's house, to build her an executive-level, heated and air-conditioned gym in the barn, she'd finally ruled against it. What if she decided to sell the farm after all? She'd never recoup her money since the whole farm would obviously be bulldozed and developed.

Even though the Chaos Room wasn't quite readied yet, she felt a huge relief to finally have Aunt Tess's boxes disbursed and the center floor space opened. She'd tossed most of Aunt Tess's papers, kept a few medical records and put the letters in a ski-boot box she kept on the upper shelf in her closet. "Out of sight, out of mind," her mom used to say. She'd determined she'd already spent far too much time on them and resolved to keep herself from obsessing.

While she stacked a few storage boxes and set two more work suits, four pairs of shoes and two objects of expensive art she'd never *really* liked into the pile for the Now and Again Resale shop — although she might give Jessica first shot at the items — *Katie's dad . . . at least see . . . his eyes . . . from a distance . . . covenant . . . CW . . . TW . . .* yammered through her mind. No matter her resolve, her mind had a mind of its own. While continuing to work, she mentally twiddled with the Core Four initials, concluding that her Aunt Tess — Tessa Martha Walker — was TW, since she was clearly in on the covenant. And since her mom's maiden name had also been Walker, then CW must be Clarice Walker. At least that seemed like a safe bet since both of the women clearly were in on it. Both of these women were now gone, taking with them whatever it was they knew. *DW. Must be another relative, but I sure don't know one* with those initials. DC . . . haven't a clue. *Two down, two to go . . .* A dated leather jacket to the resale pile, a wooden wastebasket to Josh's room, a picture downstairs to the living room. *Might work with my decor. Have to ask Jessica.*

She surveyed the room, stepping off floor space and spreading her arms to at least form a vague measurement as to how much room she'd have — or not — for the treadmill. She grabbed a pencil and paper from her bedroom, took a few notes, donned her jacket and walked to the barn to see what, if any, of the miscellaneous items temporarily stored there might fit. *Be ruthless!* she thought on the way up the slope to the big barn doors. *Any piece of equipment that won't fit doesn't stay. And what if none of it fits? Then join a health club in Hethrow. Bet they've got several to choose from.*

Several times throughout the day she'd picked up the phone to call Jessica or Dorothy, then set it back down again, realizing she needed to stay on task. And truth be told, between her goals to get this project done and her haunting speculations about the Core Four's secret — about *her* — she wasn't in the mood for small talk.

Dearest Dorothy, aka Outtamyway,
I know I haven't phoned or emailed you lately, but Help! I've lost myself! (Will explain later.) Let me know when I can stop by and I'll see if Sergeant Mom, aka She Who Yells, will let me borrow the car, since she won't get me one of my own. (Hey, how about next time you see her you put in a good word for that, okay? Too bad The Tank's tanked!) Whenever we can get together, I'll pick you up and we'll speed down a few roads. (Nothing like bribery!)
Joshmeister

Dear Lost Joshmeister (although I see your new email address says Josh-o),
I can't imagine how you've already lost yourself since you are too young for Alzheimer's, but I'm rearin' to listen. Funny how you've lost yourself just when I've been found out! (Won't explain later . . . I don't think. Although maybe I'll have to. Yes, probably will — *absolutely* will, maybe, now that I think about it — but not right now.)

Since I can't go much of anyplace without a car, and the only things I go to on a regular basis are band practice and to get my pink scalp "done," give me a call, an email or drop by. If I'm here, I'm all *yours*! And boy oh boy, speeding anywhere sounds great, as long as we can have the windows open and Sheba comes with us, but what I could really use is a hearty dose of Crooked Creek Farm! Maybe you could speed us there?

As for putting in a good word about you and a car, I haven't caught a glimpse of you *or* your mom lately. Maybe the two of you have plucked the creek plumb out of crawdads by now? However, I'm sorry to hear it sounds like you've been "at it" again. Like they say on the television (although I imagine that phrase has already come and gone), Whassup with that? (You should hear how that comes out of my mouth when my partial plate isn't seated right!)

Looking forward to a fast ride and a good visit, Dorothy, who feels more in the way than out of it lately.
PS Sheba says HI!

Dear Outtamyway (sorry, Dear Intheway doesn't work for me, plus you could never be that) and Sheba,
BAD NEWS! Won't see you right away to find out what you're not going to tell

me yet (okay, you've got my curiosity pumped) since Mom said we're going to Chicago this weekend. She said her roots need to be done and she needs a city fix. Mumbled something about the deli (don't know why; all she eats is tasteless stuff anyway), the city energy and a "distraction from obsessing about the core four," whatever that is. Sounds like one of her video workouts.

Will contact you soon after we return and I can escape,
Joshmeister
PS Notice email address is changed back to Joshmeister. Forget Josh-o. He's lost too, for good hopefully.

Dear Joshmeister,
No wonder you're lost: sounds like there's been too many of you to keep track of! HA!

Although it's bad news for me we can't get together (but I understand), it's good news for you and your best friend Alex since I'm sure you're anxious to see each other. Won't you two have a big time catching up! Please tell him I said hello! Maybe he could come visit for the Pumpkin Festival or our "grand" 130-year celebration . . . or . . . *whatever*?

Lord willing, I'll be here when you get back, and will hear from you when I hear from you.
Peace and grins,
Dorothy

Josh started to reply that Alex didn't even know he was coming to Chicago, but decided he'd rather not get into that. Truth was, he *was* anxious to see Alex, but he wasn't sure if Alex would want to see him. Since they no longer owned the brownstone near Alex's home, he wasn't even sure where he and his mom would be staying during the trip. He figured odds weren't high he'd accidentally run into Alex, though.

After his runaway visit with Woodsy, just out of curiosity, Josh had spent some time going back through copies of his "sent" e-mails to assure himself he hadn't turned into the jerk Alex implied he had. As if his day hadn't been bad enough, he'd discovered that Alex had been right: every one of his e-mails was all about him and how "popular" he'd become, how swell Kevin was, how girls seemed to dig city guys, and on and on. They sounded more like Kevin talking than himself. Not one single time had he asked Alex what was up with him or commented on anything Alex had told him, which had become less and less. Not once. And not once had he even mentioned Shelby either. *GREAT! Kevin was right, too.*

Perhaps even more troublesome was the fact that now *Kevin* was taking Shelby to the dance. When *was* the last time he'd talked to her himself? Shelby, who had befriended him and dazzled him with her smile. Shelby, who had introduced him around to everyone, only for him to leave her in his "popular" dust, falling prey to the likes of Kevin! He held his right hand up to his forehead, pointing his index finger straight up and his thumb at a ninety-degree angle, forming an L. "You, Josh, *are* a loser."

"You did WHAT, woman?"

"You heard me, Arthur Landers. After all these decades of marriage, I know when you hear me and when you don't, and when you don't, it's usually because you don't want to — although your hearing is no doubt NOT" (and she yelled that, just to prove her point) "what it used to be either. And since this is one of those don't-want-to times, I will repeat myself, even though I know good and well you *heard* me. I said I signed you up to be on the Centennial Plus Thirty committee since what else have you

141

got to do now that you don't have The Tank to mess with — aside from torment *me?*"

"I got my La-Z-Boy. I got my TV and football season. I got you to put up with, and right this minute, that's bout more than I kin stand, woman!"

Jessie harrumphed around the kitchen, clearing the lunch dishes from the meal Arthur had not helped her prepare, and the table he had not helped her set, and the dishes he would not help her do. Parking his butt in that dang La-Z-Boy was about all he seemed interested in tackling lately. By the time she'd put the dishes in the drainer and wiped down the table, she'd worked up a full head of steam. She marched into the living room, grabbed the remote control out of his hand, turned off the television, then stood looking down at his reclining self.

"Here's the deal, Arthur, and I'm only going to say this once: you have *got* to do more than move from this chair to Harry's and back. When you came home this morning and told me what Gladys said about folks putting their actions where their mouths were, or something like that, I thought, you know, it's time Arthur did just that. And you know what, Arthur?" She didn't wait for an answer. "You would be a good person to have on that committee since I reckon you know about as much about this town as anyone who's lived in it as long as you have — and those folks are dying by the minute."

"Now jist a gol' dern minute!" he said, snapping down his leg rest and planting his hands on the chair arms to boost himself up, since his knees weren't what they used to be, especially after all the bending over, kneeling and crawling around under cars he'd done over the decades. About halfway up he said, "Why I ain't even . . ."

Jessie reached out her hand and gently pushed on his chest, causing his back side to thunk back down in the chair. "I don't give a hoot what you *ain't even* because what you *are* is going to that meeting, and it starts at seven P.M. tomorrow in the hospitality room down at church, so you still got thirty-six hours to get your precious chair-time in." She disappeared out of the living room before he could respond. By the time he pried himself out of his chair, he heard the back door slam. It wasn't long after that he heard the sounds of something whapping into the side of the old outhouse. Throwing things at the outhouse was what she did when she was as mad as a hornet, especially if Arthur had retreated there to get away from her when they were in the middle of one of their storms, which blew in quite often. Since in her heyday she'd been a semi-pro softball catcher with the best pickoff arm in the traveling league, and since she now pitched for the Wild Musketeers (like Arthur, her knees weren't what they used to be, what with all that squatting), she needed to keep her arm in shape, so she'd hurl anything at hand. This time it was a wad of acorns she'd collected from the ground on her way to her target.

"I'm the one who oughta be throwing somethin'!" Arthur mumbled to himself. He settled back in his La-Z-Boy, lifted the leg rest, picked up the remote and turned on a soap opera. Although he never watched those types of "stories," after a few minutes of viewing the likes of the troubles those folks were having, he decided the whole world had gone plumb goofy.

9

May Belle had arrived at church early to get some coffee going and set out a plate of her oatmeal raisin cookies. When she'd read that a Centennial Plus 30 committee was forming and that all interested parties should show up at church by 7:00 P.M. Thursday, she didn't ask a single question or even let anyone know she was interested; she just fired up her oven and began lining up her ingredients. She always kept her flour, baking soda, baking powder and salt stored right next to one another since she so often sifted combinations of them together with her noisy old metal hand sifter whose blades whirred round and round as she cranked the handle.

"I have no idea how many might show up tonight, Earl," she said as she moved a few things aside on her counter, clearing space for the procedure, "but it never hurts to have extra. Funny how committee members are more likely to keep showing up when they know there'll be food in front of them. Yes, nothing like a little sweet enticement." She laughed, although Earl didn't understand at what. Just the same, he loved to hear the lilt of his mother's laughter, which always made him smile. "I don't imagine I'll be able to add much more in terms of a contribution, but I guess every little bit will help since time is short. Of course, if they decide to have a bake sale, I can contribute to that. . . . Would you please get out my cookie sheets, honey? And grab me a stick of butter from the ice box, and the box of raisins out of the top cabinet over there," she said, nodding her head in the appropriate directions while tying the long strings of her faded blue gingham apron in a neat bow behind her back. Although it was really her laundry day, no amount of routine would or could ever interfere with the opportunity to bake. She didn't need to look at recipes; they seemed to come engraved in her memory along with her gift for creating new ones. She loved experimenting with ingredients, adding a pinch of this and a dab of that — as long as they were this-and-that staples she usually stocked, since funds were always tight.

One of her favorite things to add "just a

bit of" to many baking recipes was coconut. She'd chop it up into morsels tiny enough so it couldn't even be recognized. She even once, being low on crackers and plentiful on coconut, found herself stirring it into a meatloaf mixture, right along with eggs, onions and a little green pepper, because if Earl saw her adding the green pepper, he'd say he wasn't hungry. If he didn't catch her, he never said a word, not even if the green specks were right there in the meatloaf when she served it. Although May Belle hadn't minded the hint of sweet coconut flavor in her meatloaf experiment, she decided it hadn't done much for the texture, and she'd quickly added crackers to her grocery list.

"Who's in here?" Gladys's voice echoed down the church hall after she'd entered at 6:45 and noticed the lights to the hospitality room were already on.

"Just me, dear! May Belle! Getting the coffee going!"

Gladys came around the corner and shivered. "Now *that* will taste good this chilly evening. How close is it to being ready?" She rubbed her hands together and acted as if she'd been expecting May Belle all along, although truthfully, she'd had no idea.

"Just another minute. Sounds like it's on its last blurps before the light comes on."

"I'm going to go hang my coat up in the narthex. I'll be right back. I'd like to get this meeting started on time — at least I *hope* enough people show up to call it a meeting." After her horrible morning at Harry's yesterday and her huffy exit, she wondered how many they'd be. She snatched a cookie off the doily-decorated plate in the middle of the table, glancing over her shoulder, somewhat relieved that May Belle hadn't caught her. *Better get one before Dorothy and her sweet tooth arrive.* While she was busy walking and staring at her teeth marks in the cookie, trying to detect if May Belle had snuck in any surprise ingredients to what otherwise looked to be an ordinary oatmeal raisin cookie, she was happy to see Sharon Teller and Eugene Casey, owner and undertaker at Casey's Funeral Home, walk in together. They were chatting up a storm.

"Go right on in! We've got refreshments just about ready."

"Refreshments?" Eugene asked. As soon as Gladys was out of earshot he said to Sharon, "This might be better than I expected!"

Sharon set her briefcase down on one of the chairs surrounding the table. "Cookies! May Belle must be on the committee!"

"Well, I'm not sure about that," May Belle said, arriving around the partition between the kitchen area and the meeting room. She set a tray of steaming coffee mugs filled right up to the brim onto the table. "I am on cookie patrol! Go right on and help yourselves. Napkins are right there and I'll be back with the cream, sugar and sweetener. Oh, and a few spoons," she said after surveying the setting. "As for actually being on the committee, that's debatable. Are you here this evening on official newspaper duty, Sharon?" she asked, wiping her hands down the front of her best apron.

"Sort of. I'll take a few notes, no doubt; can't help myself. I'm sure we'll at least run a blurb about the formation of the committees, report contact names and such. But mostly I just want to take part. Besides, my social calendar hasn't exactly been filled up lately with much more than band practice, so, why not!"

"Perty thing the likes of you ain't got a filled-up social calendar? What's a matter with these dern fellas today?" Arthur stood in the doorway to the room, not really wanting to enter, but happy to see Sharon

Teller's cute little self, giving her a longer-than-usual once-over. He could be a hopeless old flirt, even though Sharon knew he was harmless. In fact, she felt rather flattered by his attention, even if he was only teasing her. It was nice to be thought of as a "cute little self" by anyone, even if that anyone was wearing coveralls and a baseball cap that looked as old as his eighty-plus years.

"Arthur Landers, you old codger! Will you please stop gawking and get out of the doorway," Gladys demanded rather than asked. "You're old enough to be her great-grandfather. And what on earth are you doing here? You're about the last person I expected to see."

"That contrarian woman of mine done signed me up, that's what I'm a doin' here."

"Although I'd like to see this evening end with many commitments to hard work, and maybe even get subcommittee assignments in place, we've had no sign-ups. I don't know what you're talking about." Pause. "Unless . . ." Her voice halted as she put the pieces together, then realized Jessie must have cornswaggled her husband. ("Don't you mean hornswoggled, Gladys?" Folks had tried to correct her for years, but she was sure they were all wrong.) "Why, Arthur

150

Landers! I do believe you've been had! Good for Jessie!" Gladys nearly laughed herself silly. She couldn't think of anyone she'd rather see cornswaggled than Arthur!

Arthur started to turn on his heels and leave, his face contorting into thunder.

"Here, Arthur. Simmer down and come sit by me," Sharon said, pulling out the chair next to her. She figured her invitation might help him save face as well as cool his jets.

Arthur looked at Sharon, then at everyone else in the room, then back at Sharon. "Well, now," he said with a newborn slyness in his voice, "maybe Jessie's the one who'll git had in the end!" His hand tipped the bill of his baseball cap at Sharon. "Ma'am," he said, acknowledging the young thing he was parking himself next to.

"This must be the Centennial Plus Thirty meeting!" Jessica's voice was filled with enthusiasm as she entered, Sarah Sue strapped to her chest in one of those cuddly contraptions, a sprawling mass of sweater-covered arms and chunky legs reaching forward like a spider searching for the fly. Paul followed close behind.

"Well, look at you! Aren't you a handsome family!" May Belle said, first removing Sarah Sue's little hand-knit cap and gently

151

kissing the top of her head, then smiling at Paul, then scurrying to get some more mugs of coffee filled up and delivered. She also unwrapped the second plate of cookies and brought them to the table.

"Paul and me, well, we decided we needed to get out and do something together for a change," she said as they seated themselves around the table. She looked at Gladys, who was staring in an unkindly fashion at Sarah Sue, whose fist was jammed into her mouth, a long string of drool dangling from her lower lip. "I figure if Sarah Sue starts acting up, one of us can just take her home."

"Good," Gladys said. She yanked her blazer back down over her bosom, noticing with chagrin that it must have been bunched up since she took off her coat. She glanced at her giant wristwatch face. "Six fifty-nine. Let's all get seated," she said, straightening her ever-present bronze nametag, reminding everyone that she was the mayor — like they could ever possibly forget that little fact. When she heard the church door open, she expected it would be Dorothy, surprised she hadn't already arrived. Surely, she'd need to be getting her twenty-nine-cents-worth into the doings. That was okay, though, because Gladys wanted to talk to her about something anyway. However, instead of Dorothy, Doc Streator sauntered in.

"Good evening, ladies and gentlemen. Looks like I made it in the nick of time."

"Well, howdy, Doc," Arthur said with enthusiasm. "Reckin it's been a long time since I saw you! Glad to know yur still alive and a-kickin', Doc."

"Arthur Landers, you old devil. It *has* been a long time. And I'm glad to know, since you don't ever come see your good doctor, that *you* haven't croaked. Then again, I imagine if a person has the power to stay alive on spit and vinegar alone, you're likely to live forever." The two of them laughed a comfortable laugh, genuinely glad to see each other.

Doc Streator had recently brought a young internist into his practice, which afforded him the ability to start taking a little much-needed time off. Very little, but nonetheless a step in the right direction. For years he'd been good at prescribing rest and relaxation for his patients, but he hadn't been quite as good at taking it for himself. The needs of the townspeople had always overridden his desire to vacation. But now, nearing seventy-five and having outlived his wife, he knew it was time to call in reinforcements and spend more time with his grandchildren. Maybe even play more golf in the summer and become a winter snowbird for a week or so — or more, if the town took to the new doctor and things worked out all right. But in this transitional period, when folks were still leery of the young ("Why, he's no more than a kid!") new physician, the least he could do was to take some small steps toward getting involved with more personal things. Why not dip into the Centennial Plus 30?

"Please, folks, let's get this meeting under way. Of course, since we have no 'official' members yet," and Gladys made quotation marks in the air to make sure people got her drift, especially Arthur, who she snickered at once again, "we have no secretary to record our minutes, or sergeant at arms to keep us in order, or . . ."

"Sergeant at arms? Whatdaya think this is, Your Highness, the military?" Arthur said more than asked, interrupting her sentence. A quiet chuckle rippled through the room, although nobody dared release a full-blown laugh since Gladys had clearly not perceived Arthur's comment as a funny one.

Gladys eyeballed Arthur a good one, sucked in her cheeks, yanked down the bottom of her jacket which was already yanked down, measured her tone and looked around the room. "Arthur, everyone . . . I'm glad you've all come. I think it would be best if we try to stick to business so we can get out of here early, setting a good standard to follow for the rest of our meetings." Jessica's hand went up in the air. "Jessica?"

"Paul and I, or one or the other of us, might not always be able to come to all the meetings since we never know when we'll have too many check-ins at the motel or the baby might be cranky or sleeping. Is it okay if we just come when we can, whichever one of us can come, if it's not both of us when we can?" Gladys had always intimidated Jessica and Jessica hated the fact she knew she had just sounded like a blathering idiot. "What I mean is . . ."

"I understand, Jessica. I'm sure I can speak for all of us when I say we'll appreciate whatever help you two can give us. We don't want any cracks in our master plan, though, so just don't accept any more responsibility than you think you can handle, okay?" Jessica looked at Paul, who nodded his head in the affirmative. Jessica passed on the nod to Gladys.

"Good. Then let's move on. Let's begin by establishing our mission statement for the celebration. I've been working on a brief one I believe can also be used in advertising. 'Celebrating Our Roots.' "

Arthur leaned over toward Sharon and whispered, "Sounds like somethin' Maggie Malone might be agin, from the sounds of her spot about her shop in the paper." Sharon giggled.

"Did you have something to share, Arthur?" Gladys asked.

"Nope."

"Please, Arthur, let's stick to business. Does anyone have any comments about my suggestion?" The room was quiet as people first weighed the advisability of speaking up. Since most of them had heard what Arthur had said, it seemed impossible to think about anything but hair roots requiring attention. They needed a moment to reframe the suggestion and look at it objectively.

"I think it's a step in the right direction," Eugene said. "Seems like there ought to be more to it, though."

"Like what?" Gladys asked.

"Like . . . Like . . . 'Celebrating Our Roots; Welcoming Our Future.' "

"Sounds like a *great* headline to me," Sharon said with enthusiasm. She began scribbling in her notebook.

"I like it, too," Doc said. A murmur of agreement left them all looking at Gladys.

"Yes. It does have a nice sound. Thank you, Eugene. And it goes along with the forward and progressive image I'd like the surrounding communities to have about us, especially Hethrow. It also is the perfect setup for perhaps the most exciting thing I'd like to see implemented during our Centennial Plus Thirty, but we'll get to that later. Well, if I hear no objections then, here's what it will be."

She stood up from the table and disappeared into the hall, leaving everyone staring at the doorway shrugging their shoulders at one another. She returned in a moment carrying an easel with the flip chart the Sunday school teachers used, setting it up next to her chair. Then she left the room again, leaving those gathered staring at a very bad line drawing of the ark, or maybe a whale . . . but then again, upon further inspection, it might be John the Baptist or Jesus, if those squiggles were supposed to be eyes and a mouth.

Gladys returned with a giant red marking pen and flipped whatever or whoever it was over the back, revealing a clean page. She wrote on the flip chart in block letters:

A rush of pride and satisfaction rushed through her, causing her to light up like a glow stick and forge ahead with vigor.

"Okay, then. Next thing will be to establish a date. I recommend the same weekend as the Pumpkin Festival and dance since we already always draw such a good crowd for those festivities and we're so short on time before the snow starts to fly. It will give us a solid foundation to build on and the duo of festivities should draw new folks to Partonville as well. My only concern is that the Centennial Plus Thirty celebration doesn't get lost in the midst of pumpkin doings, but I think if we handle it properly, we can capitalize on some things that are already in place."

"I think before we can decide on a date," Doc said, "maybe we should consider what type of special activities or . . . Just what *is* it we're going to do to celebrate? I mean *how* are we planning on celebrating?" He'd voiced a question that had been at the top of everyone's minds.

"That is a fine question, Doc," Gladys

said. "Here's what I've been thinking." She flipped to another clean page on the flip chart, then uncapped her marker and wrote:

1) PUBLICITY, PUBLICITY, PUBLICITY!

"I can't think of anything more important than getting the word out that we *have* something to celebrate and that we are *proud* of it! If we work hard at press releases and cause enough buzz, we can hopefully even get the Hethrow *Daily Courier* to run a full feature article!"

Her head spun to Sharon Teller. "No offense, Sharon. Of course, the *Partonville Press* is of *utmost* importance to all of us. It's just that something in a major daily paper would be good." Sharon nodded her understanding; even she read the *Daily Courier* to find out what was going on in the greater area, not to mention get all the sale flyers for the discount stores.

2) HISTORY.

After bonking the marker to create the period, Gladys set the marker down in front of her, first on its end, then resting it on its side so it didn't fall over and roll to the floor. "I'd like to see us get some town history in print, you know, like the 'Meet Your Neighbor' column but with a few stats on Partonville."

"Meet Your Town," Sharon said. "I like it!"

"Brilliant!" Gladys was becoming more energized by the moment. "We have so many people who were born and raised here that I'd like to read about some of their family stories as well as tell my own, what with Jake and myself both having been mayors. That would make a nice tribute to his memory, too." She worked to keep her voice steady, feeling a surprise rush of longing for her husband. "Maybe print a book of oral histories, you know?"

Sharon recalled her brain-numbing interview with Cora Davis and started to say something, but thought better of it. Surely there were more interesting stories than Cora's, and she hoped one of them was the McKerns' since no doubt Gladys would, as mayor, claim premium space in any kind of a publication.

"I reckon I kin tell a few stories alright," Arthur said, "although I'm not sure some of the folks involved would want me a tellin' 'em."

"I reckon you could, Arthur," Eugene said. "I reckon a few folks I've buried the last decade alone just rolled over in their graves thinking about stories that could be told on them!" Everybody laughed but Gladys. Although she wanted to, she thought better of laughing at the dead, especially since it was the departed who had founded this town.

Jessica raised her hand again. "Yes, Jessica. You have something to say?" Gladys worked extra hard at being congenial to Jessica. After all, things were going her way, for a change.

"No, ma'am. I have a question." Everybody stared at her, waiting.

"For goodness sake, Jessica, what is it?" Congeniality had its drawbacks, Gladys quickly decided.

"Who's going to pay for us to print a book of history about our town? Do we have a budget for something like this? I mean I really don't know how government works."

"Good question," Doc said. "*Do* we have any funds to get us going with this whole Centennial Plus Thirty project?"

"I'm hoping we can solicit advertisers and underwriters for the entire celebration," Gladys responded with authority. "Like folks on the square who might benefit from extra traffic in town, or perhaps even undertakers and doctors, who certainly make their fair share from the community." She didn't look at either Eugene or Doc when she delivered this line, but her words were received . . . like the subtle two-by-four she'd intended. "Maybe even place ads in our book, or booklet, or whatever we decide. Maybe we could encourage some private individuals to be patrons, you know, like they do for the arts and such. Instead of being a patron of the arts, they would be a patron of the Centennial Plus Thirty. Be publicly thanked at some kind of ceremony or have patron pins made up or such. Which brings me to the next item of celebration."

3) CEREMONY.

"We need to have some kind of ceremony of dedication." She popped the lid back onto the marker.

"To dedicate what, exactly?" Sharon asked, pen poised over her steno, having copied down everything Gladys had written on the flip chart and most of what everyone had agreed upon.

"You know, I cannot imagine why Dorothy Wetstra has not shown up for this meeting!" Gladys realized the tone in her voice had been a little too convicting; she reined herself in, softened her voice and forced herself to smile, knowing perfectly well that to pick on Dorothy *now* would be to immediately dampen folks' enthusiasm for *her.*

"If you will all recall, some nearly twenty acres of Crooked Creek Farm were donated to the conservation district when Dorothy sold her farm to Ms. Durbin, at least that's what we were told. The donation was to include the portion of the land where the creek makes the bend, down there by the wooded area, and of course an access road from the gravel road. It was to be named Crooked Creek Park, and be open to public use. I haven't heard another word about it since the sale, nor have I seen any evidence of any official activity."

Between the end of her workday and this evening's meeting, Gladys had taken a drive out to the farm just to make sure she hadn't missed something. She'd even driven up the lane to inquire of Ms. Durbin if she knew when work might begin on the project, but her fancy vehicle was nowhere to be seen. Gladys hadn't contacted Dorothy because she expected her to be at the meeting. "But wouldn't it be perfect if we could make *that* official for our Centennial Plus Thirty! Have a dedication of the park to celebrate! Maybe even have a plaque made and posted at the entryway to the park saying something to that effect. We could have a ribbon-cutting ceremony and. . . ." Gladys stopped talking, mouth open, as visions of a photo of her on the front page of the *Daily Courier,* holding a big pair of scissors, danced in her head — not the first time she had beheld this vision. She smiled, then snapped back into now.

"May Belle, do you know why Dorothy isn't here?"

"No, Gladys, I do not." In fact, she wondered herself and was trying not to fret about Dorothy's absence, especially in light of the fact that she'd seemed a little distracted lately, although thankfully May Belle hadn't seen her have to take a nitroglycerin tablet recently — even though she knew Dorothy wouldn't tell her if she had.

"I'll be checking with her before our next meeting to consider these possibilities," Gladys said. "Or maybe I should just contact the conservation people myself. Whatever, I'll have a report by then. And if we cannot yet dedicate Crooked Creek Park, then we'll just have a dedication ceremony to our founding forefathers. How about that?"

"That sounds good to us, right, honey?" Paul put his arm around Jessica and gave her a quick squeeze as she nodded her approval, both of their families having age-old Partonville roots. Since Paul Joy was a man of few words, he had silenced the room when he'd spoken.

"Good," Gladys finally uttered. "Good! Let's see, what's next then?"

"Dates, I believe," Doc said. "Unless there's going to be more to our festivities than, let's see, publicity, history and ceremony."

"Well, actually, there is," Gladys said. "That's the surprise I talked about earlier. But let's get the dates set first, then we'll see if we can't assign committee members — and I am hoping volunteers step forward for each of them so I don't have to point fingers — and we'll close with a grand finale."

Out of habit and nervous energy, Sharon tapped her pen on the table a few times. "I think we all agree we should combine the elements of our celebration with the Pumpkin Festival. Maybe just add a day to it. We already have the chili dinner on Friday night, followed by the talent show, so risers and a stage will already be set up. Great time to have a kickoff ceremony of sorts for both events."

"Yes! I like that idea!" said Gladys. "I

could make a proclamation that the Centennial Plus Thirty is officially under way, along with the Pumpkin Festival!"

"If we can get this program, or magazine, or *whatever* we're calling our history, produced, we could also make announcements about them being on sale," Doc said. "I imagine plenty of folks might want to buy extras and send them to relatives, especially if any of their kinfolk have been mentioned. That would also help fund the thing. Plus we usually draw a nice crowd for the talent show, so . . ."

"And since Saturday is pretty full with the craft fair and then the dance, maybe we could have the park dedication on Sunday, if it's a go. Otherwise, we could . . . What's left?" Jessica had lost track.

"I was going to wait until we wrapped up to make this exciting announcement, but it seems like now is the perfect time. Whether the Crooked Creek Park is ready for dedication or not, Partonville is about to take an intentional step into the future." Gladys stopped and withdrew a sheet of typed paper from the bottom of the stack of notes in front of her. She was beaming. She cleared her throat, held the paper up, extended her arms a little, adjusted her glasses, then extended her arms a bit more.

"Whereas we now must admit that our town spends its days moving counterclockwise around the square rather than forward in time, I therefore commit to reversing that order, progressively ushering us toward the Centennial Plus Forty!" She folded the paper in half, then looked up to receive the committee's joyful affirmations, probably even their applause.

Blank. Looking from one face to the next — including May Belle's, who had frozen in place while refilling coffee mugs — they looked like a room of painted people. "Well? Cannot *one* of you imagine how important this is in terms of symbolism?" her voice exuding rivers of positive energies.

"Could you please read that again, Gladys?" Jessica, who was now standing behind her husband to allow Sarah Sue more wiggle room, shifted her daughter slightly toward her right — as though her off-center child might have interfered with her original comprehension — then stuck out her chin toward Gladys as an earnest sign of concentration.

"I'd like to hear that agin myself," Arthur said, "since I don't have a clue what yur talkin' bout, woman."

Gladys swallowed, sighed, licked her lips,

once again adjusted the paper just so, then read very slowly. "Whereas we now must admit that our town spends its days moving counterclockwise around the square rather than forward in time, I therefore commit to reversing that order, progressively ushering us toward the Centennial Plus Forty!" This time when she was done reading, she looked at their faces a bit more tentatively.

"Reversing what order?" Doc asked.

"It's perfectly clear! The order of traffic on the square!"

Before her very eyes, blank faces now transformed into a mix of squints. Then pure shock.

"Mayor McKern, you're not suggesting we have the traffic on the square reverse directions, are you?" Paul, always being one to show respect for office, just wanted to be sure he understood what was beginning to be envisioned in nearly everyone's heads as a complete disaster. "Your statement more or less sounds that way."

"Of course I am, Paul. That's *exactly* what I'm saying. And if you'll all think about it for a moment, I'm *sure* you will understand my point. The direction we travel now is counterclockwise, as though we're trying to get back to where we came from rather than moving with the clock into the future."

Jessica reached her arms in front of her, around Sarah Sue, and, with the pointer finger on her right hand, began drawing a circle on the palm of her left. "You're right! That *is* counterclockwise! We *do* go counter-clockwise around the square!"

"Course we do," Arthur said in disgust. "Nothin' else makes a lick of sense."

"What do you mean nothing else makes any sense, Arthur? Just because that's the way we've always done it, does that mean that's the way we have to keep doing it, even if it's backwards — which many folks would like to, and already do, accuse us of being?" Gladys's mind flicked to Katie Durbin, who always seemed to radiate a disdainful air about Partonville when she was in town.

"Gladys, I hate to be negative here," Eugene said, "but I can't imagine trying to change the flow of traffic on and off the square. Just going around a circle in a different direction isn't that big a deal, but people have to get on and off the square, and that would be trouble."

"How can it be anymore trouble than it already is?" she asked defensively.

Doc considered his thoughts, then presented them carefully, trying to sound reasonable rather than just reactionary or accusatory. "I think it's a fine idea you want to have Partonville move intentionally into the future, Gladys, and that you want to make sure that not only us, but those around us, know we are serious about ourselves . . . proud of our heritage. But I think there are better ways to do this than what you're suggesting here. You've presented many fine ideas this evening, but I can't agree that this is one of them."

"It's dern crazy's what it tis!" Arthur glanced over at Sharon, who had been drawing squares and arrows in her steno a mile a minute, trying to figure out for herself how the proposed idea might or might not work. Her overall schematic looked like a bowl of spaghetti. Without asking Sharon for permission, he withdrew the steno right out from under her moving pen and tossed it in the middle of the table. "Jist look at that!" Arthur yelped. "Bedlam!" Sharon's face turned beat red. Before she could retrieve it, Eugene had pulled the steno over in front of him. He turned it this way and that, then traced some of her flip-flopping arrows with his finger. "I think Arthur's right," he said. "Bedlam."

Gladys flipped to a clean page on the chart. First she drew a square, then another larger square outside of that one, then she drew dotted lines down the middle space between the squares to indicate the two lanes of traffic. Like in a movie theater, heads jockeyed for position to get a clear view of what she was doing. She then drew arrows around the outside of the larger box indicating the way traffic now flowed on the square, which was, indeed counterclockwise. Next she drew a small rectangle in the outside lane toward the right of the top block. "This," she said tapping at it with the end of the marker, felt tip making little red dots in the hood area, "is a car now getting ready to get off the square." She made a line of dashes, occasionally inserting an arrow in their midst, to show the traffic pattern the cars now used to exit the square.

She stood back and contemplated her schematic a moment, then began to draw arrows around the outside of the squares again, only this time going clockwise. She shaped the arrows slightly thicker to indicate her new plan. Next she drew another rectangle, but this time she carefully filled it in, like a child trying to stay within the coloring lines. This vehicle was also in the outside lane at the top block, but to the left side. To further indicate the difference in the plans, she drew an arrow, to match the newly designed clockwise arrows around the squares, on the front of the car, then proceeded to draw another series of dashes showing how this vehicle could also just cruise off the square, making a left-hand turn rather than the right-hand turn vehicle number one would have made. She set the pen down and brushed her hands together, as though eradicating them from chalk dust and any further confusion. "There! Simple. Now, going counterclockwise, we turn right veering off the square. Soon, moving forward in time, we just turn left off the square. That's all."

Doc, who was sitting straight across from the easel, began to chuckle. "Gladys, I'm sure you didn't mean to do this, but since you have used the top block of the square to show us both situations, those two autos are about to have a head-on collision!" He busted out in full-blown guffawing, as did everyone else.

Gladys was steamed. "Well of course they *won't* because that's not how it will *be!* ALL traffic will be going in the same clockwise direction!"

"Ms. Mayor," Paul said in his quiet voice, often mistaken for shyness. "Trying to get people to remember that is going to be the problem. After all of these years, that kind of a change won't come easy, and I fear we might just end up *really* looking like your current chart's coming disaster."

"It's plumb crazy, I tell ya. Plumb nuts. Why the only folks to benefit from that mess is liable to be either the good Doc here, or worst yet, Eugene!" Arthur backed his chair away from the table and leaned back until it tilted on its hind legs. He folded his arms across his chest, intending this gesture to show his withdrawal from any such wild ideas — and that's exactly how it was perceived.

"I think you're all being a little too dramatic," Gladys said. Sharon nudged Arthur, having intuitively guessed (since she felt herself doing the same) he was opening his mouth to ask just who was being dramatic here. But Arthur was liable to do it. He looked at Sharon, who furrowed her brows at him, and he kept his mouth closed — but just for her.

"Let's give this some time to sink in. I'll table the issue until our next meeting. I'm sure as you go about your business this week, traveling backwards around the square yourselves, what I'm talking about will soak in and you'll all be as anxious as I am to step into the future. For now, let's get our committees set up. As I've listened to each of your comments throughout the evening," she said, barreling right along in order to prevent any more discussion, "it's become clear who would work best on which committee. For the sake of expediency, I'll go ahead and make assignments. If anyone objects, before you object out loud, give yourselves time to think about it first. I'm sure you'll realize I'm right. . . . The obvious person to head up publicity is Sharon. She's got all the skills and talent we could possibly need to put together press releases, and I'm sure she's got a little pull, at least to help us get good coverage in our own paper." Gladys smiled at Sharon, who was suddenly wishing she'd stayed home and worked a puzzle. "Arthur can work with you on those, Sharon."

"I second that!" Arthur just grinned; Sharon smiled, too — mostly because she didn't know what else to do, although taking her first trip to Las Vegas entered her mind.

"Eugene and Doc can work on gathering our history. I know Sharon would be good at that too, what with her reporting skills, and maybe she can lend you two a hand in typing up what you find. But for now, I figure since you two gentlemen have been around about as long as anyone else, you'll know who has the most interesting stories, not to mention all you can come up with between the two of you about birthing and burying." Doc and Eugene nodded at one another, both of them already rifling their memories for the "best of" memories they housed in their own personal story logs.

"Paul and Jessica, you two can be in charge of the Friday night declaration and dedication ceremony. That will probably take the least amount of time and will mostly include setting up a special place on the platform and decorating it for me. Shouldn't be that much work, and won't matter if you have to miss a meeting here and there." Jessica looked to Paul, just to make sure they were on the same page. He nodded his approval, then they both nodded at Gladys.

"I propose you all immediately set about your tasks, gathering more folks as you need to, and we'll meet back here at the same time and place next week with reports," Gladys said, flipping all of the pages on the flip chart back to their starting positions, which left them looking at *whatever* it was — and just in case it was Jesus, they thought they should at least look at it respectfully.

"I, as mayor, of course, will be on all of the committees and make any and all public proclamations, dedications and declarations. May Belle, if you'd like to jump onto one of these committees, let appropriate folks know. Otherwise, I figure you can bring weekly refreshments and crank up the coffee for us. This meeting is adjourned."

"WAIT! Who's going to do an actual study of this proposed traffic . . . um . . . suggestion?" Eugene felt there'd been a giant dangling end left waving in the breeze that had blustered from Gladys's mouth.

"Me," Gladys said with finality. "If I need help, you'll be the first one I call, Eugene."

10

"Hello, Dorothy. It's May Belle."

Dorothy smiled. May Belle always announced who she was, as though Dorothy wouldn't recognize her voice after eighty years of friendship. "Yes, dear. How are you this bright sunny morning?"

"My, don't you sound chipper today! That does a body good to hear. You know, that first Centennial Plus Thirty meeting was last night, and when you didn't show up, I have to admit I was a little concerned. But you sound mighty fine. I trust our rainbow-connected prayers are working and that you're feeling better about whatever's going on?"

"Everything is relative, isn't it? And pish-posh! I'm sick of thinking about me. What about you? I didn't know you were volunteering. I imagine you arrived bearing good-ies, though, right? What kind of cookies did I miss?"

"I guess you know me pretty well. Oatmeal raisin. Don't worry; I saved you a half dozen or so. You mentioned the leftovers in your refrigerator were starting to add up to a smorgasbord night and I've got a few tidbits myself. How about we combine forces for dinner. We'll eat in your cheery kitchen and I'll bring you your dessert. Why *weren't* you there though, dear?"

"I thought about attending, but at the last minute I decided to take a pass. I've already got a few things to do for the Pumpkin Festival, like play in the band, which is already practicing twice a week now. And I always help with the talent show, too. That takes a heap of phone calls and coordinating, not to mention begging and cheering. I think that'll be enough doings to keep me plenty busy. I'm sure Gladys can handle everything just fine without me there sparring with her anyway. Besides, that personal *issue*" — and she said the word *issue* with the same tone of voice one might use to respond after smelling a rotten potato — "I'm dealing with is sapping enough of my emotional energy simply thinking about it, in case you can't tell by the way I just, within the last minute, *pish-poshed* it, but looped right back to it again. If things bust loose . . . I need to conserve at least a few of my resources, my time and my energy, not to mention asking God to give me more than I can muster on my own. I can't go into details, but I can tell you this: it's going to deal with a whopping issue of forgiveness, May Belle, and you know how hard those can be. I'm afraid the worst is yet to come. Knowing you're praying for me is a good comfort, dear. But that's for *sure* enough of that. There's something about the sunshine beaming brightly through the windows that makes a person feel good after so many days of mostly gloomy chill. I just wish the sunbeams landed on crystals here rather than on my dust! That is one thing about cloudy days, I've determined. The house always looks cleaner in the dark."

"I would one hundred percent agree with you about the sunshine making you feel better, although I don't much care about the dust one way or the other anymore. I'd rather bake brownies than dust." While May Belle was making that statement, Dorothy grinned, knowing she'd never once seen as much as a speck of dust in May Belle's house. Not ever. "I even hung a load of wash out this morning, it was so nice. I can't wait to bundle those sheets up in my arms and smell the fresh air on our beds tonight!"

"Already you've got laundry out? Goodness! It's only eight-thirty."

"I nearly phoned you at seven, but thought better about it. I know you're nearly always up at the crack of dawn, but I even found myself sleeping in lately, what with all the cool weather that settled in for so many days. I was beginning to think for awhile we'd missed fall altogether and were heading straight into winter."

"Now wouldn't that just frost Gladys's cake, to think we were going to have to have the Pumpkin Festival without a fall!" The two of them chuckled.

"Speaking of Gladys," May Belle said, shifting tones, "she did ask me if I knew why you weren't there last night. She was expecting you. Consider yourself forewarned, though: she's wanting to have a ribbon-cutting ceremony for Crooked Creek Park as a part of the Centennial Plus Thirty celebration. Said she hasn't heard a word about the park and was needing to find out what was holding things up. And you'll appreciate this: although you weren't there to spar with her, I reckon Arthur will be enough to keep giving her a run for her money!"

"Arthur Landers showed up for the committee? I can hardly believe my ears."

"Seems Jessie tricked him into it, telling him she'd signed him up, when really, there wasn't any official sign-up. I imagine she just wanted to have a night of peace and quiet."

"Goodness! I hope those two don't knock each other out before the doings."

"They are a pair who has their own way of communicating, that's for sure."

"I mean Arthur and Gladys!"

"Oh!" May Belle laughed out loud, covering her mouth out of habit when she did so.

"As far as Crooked Creek Park, Gladys does get ahead of herself, doesn't she? There's lots of things that have to happen before a park will be in place, and Katie and I requested, as part of our official donation documents, that no plans move forward for the actual park until next spring. Those two have barely gotten settled into the farm themselves; they don't need a bunch of construction going on around them right now. Besides, to plan a park takes some thought. We talked about playgrounds and what types they're putting into parks these days, and maybe wood-chipping a few walking paths through some of the area down there. But I don't want to detract from an ounce of God's natural glory and peace and turn it into something that might as well be in the middle of Disneyland. I think to bring *too* much planning in would defeat the purpose of it preserving nature.

"Of course there's a part of me that's anxious to see it come to life, and I occasionally verge on telling them to just do what they will — which, come to think about it, I suppose they can anyway. I'm not gonna live forever. But it would sure give me satisfaction to see that piece of my family's history being enjoyed by folks before I pass beyond the yonder. Still, no need for everybody to rush things just because my old ticker is ticking slower."

"Dorothy Jean Wetstra. I do not want to hear any more of that kind of talk, especially since your old ticker is only a few months older than mine!"

"*Old* being the key word for both of us, right?"

"Oldsters. We're two oldsters. Isn't that the word you use?"

"Yes, ma'am. We are oldsters for sure. Kinda has a zesty ring to it. Sounds much more glamorous than just saying we're old bags."

Tsk, tsk. "Oh, how you talk! But back to

last night's meeting for a minute. Wait until you hear what Gladys has dreamed up for her idea of a grand finale to the Centennial Plus Thirty!" The women talked and laughed for a good ten minutes, speculating on all kinds of disasters in the making. If Gladys actually pulled this one off, it would be the first time Dorothy might be glad to have given up driving!

"Grannie M, how do you think I should wear my hair for the Pumpkin Festival dance? Think you can make it glamorous? This will be my first honest-to-gosh dance, you know!" Shelby spoke loudly as she swiveled this way and that in the salon chair while her great-grandmother moved salon towels from the washer to the dryer in the utility room at La Feminique Salon & Day Spa. "Oh, and by the way, I loved your picture in the newspaper! Maybe I should wear my hair up like that. Think an up-do would look good on me?" She ripped the elastic band out of her ponytail, raked her hands through her hair to smooth out a couple tangles, then picked it up and piled it on top of her head, holding it there, turning her head from the right to the left. Maggie walked up behind her and began pumping up the chair, studying Shelby's makeshift hairdo.

"Let me have at it a minute," she said, grabbing a wide-tooth comb out of the sterilizer. She began carefully combing Shelby's long, fine golden locks so as not to yank them and cause her any pain. It was a moment of déjà vu for Maggie, Shelby's hair being the same color and texture as her own daughter's used to be. She continued combing, long after it was untangled, her mind drifting back to her daughter at age four.

"Oooowwwww! You're hurting me, Mom. STOP PULLING!"

"If you'd sit still like a young lady, this would be much easier for both of us."

"But, Mom, why can't we just leave it the way it is?"

"Do you want people to think your mother let you go to sleep last night with an entire rodeo of rats in your hair? Who'd come to the salon then?"

"Hey! I'm more important than your dumb beauty shop!"

Maggie stopped combing and got right in her daughter's eyes. "Yes, dear, you certainly are." She kissed her on each cheek and the tip of her nose.

Now, in a seeming fingersnap, that same

daughter's hair was not only snow white, but *she* was a grandmother to this beautiful girl whose hair Maggie now ran her fingers through.

Maggie picked up a switch of her great-granddaughter's locks and twisted it up and off to one side. She grabbed a couple hairpins and stuck them in this way and that. Immediately she pulled them out and combed through her hair again, like an artist wiping the canvas clean before her next attempt to create a masterpiece. This time she began a French braid that wrapped around Shelby's head. Old-fashioned. Feminine. "You could put a sprig of flowers right here," she said, wiggling the spot where she was holding the ends together. "I don't know if it will stay up, though; your hair is awfully fine and slick. Pretty, but maybe not best for a total up-do. You don't want the evening to end with you looking like Cinderella stayed a little too long at the ball. Is Josh getting you a corsage? Maybe you could ask him to tell the Floral Fling to leave off the wristband and forget the pins; I could secure it to your hair like so . . ."

"I'm not going with Josh. He's a stuck-up pig. I'm going with Kevin Mooney."

Maggie tried not to reveal her surprise. She knew Shelby had had a huge crush on

Josh Kinney since she'd laid eyes on him. And she couldn't recall the last time she'd heard Shelby talk so harshly about anyone. "Kevin Mooney. Is he the young man I'm always reading about in the sports section? Runs track for Hethrow?"

"That would be him. We've been friends for years."

"How nice for you. Do you like him?"

"Grams, I wouldn't have said yes if I didn't!"

"Is Josh going to the dance, stuck-up pig that he is?"

"Who cares." It was definitely a statement and not a question. The tone in Shelby's voice had revealed alot to Maggie: clearly, Shelby cared, and a great deal. Maggie continued to fiddle with Shelby's hair, then she spun the chair to face her.

"How about we give you a complete makeover? New hairdo, a little eye shadow, blush . . . maybe even some lip gloss? Not that you're not naturally beautiful just the way you are, but for the dance, let's turn up the glam a notch. Want to?"

"Just don't get me in trouble with Mom, okay? She won't let me out of the house looking too made up. And don't give me very much makeup because I won't know how to use it anyway. I want to look beautiful, not like I'm wearing a Halloween costume!"

"How about we give the entire head a practice run right now? You can tell me what you think and we'll get the fine-tuning over with. That way you'll have a couple weeks to practice any or all of it, and we'll be ready for action when the big day gets here. And that is . . . when, exactly?"

"The dance is the last weekend in October during the Pumpkin Festival. Saturday night."

Maggie knew darn well when the festival took place since next to the annual hair convention in Chicago, it was one of the highlights of her entire year. Twirly skirts, extra sparkling accessories, romantic lights, music, husband Ben looking so dashing in his dressy country western shirt and string tie . . . smelling so good . . . After all these decades, that man still ignited her passions. Had from the very beginning.

"Grannie M? You on the planet? Where'd you go?"

"To Cinderella's ball, my dear!" Maggie, who had frozen in place, dropped Shelby's hair, letting it fall around her shoulders. She went over and started flipping through the giant pages in her booking schedule. "Let's see. Hm." She ran her hand up and down.

"Looks like several of my usuals have changed their appointments to that Saturday. Must have hot dates themselves!" Maggie and Shelby both laughed, trying to picture the likes of Cora Davis and Gladys McKern with hot dates. "How about three-thirty?"

"Sounds good to me, Grams." Maggie filled out an official appointment card, although she knew neither of them would forget.

"Now, let's see what we can do here," Maggie said as she whipped a salon shawl around Shelby's neck, grabbed her scissors and snapped them a few times. "We'll start with the hair, then move to the makeup. Before we're done, any man in his right mind will wonder why *he* wasn't the one escorting you!"

11

Katie had booked two rooms for her and Josh in Chicago at the Four Seasons Chicago on the Magnificent Mile. As she checked in, it struck her that a room here cost more than ten times per night than the Lamp Post, plus another chunk of change per evening for parking fees. Although the high sticker didn't surprise her and was, in fact, what she was used to — five-star hotels had been her comfort zone — she now realized her comfort zone may have changed, since she and Josh had spent, on and off, so many weeks at Jessica and Paul's during the estate sale and move.

While they rode the elevator up to their rooms, she considered how handy it had been at the Lamp Post to be able to park right in front of her door. No waiting for a "ride" to get to your floor and bed; no loud dings outside your room if you got stuck with sleeping quarters next to the elevator.

Although the room in Chicago was considerably larger, more luxurious and better equipped than the Lamp Post for a businessperson to set up shop, there was nothing more functional, really — aside from the fact that the Four Seasons Chicago wasn't within a mile of a cornfield and a couple blocks from Harry's Grill. *Is that good or bad?* Of course, this hotel offered a stunning view of the lake and access right into her favored high-end shops, but she concluded since the Lamp Post had Jessica, nothing could be better than that, not even a top-notch concierge. She was missing her new friend and decided to make it a point to get in touch with her soon after they returned home.

Katie stood in Josh's hotel room doorway at 9:00 P.M. She'd stopped by for a moment to comment on how mopey he'd been all the way to Chicago. He just shrugged and said he guessed he was tired, too. Even though his mom had picked him up from school on their way out of Partonville, Friday night traffic had been horrible. By the time they'd checked in and had a bite of dinner in the hotel dining room, it was already late. "Now remember, you're going to have to entertain yourself all day tomorrow. Feel free to have Alex come spend the day with you. He can spend the night then too, if you like, since you've got the room. The El comes two blocks from here. Maybe the two of you can take in a movie or something; I'll probably be too dead to the world to do much of anything else after all day at the spa — at least I'm hoping I am. Then we'll have breakfast Sunday morning before we head out. We can drop him off on the way."

"Fine," Josh said as his mom left his room. Her references to Alex, which should have made him happy, stabbed him with guilt. As soon as she was out the door, Josh turned on the television and watched a premiere show on one of the network channels. "Dumb. Waste of time," he said as he flipped off the television and set up his laptop to check his e-mail. Nothing but SPAM. He e-mailed Dorothy a quick note to tell her he was available to cyber talk, but she went to bed pretty early and he figured she wouldn't read it until the morning. Then he began to fret about Alex. After a brief session of arguing with himself, he pushed through his pride and clicked on "Create New Mail." Two failed drafts later — the first being kind of flip and funny; the second, too drawn out and intense — he finally wrote a third version and pushed "Send" before he lost his courage.

Dear Alex,
Where do I begin? How about this? I am sorry for being a loser of a friend. You deserve better and I won't be surprised if I don't hear back from you, but I sure hope I do since I'm in Chicago right now and would like to see you tomorrow, if you can stand me. We're staying at the Four Seasons. I'm in room 345. Email or call. I'll be glad to hear from you and hope I do.
Josh. Just Josh. Not even the Joshmeister right now.
PS I am especially no longer Josh-o either. That guy was a HUGE jerk! Thanks for letting him know.

Originally he'd typed a closing that said "I miss you," but after deleting it, then adding it back in, he ultimately decided that even though it was true, it made him sound like a complete sap and Alex would be the first one to point that out, should he answer him at all. The sentiment went unexpressed, although nonetheless felt.

Four times before he finally turned off the

light after midnight, he checked his e-mail to see if Alex had responded. Nothing.

Katie began her spa day with a short rest in the oh-so-aqua-blue, cocoon-like whirlpool, the piped-in sounds of a bubbling brook and lightly tinkling wind chimes quieting her anxious self. Next came the massage room. Always sensitive to fragrance, she'd asked for essential oils to be added to the massage lotion. "A soothing scent," she'd said. "Something . . . soothing."

Eyes closed, face down on the massage table, tucked in beneath the soft flannel sheets, head comfortably resting in a face cradle, Katie heard the familiar sound of warm, flat river rocks clicking together as the masseuse gathered them from a small warmer. Katie drew and released a deep, cleansing breath in anticipation of the benefits she knew were to come. Michelle gently placed the various-sized stones exactly on target — over the knots inside Katie's shoulder blades, alongside her spine and way down on her lower back — allowing them to rest there, each stone matching the size of the tension. Her body received the warm pressure as eagerly as a child receives a goodnight kiss. Senses quickened, Katie heard the faint *whoosh* of a pump dispenser infiltrating the moist lotion with lavender. *Ah, yes, something soothing.*

Michelle rubbed the potion between her hands, warming it to body temperature. She began the ninety-minute therapeutic session by carefully withdrawing Katie's left arm from beneath her nest, softly stretching, firmly gliding her hands in long sweeping motions up and down taut chords of muscles, working from shoulder to fingertips before tucking her arm back under the cover and beginning on the next needy append-age — harp music drifting, rolling over and around Katie in the dimly lit room.

Arms and legs now at peace, the warmth of the rocks had, with weighted assurance, drawn blood to her clenched torso muscles, preparing them for this moment when they were removed and Katie's back was un-veiled, readied for the rhythmic kneading, the rolling, the heel of a hand coupled with Michelle's instinctive gift to discern hidden pressure points that could gently force the strains of life to loosen their hold on a body, at least for now. Katie melted into the table, allowing herself to concentrate solely on surrendering her body into the hands of her skilled masseuse. Her very being drank of the intoxicating healing blend of touch laced with the scent of lavender and the beauty of music as she lost herself to the welcome *present,* where nothing existed but a body made whole.

What, Katie wondered, could one do to receive such a sense of wholeness in the deepest part of their soul?

After a brief respite in the Quiet Room, first drinking replenishing spring water and then enjoying a cup of herbal tea, Katie moved into a facial followed by a pedicure and manicure. She all but oozed her way to the hair coloring station, first enjoying another brief break in the Quiet Room to allow for more thorough drying of her nails.

Swathed in a bountiful, ultra-soft, white terrycloth robe, eyes closed, she rested comfortably in the salon chair. Although she usually, with an eagle eye readied for critique, watched Jeffrey's every smear of color and treatment to her hair — even though he was the top colorist at Gregory's, Chicago's poshest salon and day spa — right now she couldn't stand to see herself in the mirror, which is the direction he insisted on facing her, coloring tray pulled up next to him. She looked like a makeup-less Raggedy Ann doll with her finger stuck in a socket, such an array of sprouts of red hair and foil and clips jutted off her head this way and that. So she'd closed her eyes in order to preserve her inner calm.

For years she'd tracked every moment of her transformation sitting in this very chair, but today . . . *eyes closed* . . . today she needed to shut out anything but order, and her massage had at least brought respite to her otherwise tense physical body. Her brain had undergone enough havoc lately . . . *keep your eyes closed* . . . without having to see the outside of its housing looking like it had exploded, too. She was grateful that Jeffrey had never been one to chat, and she didn't have to explain what she wanted; she was in their computer's database, everything exactly the way she liked it, right down to a head shot taken with their digital camera the day her entire color, cut and do had come out perfectly. Quietly, Jeffrey had gone to work on the last phase . . . *I'm melting* . . . aside from styling, of her all-day salon and spa treatment.

Katie had always purchased "The Total Body Experience" package, even though she received it in parcels, one element per visit, stringing them throughout the month. She used to frequent the salon weekly to receive either the massage, facial, pedicure and manicure, or color and style. But that's when she lived nearby. Now that she had a drive long enough to require an overnight stay, she decided she'd just spend the day getting the works. Although it had taken a little jostling on the salon's part — which, since she'd been a longstanding customer who'd always tipped *very well,* they were willing to do — they finally got it worked out. While she was clearing her bill this visit, she went ahead and booked herself a day a month for the next three months, working around her standing colorist appointment since Jeffrey booked eons in advance. This would be something wonderful to look forward to in the midst of her . . . *whatever* it was she was in the midst of.

By the time she headed for the coat rack, she was grateful no one but the salon workers had recognized her, which was a first. In the past she had enjoyed not only the services, but being seen. As business was conducted on the golf course, so contacts could be made anywhere, including the spa, aside from the Quiet Room, of course. But now, oddly — especially since she'd been so craving the city experience — she'd realized the revitalizing benefits of silence, and particularly her desperate need to cling to the calm she'd just purchased for premium bucks. It flicked through her mind that she might be adapting to the solitude at Crooked Creek, even in the midst of her isolation. *Surely not!* But just as she slipped her coat off the rack, unfortunately she ran into Zeda, Mac Downs's wife.

Immediately after Katie had been ousted from her commercial real estate firm in a hostile takeover by Keith Benton — who had called in some of his markers — Mac, a bigwig at Strong, Hart and Cleaver, her previous employer's top-dog rival, had done everything in his power to get her to come to work for him. Katie had a reputation for being a fearless, kick-butt deal closer, just the kind you'd like in your court. In fact, Strong, Hart and Cleaver had been trying to steal her away for years. When, in a sudden surprise tactic, Katie had moved to Partonville, and onto a farm, no less — which was completely out of character for her — they'd all concluded she was setting herself up for the independent real estate kill of the decade, having purchased the largest plot of land contingent to Hethrow, the fastest growing town in the northern part of the southern Illinois rural area — which was being developed by none other than Craig & Craig, a firm Keith Benton had partnered with on more than one occasion. If ever there would be the ultimate revenge, this could be it, since Katie had stopped the Craig brothers' advance into Partonville dead in its tracks. What, many in the industry wondered, was she planning to do with her pearl?

Mac had finally gotten tired of leaving messages for Katie and stopped calling, figuring she'd decided to keep the booty to herself rather than join forces with *anyone.* He knew she had enough of her own money to pull it off, too, which she did, and her silence on the issue could only mean one thing: she was keeping the property secured until the most lucrative moment arrived.

Since Zeda had attended many business dinners with Mac and Katie over the years, she was familiar with her husband's quest to land "Kathryn Durbin, Development Diva." Although Katie's given name was Katie Mabel Carol Durbin, not a living soul, not even her own son, knew the whole of it. She had never gone by anything in the business world other than Kathryn Durbin. It was her opinion that Katie sounded too informal, and Mabel was unthinkable, even though her mother insisted it was a strong name, which is why she had given it to her. When she'd asked her mother why she had two middle names, why Carol, all she'd said was that her dad liked it. Katie Mabel Carol Durbin. "Could anything be more Partonville?" she'd once asked her mom in disgust. "Like it or not, honey, Partonville is in your blood." And now, she lived there!

But seeing Zeda, Katie determined to bid her a quick hello and good-bye before she could entrench her in conversation and start asking too many questions. Mystery and mixed messages, which she knew would get back to Mac, would help keep all her potential options alive.

"Why, Kathryn Durbin! How wonderful to see you! Have you come to your senses and moved back to the city?" Katie extended her perfectly finished French-manicured hand; Zeda received Katie's with her own, newly painted with bright red polish that gleamed in the salon lighting.

"No, I haven't, Zeda." Katie swiftly let go of Zeda's hand and slipped it into her jacket sleeve, thinking how glad she was that she'd taken a few minutes to apply some makeup and put on her earrings when her hair was finished. "That is, I haven't moved back to the city; I'm just here for a spa day." She slipped the shoulder strap to her handbag in place, opened the clasp and retrieved her car keys. "And for the record, I never lost my senses. I finally just realized there was more to life than real estate, although my residence *is* parked on a goldmine, I must say." She beamed her high-beam smile at Zeda, whom truthfully she'd always enjoyed, even though Zeda had always seemed a tad too "domestic" for Katie.

"Please tell Mac I'm taking my time deciding what I'm going to do next. I'll phone him if and when I have any announcements to make that might pertain to him and development. And please give him my best regards," which she sincerely meant. She pushed her jacket sleeve back and looked at her wristwatch.

"It was nice to see you, Zeda, but I've got to be moving along." *Before I lose the calm I just paid for.* "Joshua's been on his own all day and I told him I'd be back at the hotel by six. I'll tell you one thing I don't miss about the city, and that's all the traffic! It'll probably take me an hour just to go eight blocks."

Josh slept in. First thing after awakening with a jolt at nine-thirty, he happily remembered it was Saturday and that his mom was off to her spa day. He checked his e-mail. Nothing, not even from Dorothy. He showered and went down to the dining room and asked if he could order lunch instead of breakfast. "Not yet, sir; we start serving off of the lunch menu at eleven." *Sir. Like Dorothy would say, HA!* It was only ten-fifteen. He decided to grab a candy bar from the gift shop and wait it out; a hamburger sounded far better than eggs. In fact, one of Lester's homespun greasy burger and fry plates sounded the best, but alas, he was left without a car — as always lately — and since it was a solid ten to twelve-hour round trip, he knew that wouldn't be a good idea, even if he did have wheels. Not to mention that he'd be grounded for life if he pulled a stunt like that. But a guy could dream about hamburgers just as easily as he could dream about a blonde named Shelby.

He poked around in the hotel lobby for a while, then walked a block this way and a block that way, deciding nothing in any window caught his interest long enough to lure him in. *Nothing half as interesting as a creek or a tree with a name.* He went back up to the room to check his e-mail but first noticed his message light on the telephone was flashing. "Alright!" he exclaimed as he read the instructions as to which button to push to receive voice mail.

"Josh. Alex. It's, um, let me see here, ten-fifteen and I just read your e-mail. I was out late last night with some friends. I'd like to see you today, but maybe you've already found something else to do. Phone me if you get in before noon; otherwise, I'll probably go shoot some hoops at the park, then . . . I don't know what. A couple of the guys are gonna hang out tonight but I don't know where yet. Anyway, wish I'd have known you were coming to Chicago. We could have planned something. Hope we at least touch bases before you're gone. Bye."

"DANG!" Josh said out loud at the sound of the click. He banged the receiver down in the cradle, then sat down on the bed and stared at the phone, as if that might make something different happen from what already had. Then he picked the handset back up and dialed Alex's number as quickly as he could, first forgetting to dial the number to get an outside line (start again), then accidentally hitting a wrong keypad one digit from the end of the number (start again), then forgetting to wait for the outside line before dialing, only to hear some recording telling him he couldn't do what he was trying to do. "NOT AGAIN!" He sat the receiver in the cradle and stared at the phone for about a minute, calming himself down. Then he picked it up as though it were breakable and slowly and deliberately pushed each button until he'd at last placed the call.

"Hello."

"Mrs. Gillis, it's Josh. How are you?"

"Fine, Josh. Fine. It's good to hear your voice. Alex told me you were in town for the weekend."

"Yea, Mom's at an all-day spa thing."

"Lucky her. I'm on my third load of laundry."

He couldn't think of a thing to say in response. "Nice to talk to you, Mrs. Gillis. Can I please speak to Alex?"

"You *just* missed him, Josh! He left not more than sixty seconds before the phone rang. Wait, let me check to make sure he's not still around . . ." Josh could hear her footsteps moving across the floor to look out the window, then come padding back. "No. He's gone."

"Do you know where he went?"

"Down to the park, I think — although I'm not sure whether it was the one a couple blocks down or the one over by the school. He didn't say. One of his friends phoned. I heard him say he wasn't sure whether you two were going to get hooked up or not. He grabbed his basketball and took off. I'll tell him you called, okay? He has the number where you're staying, right?" Silence on the other end. "Josh? You still there?"

"Sorry, Mrs. Gillis. I was just thinking how I might not have missed him if I wasn't such a dialing dummy."

"Dialing dummy?"

"I was trying to . . . Never mind. It doesn't matter. Yes. He knows where I'm staying. I'm gonna go get something to eat now. Tell him if he gets the voice mail to either e-mail or leave me a message and let me know if he can stay overnight with us; I've got my own room with an extra bed. It's okay with my mom if it's okay with you. I'm kinda stuck here, so I'll probably be around all day. But if I do miss his call, and if he's coming, tell him to let me know what time he thinks he'll get here. Oh, and Mom said we could drop him off in the morning on the way out of town."

"I'll give him the message. Tell your mom I said hello. Good-bye, Josh."

"Bye."

Josh hung up the phone and punched his bed pillow. "If I don't get to see him . . . it will be nobody's fault but my own!"

■ ■ ■ ■

When Katie got back to the hotel, she was surprised to find Josh alone. "Where's Alex?"

"He couldn't come . . . I guess."

"What do you mean 'you guess'?"

"I never actually talked to him. We played phone tag, and then he must have ended up going out with the guys."

Katie studied her son's face. *Lost and lonesome.* At least she'd had a spa day. From the looks of him, he'd had nothing but nothing.

12

May Belle and Dorothy usually flanked Earl in church, although Dorothy tried to change seats each week. She rotated from front to back and side-to-side so she could stay familiar with the congregation and not appear as though she'd staked her claim to any particular slot. She believed when people became creatures of habit in church and sat in the same exact spot every week, they developed blinders to newcomers and neighbors. May Belle was always on the lookout for visitors anyway, presenting them with a half dozen of her cookies, brought along every week on a paper plate wrapped in cellophane and decorated with curly ribbon — just in case.

The whole rotating-seats routine was important to Dorothy. She sometimes felt that people who sat in the same place every week radiated a prideful message that they had "paid" for their permanent seat in one way or another, and that their family was therefore entitled to that particular row. She'd gotten this perspective from her parents, who always went out of their way to "stay alive and alert to the message," and those whom God would send to sit beside them while they received it. She'd also been raised up to chat with everyone in her pew about the message as they filed out to see how uniquely God spoke to each of them about the same topic. "Dorothy Jean, it's important to stay open to different opinions; otherwise, a mind can get too set in its own ways for its own good," her dad used to say. No doubt he had tailored that message especially for his stubborn daughter.

Then again, as Dorothy occasionally examined her own habits and realized how easy it was to fall into a judgmental spirit herself, she remembered hearing a journalist say that we should always question our assumptions. If one assumed it was bad to sit in the same pew every week, one could, she concluded, rightly be challenged on *this* basis: at least when folks did do that, it was easy to notice when they were absent, which was a heads-up that perhaps they were ill or needed a call. For instance, Gladys always sat right in the first pew in front of the pulpit where she could be seen, and where her every *harrumph* could be heard by Pastor Delbert Carol, Jr. ("Somebody needs to let that man know he's being scrutinized by *somebody* other than God!") But thank goodness she did, because it had perhaps saved her life back in 1987 when she'd been stricken with bacterial pneumonia.

That Sunday Dorothy had noticed — for the entire sermon, since Gladys did sit right up front — that Gladys was missing. Jake was on the road and her son attended St. Augustine Catholic Church with his wife and family every week, so it wasn't unusual for her to be alone. It was highly irregular, however, for her to be absent, so Dorothy drove directly to her home when church dismissed. Turns out the pneumonia had washed over her so quickly, it was as though she'd literally been slam-dunked into immobility and all she could do was pray she didn't die before help arrived. When Dorothy'd found Gladys's car in the carport and got no response to her knocking and endless ringing of the doorbell (she tried the door but it was locked; Gladys tried to holler and get out of bed, but she couldn't), she drove straight to St. Augustine, which didn't let out until later than United Methodist, to find Caleb, Gladys's son, who, wouldn't you know, was seated all the way in the front pew — chip off the old block that he was. Although Dorothy had tried to flag an usher, she couldn't catch his eyes. She didn't want to be disruptive, but she worried time might be of the utmost if Gladys was in trouble, so she quietly walked up the side aisle, tapped the person sitting at the end of the pew on the shoulder and motioned toward Caleb.

"What?" The older gentleman's voice belted out of him; he was obviously hard of hearing and thought he'd missed an instruction since Dorothy's pointing made no sense to him. Realizing anything short of yelling would be futile, she leaned forward and quickly walked in front of the row until she reached Caleb, then whispered in his ear. As Caleb rose from his seat, encouraging his wife and family to stay seated — which they did not — Dorothy turned to Father O'Sullivan, a longtime friend of hers, who had been, up until this moment, right in the middle of his homily.

"Good Father, I beg your pardon. But we might have an emergency situation here with Gladys. Might." As they were exiting the church, Dorothy heard Father O'Sullivan begin, "Lord, we take a moment to thank you for being with Gladys, knowing exactly what she . . ."

Gladys had been hospitalized within thirty minutes of her family's arrival.

Dorothy, Earl and May Belle were finally seated in the third pew from the back on the left side next to the Carters, Challie Carter being the one who both leased and farmed acreage on Crooked Creek Farm and that of the Landerses. He also had his own hearty spread. The Carters always sat in the back pew, usually arriving a few minutes late and scooting out at the sound of the last *Amen*. Dorothy had intentionally meandered around in the narthex awaiting their arrival, Earl on her heels, since they usually occupied that pew alone and she hadn't visited with them for quite some time. Thankfully, they'd arrived today just before Chester rang the church bell.

After a few friendly greetings and inquiries about when Challie speculated the corn would be ready for harvest this year, Dorothy opened her bulletin. When she saw that Pastor Delbert Carol, Jr., who had succeeded his deceased pastor father upon his death some eleven years ago, had named his sermon for the day "Ready to Forgive," she gasped and clasped her hand over her mouth, believing God had a message not only for her today, but that unquestionably, His hand was already going before her situation with the Core Four Covenant. *I can't believe I'm surprised! You did recently assure me with all that holy chirping and color! Why, God, is it so easy to forget, even Your signs and wonders?* Nothing but God and the Holy Spirit could have nudged *Pastor* to preach on this very subject, especially now. And okay, maybe there was a church calendar Pastor had to follow, but for this to now be the . . . It gave her goose bumps.

She leaned over to May Belle and pointed to the sermon topic. May Belle's eyebrows raised, then she smiled and said, "Isn't God always just so faithful!"

Although Dorothy still hadn't revealed any particulars to May Belle, she'd made it clear that *whatever* it was had been held inside of her for a long while, and that it was B-I-G, and that it involved several people, and that she trusted that in the long run, God would heal her and everyone involved, but that it might, indeed, be a long run. She'd also shared that she was the last living person to know the details (at least those that she did know), which seemed more and more likely to soon be discovered. "The tough part's going to be the forgiveness, May Belle, and I'll be needing as much of it as anyone. Many folks — possibly a snowballing *lot* of folks — are going to have to find it in their hearts to forgive other dear souls even more so, and they have already passed on."

May Belle had spent extra time in prayer for Dorothy, praying for her ability to trust God the way Dorothy had always trusted Him. She'd also prayed that she herself would be a good, sensitive friend, and a safe harbor to which Dorothy could turn if she needed to talk more.

Pastor went on to preach his message of forgiveness from Psalm 86:5, *For Thou, Lord, art good, and ready to forgive, And abundant in lovingkindness to all who call upon Thee."* He delivered the sermon with eloquence and conviction. As usual, she took plenty of notes on the back of the bulletin and in the margins of her Bible, especially noting today's date near the passage when she underlined it for the third time, and she could tell by the different color of ink in each underline how many times that passage had stood out to her during her personal studies over the years.

But every once in a while she'd squint up

her eyes and stare at Pastor, appearing as though she really wondered about something he was saying. Twice he'd caught her doing so, the second time having to clear his throat, the look on her face so broadcasted her . . . questioning, disapproval . . . what? Pastor was used to seeing Dorothy nodding affirmingly at his words. Although he'd learned to ignore most of Gladys's tsk-tsking, this look coming from Dorothy caught his attention and he had to shift his eyes away from her so he wouldn't become distracted. After all, he was preaching!

He pressed on and closed by repeating the scripture verse. "Yes, friends, our Lord is always good, and ready to forgive. Whether you read that as good . . ." and he paused for dramatic effect where he saw the comma in his bible, ". . . and ready, or good-and-ready," and this run-through he'd spoken the phrase as one word, "*forgive* is what He does."

At the *Amen,* Dorothy leaned past May Belle and grabbed hold of Challie's sleeve before he could escape. "What did you think about Pastor's sermon today, Challie?" Challie looked more like a busted sheep than a fed one.

"Um, I . . ."

"Go ahead, Challie," his wife said, smiling and gently leaning into him, nudging him with her shoulder. "Why not just admit you slept through the sermon, as usual." Then she looked at Dorothy. "Poor Challie. I know how much he loves the Lord, but try as he might, he just can*not* stay awake once the sermon begins. Now you know why we sit in the back every Sunday."

This "news" would surprise nobody since Challie's snores occasionally rippled clear up to the choir, who sat behind the pulpit. No amount of fierce staring at Challie — not even by the entire choir — had ever awakened him, not even for a nanosecond. Although his wife used to elbow him until he'd at least change positions enough to lessen the sound, she'd finally just given up and decided to concentrate herself on the sermon so she could tell him about the message on the way home. It wasn't usually until the choir started leading the congregation in the last hymn that he'd come back to life, just in time to beat it out the back door.

"As we were told today," Dorothy said, looking kindly at Challie, "the good Lord is always ready to forgive, even sleeping through a sermon, I'm sure." She laughed a nervous laugh, working to lighten her own mood and kill enough time for others to depart so she could have a few private words with Pastor.

With true affection, Pastor bid each of his Sunday morning parishioners at United Methodist Church a farewell for the week. One after the other, they congratulated him on his "*sterling* sermon about forgiveness," a couple even going so far as to say his daddy would have been proud since this had always been one of his favorite topics. "Chip off the old block," Rick Lawson, Attorney at Law, had told him. More than once, Pastor responded to their accolades with "Just preaching what the Good Book says." *Just like you, Dad. Not only what the Good Book says, but what you, by the grace of God, taught me to believe. What you so clearly knew in your heart to be true.* He gave private thanks to God for the accolades, which surely belonged to God, not him. After all, it was God who'd nudged him to dig deeper and deeper into this sermon topic, checking just one more book, one more concordance, one more biblical cross reference only to rewrite several thoughts a few more times. He couldn't remember when he'd spent more time preparing for any sermon, not even on Easter Sunday.

Pastor Delbert Carol, Sr. had been a stalwart and respected shepherd right up until the heart attack that had claimed his life. Although by the time he died his son was already well into seminary in a second career move ("God yanked me out of my accountant's chair," he was fond of saying), it had always grieved Delbert Junior, as well as the entire congregation, that Delbert Senior never got to hear his son preach. They'd allowed Delbert Junior a month to get through all he'd had to handle after his dad's death, since he'd lost his mom when he'd been only six, and he was their only child. Then after local licensing, Delbert Junior was blessedly appointed by the Conference to serve as their pastor. Congregants were relieved, knowing that permitting his honest and continued grief as he ministered to them would also help them to walk through their own.

After the Carters finally made their way out the door, Dorothy pretended to be rearranging hymnals — something Earl usually liked to do and could sometimes be found doing, even in the middle of a weekday — then she feigned trying to organize her coat and handbag, which really only needed picking up. At last, everyone was gone but she, Earl and May Belle. "You two run on along. I've got to stay today and clean up the altar anyway. I'm sure I'll see you soon."

"We'll help you, dear, won't we, Earl? The more hands, the quicker it will go!" May Belle started to remove her coat.

"No!" The word came out with a harshness Dorothy hadn't intended. Earl looked wounded. Dorothy settled her palm on his arm. "I'm sorry, honey. Dorothy didn't mean to be so sharp. You know how I love your help. But today, to be perfectly honest with you, I'd like a moment to talk with Pastor and this seems like as fine a chance as any."

"Good," May Belle said, nodding her head in approval. She buttoned her coat back up and reassured Earl that Dorothy meant what she said about enjoying his help, then they said their good-byes to Pastor and made their departure. Dorothy looked all around the sanctuary to make sure everyone else was gone. When she looked back, Pastor, his wife and their children were just about to take their leave.

"Pastor Delbert! Do you have a moment for a question?"

"Certainly, Dorothy. What is it?" He turned to his family and told them to head on home, assuring them he'd be right along. "Promise," he added like a ten-year-old. He and his wife had engaged in more than one discussion the past few months about the lack of time they'd had for each other, even though they lived in the rectory that was right next door to the church.

"It's about forgiveness," Dorothy blurted as soon as they were alone.

He walked up and stood in front of her, waiting for the question, wondering if it had something to do with her facial expressions during his preaching. "Yes?"

"Do you believe what you preached today?"

"Dorothy! Of course I do! God said it and I believe it! What kind of a question is that coming from you, who I know believes what God says in His Word?"

"I'm sorry; I didn't phrase that just right. Seems to be a lot of that going around for me today." Pastor furrowed his brows, not having a clue what she meant, but she waved her hand to dismiss whatever it was. "Of *course* you believe what you preached; that was evident. But let me ask you this: Do you believe because the Lord is always ready to forgive that we are too?" She stared hard at him, searching his very depths, something Dorothy was good at, no matter whose face she stood before.

He raked his fingers through his reddish-brown thinning hair, made an attempt to straighten his crooked glasses, which only made them lopsided in the other direction, then paused to collect himself. He could tell Dorothy, who was not only one of the solid rocks in his flock but one of his favorite people, was asking a sincere spiritual question that called for an earnest examination and answer. Although he was grounded in his faith, he sometimes wished he felt less mortal when he was trying to address folks who had outlived him by several decades, their wealth of experience often lending them insights no amount of books and study could supply.

With measured words, he finally responded. "I believe we are human, Dorothy. I believe God asks us to forgive, and He *intends* for us to forgive. I believe He empowers us to do just that through His son's example on the cross when he said, 'Father, Forgive them for they know not what they do.'"

Dorothy sighed, her shoulders slumping forward. She glanced at the floor, then at the cross behind the pulpit, then locked eyes with Pastor again. "Having lived nearly nine decades, Pastor, and watching first my mother, then my own Caroline Ann go through those horrible treatments for breast cancer, only to finally succumb to the ravages of such a terrible disease, I find each encounter has only made me stronger in my faith since God is the one I cling to during such times. Our sovereign God never fails us — although it sometimes might appear that way when we're angry that *anything,* including disease or darkness, or . . . *whatever,* can still seem to have rule over our earthly lives." Her voice cracked, and although she stopped speaking for a few moments to gather herself, she never broke her eye contact with Pastor, who was taking into account her every word.

"Are you angry with God about those things, Dorothy?"

"Goodness me, no! Not anymore. I must admit, I did walk — and occasionally even *stomp,* you might say — through the anger phase of grief, even in the midst of my faith. But thankfully God is a God who can take our railings, and, with God's help — which was as gentle and patient as any mother's, I might add — I finally came out the other side of my rage. I'm thankful to God for holding me so close in *all* phases of my pain when I've lost some of my dearest ones along the way."

"How does this relate to forgiveness then, Dorothy?"

"It's just that sometimes, sometimes words and messages, whether they're about death or forgiveness, or delivered by pastors or friends, are much easier to say than to live. You know what I mean? Just because Jesus is always ready to forgive us, does that mean *we* are always that ready to forgive one another . . . or ourselves? Do you believe we are, Pastor Delbert? Do you believe we humans, we children of God Almighty, can and are readied and *able* to forgive what we can't even fathom? Actions that seem unthinkable . . . unforgivable, even by those we thought we knew very well?"

Pastor swallowed hard, then shored himself up and said with confidence, "I believe, Dorothy, that if we cannot, we need to trust the Almighty to work that work in us."

Dorothy drew a deep breath, such a deep breath as to indicate she might not have been breathing at all up until that second. Then she exhaled with a whoosh. "Yes. Thank you, Pastor. That is a good, affirming answer I needed to hear and a good thing for us to remember." She leaned into him and gave him a hearty hug. Close into his ear she whispered, "I'm glad you're grounded in trusting God for human forgiveness, Pastor, because sometimes the sudden need to do so can surprise us." She patted his cheek with tenderness, and with the same look he'd seen in her eyes while he was preaching.

What was that look? He decided it almost looked like one of sympathy. A chill ran down his spine, as though the building had suddenly become drafty. While Dorothy headed off to clear the altar, Pastor Delbert looked for the open window that was allowing such a sudden and cool wind to penetrate the building, although he found none.

Dorothy finished her altar duties and looked at her watch. It was nearly eleven. She sat down in the front pew, feeling weary, strained and needing to crawl up, then curl up, in the lap of her Lord. She closed her eyes, and that's just what she did, not only in her mind's eye, but in the safety of God's familiar house.

Lord, me again. No surprise there, huh? She reflected on her days since that evening in the Lexus with Katie, who had first mentioned the Core Four Covenant. *This is what happens when we weave tangled webs of dishonesty, isn't it? God, forgive me. But like the good shepherd You are, You stick right with us while we fumble, fumble along. Patiently waiting for us to fall into our own pits, then, there You are! WHAT A GRACIOUS GOD! Reaching down into our dark secrets and bathing us with Your light. . . .* Dorothy let go of words, eyes closed again, imagining for a moment bright, warm rays of welcome sunshine landing on the top of her head, her face, her shoulders, arms, lap, toes . . .

Help me be Your eyes, Lord, so Katie knows You are with her. Dorothy tried to imagine what Jesus might say to Katie, should the secret come out and He were to appear to her in the flesh, looking full in her face.

Help me.

A surprise smile rumbled within her as she recalled the song she and May Belle used to sing as girls down by the creek. Something about a rabbit needing to be rescued from the hunter. "Help me! Help Me! Help me he cried . . ." Next thing she knew, the rumbling smile let her lips know about it. "Thank you, smile," she said aloud. "Thank you, God! Thank you, May Belle.

Thank you, . . . Mom." She focused on the wonder and balancing respite one receives when one gives thanks in the middle of a crisis.

Dorothy sat as still as a post for a long while, eyes open, just listening. Listening for the sounds of His words, His thoughts to come into her.

Then she knew, as well as she had ever known anything, that she was the one who needed to pry open the box, to speak the first word, and not wait for Katie to figure it out. If she was the one with the key, she's the one who needed to use it.

Katie and Josh both awakened early. They decided they'd just get out of the city and catch a drive-through breakfast on the outskirts before Sunday traffic bottlenecked. She pulled over and let Josh drive after the halfway mark, figuring it was best to keep him comfortable driving long stretches of multilane highways rather than just country roads. They were mostly silent. Katie was physically still pretty relaxed from her spa day, although thoughts of the Core Four Covenant were beginning to once again gnaw at her peace. She'd think about the Core Four and her heart would zing, like when you suddenly remembered something important you forgot to do. When that happened, she would close her eyes and try to mentally put herself back on the massage table, feeling the soothing touch of healing.

As a passenger, which she almost never was, it was fascinating to her to watch the landscape change as they traveled farther south along the highway. Long stretches of field after field that had looked so terminally boring to her now appeared oddly appealing. *Is it being the passenger, or because I really am getting used to the farm?* Although she'd found herself in one way anxious to leave the city, she realized she also wasn't ready to arrive home yet either, what with all that . . . *Home. Yes, it feels like I'm going home. How's that for a shocker? First you can't wait to get "back" to the city, then you can't wait to get out of it. And yet, you can't stand to deal with what awaits you.* She wondered if this was why gypsies throughout time had continued to wander. Maybe they didn't feel like they really belonged anywhere either.

Her mind began to twiddle with the initials again. *Tess Walker, Clarice Walker, somebody D Walker and DC.*

DW. Somebody Walker. Dave. Dick. Don. Darlene. Debbie. Dolores. For several miles she toiled with every D name she could come up with. None sounded familiar. She wracked her brain to recall her mother ever having mentioned other Walkers. Nothing. *Has her father's eyes. Hope he can see her.* Maybe having set the letters aside for a couple of days, distance and some fresh perspective would shed enlightenment when she returned to them.

She glanced over at her son, wondering what was up with him, why he'd been so sullen all weekend. And why hadn't he and Alex gotten together? As close as the boys had been for so many years, this seemed very odd, even though Josh had obviously made new friends at Hethrow. Whatever the reason, it was clear Josh didn't want to talk about it, and that he had been disappointed. He'd once even knocked on her hotel room door to ask if she had received any phone messages, needing to see for himself that she hadn't overlooked the blinking light, just in case the hotel had patched Alex through to her room instead of his. "Joshua," she'd said, "we don't have the same last name, remember? If somebody called asking for Josh Kinney, they wouldn't put them through to Katie Durbin." He'd told her that if Alex had forgotten the room number, or his mom had thrown it away while he was out, that Alex was smart enough to know to ask for her if the desk told him there wasn't anyone registered by the name of Kinney.

Divorce could offer odd and ongoing complications to lives. She'd felt a pang again, sad that divorce had to become a part of her son's life. *How can a child form an identity when he carries a father's name, a father he doesn't live with, and doesn't share a mother's last name, a mother with whom he does live? And if I myself . . .*

Josh looked at his mom, wondering why she was staring at him. "Yes?"

"Just wondering where the time has gone that I have a son old enough to drive" was all she said. "Watch the road."

Like yesterday, her thoughts again flashed to Jessica, whom she'd been sorely missing lately — avoiding, really, in the midst of her Core Four angst. She adored Jessica, but could she be trusted with wild speculations and vulnerabilities? It occurred to her that Zeda was something like Jessica, in terms of temperament and her love for home and family. Katie wondered if she'd given Zeda half a chance years back if they, too, might have become friends. But then, that would have been too difficult with Zeda's husband being so involved in the same competitive business. Katie wouldn't have felt free to share any personal things the way she did with Jessica. Not good to mix business and friendship. That was her personal law.

Katie suddenly understood she'd needed to come to Partonville to learn that the type of friendship she had with Jessica even existed.

Friendships. She'd missed talking to Dorothy, too, who always seemed to be able to cut to the chase with her. She hadn't talked to Dorothy since after bunco, when Dorothy had recommended Katie pray. What had she said? "Some things we need to plow through and pray over before we can *get* over them." *She also said she'd pray for me. Move me to the top of her prayer list. She could be praying for me right now, for all I know, while I'm busy sitting here thinking about her. What good would it be doing anyway? NONE! Just the same, I'd like to see her.*

While Katie's mind had wandered from this to that and back again, Josh had been composing a new e-mail in his head, the one he would send to Alex as soon as they got home. He figured he'd had it coming and couldn't blame Alex for not seeming to work very hard to get in touch with him. He was going to try to patch things up one more time.

And Shelby. What was he to do about *her?* He couldn't just stand by and watch her succumb to the clutches of Kevin, who clearly didn't seem to respect *any* girls, let alone Shelby.

But then what *about* Kevin, who had befriended him? Was this something to dump a friendship over? And what, exactly, was the "it"? His own stupidity and ego to begin with? And if he did quit hanging around with Kevin, no more cool table at lunch. Probably no more friends at all.

He couldn't wait to talk to Dorothy and get her perspective. She always seemed to have a few wise words, and it was easier to talk to her than it was to talk to his mom, especially about stuff like this. Maybe, since they were getting home so early, he could still see her today.

"Mom, do you think I could borrow the wheels to visit Dorothy this afternoon?"

Katie stared at him in disbelief. "What made you think about her just now?"

"I don't know. I just did. Why?"

"I was thinking about her, too. Just now.

Just when you said that." Katie stared out her passenger window, and without turning her head toward Josh, she casually said, "Maybe we ought to stop by and see her on the way through town. If you want to see her alone later, that's fine, but we could just stop together and say hello."

Although Josh really did want Dorothy all to himself, at least a brief *Howdy Ho,* as Dorothy would say, would be a beginning. He decided he owed her an apology, too, for not keeping in better touch. And after all, Dorothy had mentioned she hadn't heard "hide nor hair" from either of them. Maybe she was missing both of them too. He glanced at the car clock. "Let's see, it's eleven. She'll probably be home from church by noon, ya think? Maybe you should call on your cell phone and ask her if she wants to come out to the farm for lunch; she e-mailed me that she could use a good dose of Crooked Creek. Maybe we could pick up a bucket of chicken or something, then get her?"

13

Doc Streator leaned back against his car, lightweight jacket unzipped, arms crossed in front of him, bald head beaming in a flash of sunlight, which felt good on his face and chest. Pastor Delbert's thought-provoking sermon on forgiveness still resonated in his mind and heart. While Pastor had been preaching, Doc had been thanking God for all the forgiveness he had been extended in his life, for surely, no man or woman was without the need. Now, though, he set those thoughts aside to chat with Eugene, who had walked out of church next to him after a short cup of coffee during the meet-and-greet session, which was mostly about having a cup of coffee — or tea, for those who had squawked long and loud enough to finally get one committee or another to donate funds toward an electric teapot. Or so they all thought. Truth was, Dorothy had gotten so tired of hearing them squawk and squabble about budgets and tea bags that *she'd* finally purchased one and anonymously donated it, along with a starter box of tea bags.

"You know, Eugene, I agree with Gladys — but please don't *ever* tell her I said so — that you and I *are* probably in two of the most interesting positions to gather and tell a few stories from Partonville's history. We're on the right committee, for sure."

Eugene buttoned the top button on his heavy, plaid Woolrich shirt, which he was using as a jacket over his Sunday dress shirt. He'd been running slightly behind schedule when he readied to leave for church this morning, and he'd grabbed the first outer garment in the front closet he set his eyes on. His wife was in St. Louis visiting her sister, which explained his tardiness. She usually laid out clothes for him each day; he was clueless and colorblind when it came to coordinating things. She would have had nothing short of a conniption fit had she seen what he wore to church. He pulled his old floppy hat out of the right breast pocket (a double conniption fit!), which he'd rolled up and stuffed in there when he hung up his jacket in the narthex. He batted it on his thigh to pop it open, then pulled it snugly down on his head. Eugene was always worried about catching a cold, and no matter how many times he'd been told over the years that colds were caught from germs, not a cool breeze, there was no convincing him. Doc smiled, knowing full well Eugene believed he was, with intent, warding off the sniffles with all this buttoning and covering.

"I wonder, Doc, how many folks you think you've delivered that I've buried?"

"I reckon a fair share of them, and many before their time, if you ask me. Although I didn't deliver Jake, I think about him every week when I see Gladys sitting in that front pew alone, knowing just how she feels without her spouse beside her. Who'd have thought, the day he pulled out in his Mac truck for his next long haul — same as he'd done for all the years of his working life — that he'd return in an ambulance straight to your funeral home? One day you're a truck driver *and* a mayor; the next day you're an obituary."

"You got that right. Course I guess when it's my time to go, I'd just as soon go out in a blink-of-an-eye crash rather than some strung-out disease, the way, say, Caroline Ann did. Now that I think about it, Doc, I guess for a guy who's birthed babies his entire career, you've watched plenty of folks die, too. Personally, I'd rather have them after they're already gone than to have to watch them suffer. Guess I'm in the right business then, huh?"

Doc grinned. "We're supposed to be working on a celebration, Eugene. I think we better cheer ourselves up before the next committee meeting, wouldn't you say?"

"You got that right, too. Gladys will be expecting us to give her a thorough report."

"What she's expecting is a whoop-tee-do to end all whoop-tee-do's. I tell you, our fine mayor is . . . is . . ."

"Sometimes there just are no words for Gladys, are there?" Eugene rolled his eyes.

"You know though, Eugene, she is on to something here. Maybe this whole shebang of a celebration will be something we all remember for years to come. Personally, I'm looking forward to reading our booklet, aren't you?"

"Where should we begin?"

"How about we each pick five families who've been here more than one generation and who we believe have contributed something special to Partonville. We can talk on the phone, say tomorrow afternoon? After we've had a chance to think about it? Maybe compare lists? We ask them for pictures and such. We say to them, 'I remember when

. . .' and that'll get their pumps primed. They'll be so flattered, we'll probably never get them to shut up. Then we'll ask them to stop talking and write up a few paragraphs, and turn it in to us by . . . When do we need this?"

"I reckon we need it within about ten days, if we're going to stand a chance of having somebody put it all together, lay it out and get it printed — and that might be cuttin' it too close. Gladys should have given us deadlines. You know, I believe we should have a talk with Harold and Sharon to see how we can work together with them, since no doubt the *Partonville Press* will somehow be involved with the printing."

"Good idea." Doc shifted positions, still leaning on his car, crossing one leg in front of the other. "Remind me who's doing the fund-raising. You know, trying to get all those patrons and such?"

"Now that you mention it, I don't recall anybody being assigned to that task! Boy, now there's *another* oversight — although I can't help but believe Gladys isn't already strong-arming everybody she sees. Probably wouldn't hurt if we mentioned it to folks. If we get any collections, we'll take those to the meeting too, until we know what else to do with them. That ought to earn our committee a few points with Ms. Mayor."

"I've been thinking," Doc said, running his hand back and forth around the back of his neck, "this town's been so good to me all of these decades, I should become one of those patrons. Get the financial ball rolling. Did Gladys say just how much it would take?"

"Don't most things like that have different levels of patrons? You know, like the silver patron for such-and-such a donation, and the gold patron level for more, then the platinum . . ."

"Then you're a patron saint!" They both laughed out loud. Doc reached for his jacket zipper, the cool fall air sinking in and a new rush of clouds hiding the warm rays, which had been appearing and disappearing as quickly as the remaining days of his life.

Eugene saw Doc's gesture as a red flag and he pulled his collar up around his neck. "And we don't celebrate saints in church until All Saints' Day, which isn't until after the festivities! No point in being one if you can't be recognized at the whoop-tee-do. I'm going to get going, Doc, before I catch a cold. I'm about to bust out shivering."

"I think we're getting punch happy now anyway."

Dorothy walked up and stood next to Eugene. "What's this I overhear about you two men getting punch happy? I tell you what, I could use a good dose of punch happy. Why don't you let me in on a round." Doc opened his mouth to say something, but nothing came out. Then Eugene thought about trying to explain it. "You know, Dorothy, sometimes you just have to be there. Let's just say it began with Gladys . . . and ended with saints."

Doc and Eugene chuckled, as did Dorothy, who did so not because the line struck her funny, but because these too old duffers just tickled her being so tickled with themselves. They each turned and headed toward their destinations. Doc opened his driver's door, then looked over his car roof at Dorothy, who was approaching the sidewalk. "Dorothy," he yelped, "would you like a ride? I know you've only got a few blocks to go, but it's getting a little chilly out here. I'd be happy to give a gal a ride in my old chariot!"

"You know, Doc, I think I'll just take you up on that. Those few blocks were feeling mighty far away to me this morning. I'm going to go straight home and take a nap. This way I can start it sooner!" Besides, Dorothy thought if anybody had aged as well as Paul Newman, it was Doc Streator. It filled her with a sudden delight to know that at her age, she still noticed things like that.

Jessica picked up her little gooseneck craft scissors and snipped off the thin, green cotton yarn next to the knot near her last crocheted stitch. She held the bookmark up and inspected her handiwork. "Perfect! Sometimes I amaze myself," she said, pleased with her ability to have duplicated the bookmark Jessie won at the last Hookers' bunco meeting. She checked the wall clock. "And in no more than fifteen minutes! I could easily make a dozen of these, honey, just using tidbits of yarn and little pockets of time like this over the next couple weeks." She determined she'd make a few more in Christmas colors and tack on a sequin or a couple of dangling beads, just to dress them up.

Then a new idea struck her. "That's it! Rather than this being the bookmark itself," she said, fingering her handiwork, "this will be the pretty part that stays *outside* of the book! I'll make them uniquely my own design by adding a long crocheted strand that goes inside the book for the page

239

marker, and attach a bauble to the end that will dangle out the bottom of the book, anchoring it all in place! Maybe use some of my fancy buttons I've collected! Won't that be perfect, Paul?" She turned to show Paul her creation, only to find him sound asleep in his lounge chair, legs stretched out on the ottoman, his book open on his lap.

"Poor thing," she whispered, removing the craft items from her lap, setting them on the end table and quietly turning off the reading light that was shining in her husband's face. He awakened when she went to pick up the book. "Hey! I'm reading!" he said. Jessica thought it was just like a man to never admit he'd nodded off, same as when she'd tried to change the TV channel during one of his snoozes, which, she had to admit, weren't very often. Nonetheless, if she ever intentionally wanted to wake him up, turning off the television would be the way to do it. She just had to be ready to hear "Hey, I'm watching that!" Right.

"I'm sorry I woke you up; I should have just left well enough alone," she said, giving him a kiss on the cheek. "You hardly ever get to take a nap, honey. It's a rare day when Sarah Sue stays down this long after church too; she must have worn herself out in the nursery! Why don't you go on in the bedroom and stretch out while you have the chance. That way I won't bother you."

"I'm sorry. I'm not very good company today, am I?"

"You're perfect company. I'm as happy as a little clam playing with my crafts anyway."

Paul decided her nap idea sounded like a good one and departed to the bedroom, which left her blissfully alone to try her new inspiration. She retrieved her button box and another clear plastic shoebox that housed her sequins and beads. She'd long ago learned that she entered another time zone — seemingly not of this world — when her mind was lost to the art of creation. She was quite satisfied with no television or radio emitting noise in the background when visiting the *wherever* zone; her own happy humming was enough.

Each year when fall approached, waves of *Must do crafts!* washed over her. Christmas would be here before she knew it, and she adored making Christmas gifts for everyone — not to mention that hand-crafting also helped the budget, especially since she always seemed to find the supplies she needed from the crafters' corner in the Now and Again Resale store in Yorkville. But first came the arts and craft fair for the Pumpkin Festival, which is why she was intent on whipping up the bookmarks.

The last couple of years, she'd had her own booth filled with everything from crocheted goodies to painted woodwork to clay beads. She'd made enough money to do nearly all of their Christmas shopping, which was, admittedly, not that much, but just the same, she'd felt proud and satisfied. This year, what with her new baby girl and motel business picking up, she decided she realistically only had time to make a few items, so she'd put them in a separate bin and let another crafter sell them at his or her booth, giving them a small commission for the kindness. Better than nothing, and every little penny helped. Besides, now that she and Paul were on the Centennial Plus 30 committee, she'd have other things to think about, plan for and create too. She hoped she hadn't stretched herself too thin. But the thought of getting to decorate the platform also gave her a rush of creative energy, which was a nice departure from diapers and bed sheets — although she figured there'd be plenty of sheets and towels and hotel rooms to clean if folks' relatives came to town for the Pumpkin Festival the way they usually did, some viewing it as more of a homecoming festivity than anything else. Who knew how many guests to expect, since the weekend had now grown into an official celebration of another color and word was just getting out. No matter what, though, it pleased both her and Paul to gather themselves up for a rare evening out, even if it was just for a committee meeting.

She attached the long tail to the bookmark and matched a button with two beads as the perfect complement. Humming "Joy to the World," she tested the new product design in the book Paul had been reading. "Perfect! Wait until I show this to Katie!"

Katie. Her heart lost some of its merriness as she considered how much she'd missed her friend. Since Katie had neither phoned nor returned two messages she'd left, Jessica could only conclude that she'd let Katie down and that Katie was pulling away from her. She was sure she'd disappointed her when she'd chosen to stay at Dorothy's and eat dessert rather than ride home with Katie after bunco last week. She kept picturing the back of Katie's SUV barreling down the road without her as she stood in the street waving. *What kind of a person opts for dessert rather than spending time with a new friend, the friend who even brought me to the Hookers' meeting?*

Intruding into her regretful thoughts, Sarah Sue began making noises that she was refreshed and ready for her own kind of play, which didn't include crochet hooks with which to gouge herself, and buttons and beads to swallow. Jessica gathered up her things, stored them back in the cabinet and removed her imaginary artist's hat. Then she donned her dairy-cow face. It was time to nurse her baby.

"Is that you, Dorothy? It's me, Katie. You sound . . . tired. Are you feeling well?"

"You caught me, kiddo. You caught me *sleeping* in the middle of the day," she said, as if to clarify her own thought.

"Oh, I'm so sorry. I had no idea you were a napper. I'll phone you another time."

"Don't be silly. And don't you *dare* hang up. I am surely glad to hear from you. In fact, I was going to give you a call tomorrow. It's been too long since we've had a chance to catch up." *And oh, child, what a catch-up it will be.* "I'm not usually a napper; it's just that by the time church was over today, then I chatted with Pastor for a spell before cleaning up the altar . . . I guess this crazy changing weather, that can't seem to make up its mind what it wants to do, is tickling my hibernating mode. Are you back from Chicago then?"

"We're on our way back as we speak."

"Goodness. You mean to tell me you're not even in town? You sound so clear. Technology is amazing. You're not talking on your phone while you're driving, are you? That scares me to death when I hear of people doing that."

"No. I sure am not. Josh is driving." (She decided not to mention that driving and talking on her phone were a common practice for her.) "It's nice to just be able to sit here and relax for a change. And while he's whisking us home, we discovered we were both thinking about you. Have you had lunch yet?"

"No, I haven't." Dorothy could hear Josh in the background saying something about chicken.

"Yes, I know, Joshua," Katie said, her hand over the mouthpiece but doing a bad job of muffling her voice.

"Josh and I would like to treat you today. We thought we'd pick up a bucket of chicken when we come through Hethrow, then swing by and get you. Bring you out to the farm with us for lunch. How does that sound?"

"Sounds perfect! How long do you think before you get here?"

Katie looked at her watch. "I'd say about an hour. Can you wait that long to eat?"

"Sure can." *I could wait a very long time, I'm sure; but God has other plans to unfold, and it seems He's kicked them into high gear.*

"We'll be at your door before you know it. Anything I need to know?"

"WHAT?" Dorothy could not believe her ears.

"Any special requests, like all white or dark meat, or certain side dishes?"

Oh, for goodness sake! "Whatever you set before me is what I'll eat since I like it all."

"Anything for Sheba?" she heard Josh holler.

"A back seat to stand in and an open window to hang her head out of on the way to the farm," Dorothy said, giving her answer to Katie. "Even though it's cool, it'll be the best treat she's had since we moved! As a matter of fact, if I can get Josh to pedal down a little, even with his mother in the car, it'll be the best gift for *both* of us!" *Although I'm sure in no hurry to get to the toughest part: that which needs to be revealed.*

■ ■ ■ ■

"Just a minute! I'll be right there!" Dorothy was in the bathroom when Katie and Josh knocked on the door. She was brushing her teeth, both in and outside of her mouth. Since she'd been awakened by the phone, she'd been praying in her prayer-chair by her bed, flipping through her bible, using the concordance to look up verses about courage. When she'd glanced at the clock, she couldn't believe how quickly an hour had flown by. She'd kicked it into high gear to ready herself before they arrived. Not that she had that much to do more important than prayer, but her mouth tasted like yuck (afternoon nap), in which case her breath probably wasn't any better. She knew the message was going to be bad enough without it being delivered on the foul winds of dragon-mouth.

Katie stood waiting on Dorothy's tiny front porch once again admiring the mailbox Jessica had hand-painted for Dorothy as a housewarming gift. Multicolored flowers, green stems, house numbers . . . all surrounded by a grapevine wreath. *Jessica is so gifted!* Katie would be contacting her tonight, she decided, to express how much she'd missed her. Apologize for the gap in their connection.

The mailbox was cheerful, just like Dorothy. She traced her finger over the green stems that ran down into the house numbers. This was the first time she'd ever noticed Jessica had also painted Dorothy's name in tiny purple cursive beneath the house numbers. The first letter of each part of her name was in a different color of paint: D (red), J (blue), W (green), with the tiniest of flower buds accentuating the tips of the letters.

"What are you doing in there, Dorothy? Hiding?" Josh's booming voice startled Katie and her body jerked. "Joshua! Lower your voice!" Josh loved teasing his feisty older friend, who knew how to dish it right back. In fact, more often than not, she was the instigator of warm kidding. "We know you're in there," he continued in a softer voice. "And we've got *chi*-cken," he said all sing-songy.

"Oh!" Katie exclaimed, this time startling Joshua. "Dorothy's initials! DJW. DW."

"What?" Josh asked his mom, who repeated the initials.

Dorothy, donning her old pink backpack in which she'd hastily stuffed her handbag, a jacket and a few extra cookies from May Belle, had her left hand on the doorknob inside her house when she heard Katie say, "Dorothy's initials! DJW. DW."

"Well, *duh*, Mom. What did you think her initials were, since her name is Dorothy Jean Wetstra?"

Dorothy slowly opened the door, heart in her mouth. Josh stepped in and grabbed her in a big bear hug, his feet over the threshold, door open behind him. Dorothy returned the hug, peering over his shoulder right at Katie, whose eyes revealed her suspicions. Dorothy patted Josh on the back and released him. He snatched up Sheba and moved inside the house, sitting down on the couch with her as she licked his entire face in a happy welcome. Dorothy moved out onto the porch and pulled the door closed behind her. She hugged Katie, and, still holding her somewhat stiffened body, very quietly said, "Yes. I am the Core Four DW. We need to talk, honey. Alone. Tomorrow, when Josh is in school. I have much to tell you, child. But for now, let's try to enjoy our chicken."

14

On Monday morning, Josh asked one of the guys to point out Deborah Arnold to him. He could hardly believe his good fortune — that is once he got over his embarrassment. "What are you, Josh, blind? She's been right next to you several times a day since school started!" Indeed, her locker was right next to his.

Twice already they'd been at their lockers together, but he hadn't found the gumption to speak. Now he was determined. His eyes flashed alternately between staring at her coming down the hall and the numbers on his combination lock. He wondered how anyone this drop-dead beautiful could have possibly been described by Kevin as "last year's news." From what he could tell by the daily attention he'd noticed her garner, from males and females alike, she hadn't lost an ounce of her popularity since being elected last year's prom queen. The only thing he had never noticed before had been her name.

He waited until she began to twirl the numbers on her lock. "Deborah! How's it going?" he asked, trying to sound matter-of-fact, as though he had talked to her every day of his life.

"It's going," she said, looking rather surprised he'd addressed her. "I think I just bombed a test, though. Honestly," she said, rearranging a few items, "I studied for hours, but when I saw the questions, I wondered if I'd even been reading the right textbooks." She retrieved a lipstick from her pocket and her head disappeared when she swung the door to an angle that enabled her to get close to her magnetic mirror. She was still pursing her lips together when she peaked back around the door.

"How's it going with you? Josh, isn't it?"

"Yup. Josh Kinney." *Hm. How does she know my name? And nice lips!* He briefly meditated on the rosy slickness of them he held in the forefront of his mind while she turned back to whatever she was doing inside of her locker. "Glad to officially meet you, Deborah." He held out his hand to shake, then noticed both of hers were already filled with the books she'd just retrieved — while he'd been thinking about her lips. He swiftly crammed his hand into his pocket as though it had just been busted running away from home. "Sorry. Which way are you going?" She nodded her head the same direction he was about to head. "Here. Let me carry those for you," he said, reaching for her stack. But at that same instant, she turned to hip-check her locker closed and he knocked the books out of her hands. The entire pile crashed to the floor in a state of disarray, papers flying out of them this way and that. "Oh, I'm *sorry!* What a klutz. Here, let me get those." He bent over — same as she — and they bonked heads.

"Owwww! Watch it!" Deborah had heard through the grapevine that Josh wasn't exactly an athletic genius, even though he sat with the jocks. Now she was more inclined to believe what she'd heard, even though she'd always been the type to see for herself before believing any secondhand information. No matter, though, he was a cutie.

Josh was now afraid to move. He sucked air in through his gritted teeth, lips parted and drawn back in a gesture of embarrassment. She thought his sheepish demeanor endearing. She shook her head and busted out laughing. "I've got it: you keep standing still. Don't move, aside from holding out your hands like so." She held her arms straight down in front of her, palms up, lacing her fingers together. "I'll pick up the books and papers and deposit them, then you can carry them to my next class, if you've got time. It's the least you can do to repay me for my pain and suffering," she said, beginning the stacking process. About halfway through, she looked at him and said, "And how'd that sound? I'd like to be a lawyer one day." Her smile was warm and kind *and oh, so rosy,* and soon her stacking task was complete.

"I'd say you'll win every case," *with that beautiful smile.* "You convinced me with your brief opening and closing argument! No trial necessary." They began down the hall until she stopped in front of her class door, which was, as luck would have it again, right next to his. She retrieved the pile and gave him a quick thanks. "And call me Deb, okay? I'm sure I'll be seeing you again," she said over her shoulder as she disappeared through the doorway.

That wasn't the way it was supposed to go, you doofus. He'd had every intention of casually chatting with her as they stood by their lockers, then inviting her to the Pumpkin Festival dance before he lost his nerve. *Why did it all sound so easy when I was talking to Dorothy yesterday?*

Yesterday. Now there was an adventure that took an odd turn. It's like everything was fine between me and mom, and then we picked up Dorothy. He shuffled into his classroom and sat down at his desk, opening his math book to the spot where he'd tucked in his homework papers. Although his brief conversation with Dorothy about Shelby and Kevin had produced the excellent idea of him inviting Deborah . . . Deb . . . and then asking Kevin if he wanted to double — assuming of course, that Deb accepted his invitation — the opportunity for that conversation had only come about after his mom seemed to mentally check out. Nearly as soon as they'd arrived at the farm — a journey during which his mother barely spoke a word — his mom said she'd developed a splitting headache and excused herself to go upstairs, announcing to both of them that Josh would have to take Dorothy home later. It was like one minute she was all perky and chatty, and the next she'd gone mute.

After Dorothy and Josh had gluttoned themselves with chicken and mashed potatoes, they decided to bundle up and take a walk down by the creek to jostle their food "down the hatch and out of our gullets," Dorothy had said. Although Dorothy at first seemed oddly distracted and worried about his mom — a little too worried about a mere headache, he thought — eventually he knew he had her full attention. He poured out another piece of his heart with each step, first about Alex (since Dorothy'd asked how his visit had gone), then Kevin, then Shelby. As usual, she'd delivered affirmations for his teenage self, assurance for his mended relationship with Alex, and the excellent double-dating idea, which would not only help him make amends with Kevin (Dorothy said, "You don't get rid of friends just because they sometimes act like jerks — no matter which end of the jerk part you're on," then she'd winked), but also give him a chance to keep an eye on Shelby. "And I've heard Deborah Arnold is a right nice young woman," she'd said. "I'm sure you'll all have a swell evening." By the time he'd taken Dorothy back to town, he'd felt renewed and ready to tackle life again.

Now, though, after knocking Deb's books

to the floor, banging her head and then never even asking her to the dance the entire trip down the hall, he was suddenly back in Doofusville.

Katie had been unable to speak after Dorothy'd revealed her Core Four self on the porch. Standing at the edge of knowing — *whatever* it was — and not being able to find out for another day was unbearable. Her emotions swung between fear for what she would learn, and anger with Dorothy for not volunteering this information sooner. Then again, maybe she would ultimately end up happier if Dorothy *never* told her the truth, if that's what she was going to do.

After she excused herself with Josh and Dorothy and climbed the stairs to her bedroom, she closed the door and locked it behind her. Walking softly, as though sneaking up on her closet — her own life — she pulled down the ski-boot box and set it on the bed. She removed the lid, then laid down on the bed next to it. Turning onto her side, she propped herself on her elbow and stared at the box for a few minutes, lightly stroking her fingertips across the top of the neat rows of letters, stopping at the notebook that also served as her marker.

Part of her was anxious to begin delving into the letters and notes with this new-found piece of information about Dorothy. Maybe putting *her* in context would reveal something new. Another part of her wanted to fling open her window and toss the entire box to the wind, which had picked up as the day had gone on. Maybe the winds would carry these pieces of her life away, the same way they'd blown them to her toes to begin with.

Katie looked at the clock. It was after two. Still lying on her side, having never touched a thing in the box other than to continue running her fingers back and forth across the tops of the letters, as though they might render soothing music if she strummed across the messages long enough, she finally reached for the lid and settled it back on the container. She scooted the box close to her abdomen, then curled her body and arms around it, cradling it to her as close as she could.

Oh, Mom. What didn't you tell me? As soon as she closed her eyes they began to burn.

Oh, God. Whose child am I?

There it was; she had uttered her growing and deepest fear.

Unbridled tears began to pour forth. An hour passed before she silently cried herself to sleep. No amount of trying to imagine herself back on the massage table — warm hands, quieting fragrances and wafting notes — could heal the deep vulnerabilities that had been laid bare within her.

Katie awakened at four-thirty. Her throat was dry, her eyelids were swollen and her arms were still wrapped around the box. She pushed it away from her and stared at it. Even though she'd faked a headache, she'd cried so long that she now actually had one. She sighed, rolled on her back and rubbed her temples and neck. Then she stretched her body, realizing how many kinks had reclaimed her in such a short period of time, her massage feeling like it had been months ago rather than yesterday. *What's the point of working on the puzzle now? I'll just wait until tomorrow.*

Slipping out of bed, she tiptoed to her closet and set the box back on her shelf, leaving the closet door open so as to make no noise. She wasn't sure if anyone was in the house or not, although it seemed quiet. She simply was not up to small talk, not even with Josh.

She stood slightly back from her window

and peaked through the curtains. Dorothy and Josh were slowly making their way up the incline to the barn, their elbows locked. Dorothy stood alone while Josh opened the large barn door. She looked older from a distance, Katie thought, when you couldn't see the sparkle in her eyes. Frail almost, even though she was a fairly sturdy woman. Katie waffled between intense gratitude for this feisty friend who had helped mend fences between her and her son, and the desire to run out and tackle her to the ground, yelling, "TELL ME WHAT YOU KNOW! WHAT'S BEEN HIDDEN ABOUT ME FOR ALL OF THESE YEARS?"

After Josh and Dorothy disappeared into the barn, Katie scurried to the bathroom, then down the stairs. Even though her stomach was in a knot, she thought it would do her good to eat a little something. Maybe nourishment to her body would help quiet her mind. Once more, she found herself peaking through a window to make sure they weren't coming. *Nothing like hiding in your own house.* She raced around grabbing a paper napkin and plucking two chicken wings — *Wish I could use these to fly away!* — from the bottom of the bucket, leaving only a thigh behind. She grabbed a container of bottled water out of the fridge and raced back upstairs. Back to her room. Back to her wondering. Back to her waiting.

Josh said he'd start the SUV while Dorothy gathered her things from inside; it was time for him to take her home. As she gathered her backpack from the chair in the familiar kitchen — which, even when relaxing in the joy of her happy new kitchen, she sorely missed — she noticed the wings were gone from the bottom of the chicken bucket she and Josh had left on the table. In Katie's haste to grab something to eat while they were gone, she must have accidentally strewn the few napkins Dorothy noticed lying on the floor. *Good. You need your sustenance, child. Lord, bless her special. Massage her heart and give her a good night's rest for tomorrow.*

Since Eugene's wife was out of town until Tuesday, and nobody had died in the night — thankfully giving all of his friends at least one more day on this earth — he'd had nothing to do since church yesterday but watch football and think about his committee duties. Sometimes being an undertaker had its happy advantages, in an odd sort of way. Of course, the more folks who died, the better his income. But Eugene never allowed himself to think that way lest people read his mind and take their business, which of course was their bodies, elsewhere. He was the only undertaker in Partonville, but he figured if they were mad enough, they'd *sure* enough make other arrangements, especially since the funeral home in Yorkville was getting a lot of attention for its new management, since the old owner had — and there was no other way to put it, Eugene thought — become his own client. And Hethrow, well, now they had nearly a dozen funeral parlors the last time Eugene had looked in the Yellow Pages. One had even been running an advertisement in the *Partonville Press* ("Does Harold Crab have no *shame* for what he allows in his paper?") promoting a do-it-yourself service, aside from the embalming or cremation, of course. "What will they think of next?" he'd asked his wife in a huff after reading her the advertisement aloud. "DIE for ya?"

He'd scribbled a short list of interview possibilities on a pad of paper Sunday during football commercials, then, after some reconsiderations, replaced two of them over a bowl of cold cereal Monday morning, right after he'd worked the crossword puzzle, which he finally quit on since he didn't have his wife there to answer his questions about seven down and sixteen across.

Eugene missed his wife. Their marriage had been, compared to some couples in Partonville — say Arthur and Jessie — a quiet and comfortable one. No career changes (housewife and funeral director, they were). No cruises or trips to Hawaii, but they did love taking a week every year to go camping, even now. They'd raised three children, never got behind on their bills and, for the most part, saw eye-to-eye on finances and politics. Even when they weren't saying anything to each other, he realized he was just more comfortable knowing she was in the house, or playing, as she called it, out in her flower garden, or sitting beside him in church. Yes, he thought, life was just more . . . interesting when she was around.

By 8:00 A.M. he'd come up with his list of five names that were sure to be town pleasers. He phoned Doc's home number and got his machine, then he tried his office, but he wasn't there either. Apparently Doc was in transit.

"Is this an emergency, Eugene?" Ellie,

Doc's receptionist asked. She was always on top of protocol and readied for crisis.

"Nope. It certainly is not. I feel as healthy as a horse." He sniffed, just to make sure that statement was still true. "Just a piece of business on which we need to touch bases."

"He's got a pretty full boat this morning, Eugene, so it might be lunchtime before you hear from him. He'll be done today at one, though, since Doctor Nielsen will be seeing patients this afternoon. But come to think of it, Doc probably won't take a lunch break since, as we all know, *he* is usually running behind. So . . . you might not hear back from him until mid afternoon."

"And I suppose you're going to tell me the young *Doctor* (he'd said the word as though he didn't believe it for a minute) Nielsen never runs behind?"

"I suppose I *am* going to tell you that, Eugene Casey. Seems punctuality is something they must be stressing in medical school. The first clinic *Doctor* (and she said that word in a way that would affirm the validity) Nielsen worked at only allowed him fifteen minutes to see a patient, and not a minute more. He pretty much sticks to that here, too, and gets the job done just fine, so that's how I schedule him."

"Who can figure out what ails a body in fifteen minutes? I'm not sure I'd trust a fella who gives as much attention to watching the clock as he does to my cranky gall-bladder!"

"Now, Eugene, we both know Doc likes to visit as much as he likes to doctor."

"Last I heard, talking with patients is how you learned what ailed them."

"Eugene . . ." There was a long pause. Just about the time Eugene thought she'd hung up on him, the terse tone in her voice having revealed her response to his comments, she began again, this time in a kinder, yet still cordially professional voice. "Eugene, Doctor Nielsen is a wonderful doctor. He graduated the top of his class and his recommendations from his previous employer were glowing. He is intelligent, careful and kind. You are not going to do this town, or Doc, for that matter — who, may I remind you, is trying to scale back to retire — any good if you assume otherwise. Do you think Doc would have hired Doctor Nielsen if he hadn't believed he would learn to care for us as much as Doc does?"

After a short pause, Eugene spoke. "You've got that right, Ellie. If there is one person in this town I have trusted enough to care for my health, it's Doc. I've always taken him to be as fine and noble a judge of character as anyone. Now is not the time to shortchange Doc's judgment, or his retirement. Just tell him I phoned, okay? I'll talk to him when I talk to him."

When Ellie hung up the phone, she wrote out a note for Doc asking him to give Eugene a call when he had a chance. She printed "No emergency" at the very top and underlined it twice. Although Eugene hadn't gone so far as to in any way approve of Doctor Nielsen, he had acquiesced when reminded about Doc's good judgment. As tired as she was of trying to talk the town into accepting Partonville's new physician by booking with him, she was at least happy to learn she'd accidentally struck on her most convincing argument yet to support him: the good Doc himself.

15

Gladys stood on the sidewalk in front of her mayoral office located in the small, one-story, dark-red brick building in the center of the Partonville square. She watched traffic passing by, more convinced than ever before that her plan to get Partonville folks traveling in the direction of the future was a must, no two ways — and especially no one *wrong* way — about it. For the life of her, she could not understand why everyone else seemed so blind to the symbolism and simplicity. From the continued banter that had surrounded her at the grill this morning — which had escalated since yesterday's *Partonville Press*'s reporting of the first committee meeting and her plans to change traffic on the square — it seemed momentum was gathering against her, at least if she listened to Cora Davis who had become a virtual flame thrower of negative comments. *Three steps forward and two steps back,* she thought as she reviewed the up-and-down emotional roller-coaster-of-a-ride this was becoming.

Since she'd learned that the Crooked Creek park would "by no means be ready until at least next spring," according to Dorothy, she was bound and determined, by hook, crook or bulldozer, to make this traffic switch happen. To her, it was simple: *Throw up a few one-way signs in the opposite direction, and there you have it!* With a beam of determination on her face and a simple plan in her head, Gladys turned toward her office to start making things happen. As she did so, her eye caught the age-old analog clock that hung from the corner of the building. Since she could remember, the hands to the clock had been stopped at one-fourteen and six seconds. *I wonder why neither Jake nor the mayors before him ever had that fixed? Then again, why haven't I?* Her curiosity was piqued as to what might have been happening in Partonville at the exact moment the clock ticked no more. *A thunderstorm? A birth? The holidays? A death? I wonder if anyone even recollects what year it stopped?*

Gladys decided she'd ask around at Harry's tomorrow morning. After all, folks at

Harry's, especially Cora Davis, looked right toward the building, day after day. Maybe this would give Cora something else to be thinking and talking about other than opinions about *her!* Or maybe Harold would know, or could scan the archives at the paper to see if there'd ever been a mention of either the clock's stopping or its disrepair. Didn't people want to check the clock as they circled the square, hustling from here to there, wondering if they were going to make it to . . . *whatever* on time? Why hadn't there been a public outcry? *Or have we all been too busy traveling backwards in time to follow through with things that matter? Maybe our lack of attention to time is why this town is on the edge of peril!*

She yanked down the bottom of her blazer, which had ridden up on her hips — *Better lose a couple of pounds before photo opportunities* — straightened her mayoral name tag and, with a heavy tromp that was distinctly Gladys's, headed for her office to make a few calls. There were not only traffic signs to order, but now signs of the TIME to correct.

Katie's phone rang at 10:30 A.M. Even

though she'd been waiting for Dorothy's call, the sound startled her. "Hello."

"Katie, it's Dorothy. If you can come to my house in about an hour, that would be good." Katie said nothing, although Dorothy could hear her breathing. "There's no way around it, Katie; this is going to be hard. I'm praying for us, and especially for you. Our God is a sovereign God. Even if it feels like others have let you down, just know that God never will." More silence.

"You can come in an hour then?"

"Yes." Katie hung up without saying good-bye.

Dorothy replayed a part of her conversation with Pastor Delbert.

Do you believe, she'd asked him, *we humans, we children of God Almighty, can and are readied and able to forgive that which we can't even fathom? That which would seem unthinkable . . . unforgivable?"*

"I believe," he'd responded, *"that if we cannot, we need to trust the Almighty to work that work in us."*

Speaking out loud, she said, "God Almighty, I am trusting you for this."

Josh's teacher was still talking when the bell rang. He'd scooted his book and his body to the edge of his desk, ready to beat it to the room next door in order to catch Deb on her way out. When they were finally dismissed, he all but butted his way through kids in the door, just in time to see the back of Deb's head mixing in with the sea of heads in front of him. "Deb! Wait up!"

As he sidestepped through and around people, he caught Shelby out of the corner of his eye. "Hi!" he said. As much as he wanted to talk to her, he needed to catch up with Deb to get this invitation in place before somebody else beat him to it, if that hadn't happened already. His ultimate goal was to protect Shelby, and he didn't want *anything* to get in his way — including Shelby herself at the moment. When he looked back ahead of him, he could barely get a beat on the former queen.

"DEB! WAIT UP!"

Shelby had opened her mouth to say hi back, but before she could form a sound, Josh had called ahead to Deb. Shelby now officially detested the . . . the . . . There were just no polite words to even *think* about him.

Deb stopped after Josh's last bellow, which had been impossible for anyone in the hall to ignore. "Hey! I thought I was going to miss you."

"You'd have seen me later at my locker, no doubt. What's up?"

"So, did you read about Partonville's Centennial Plus Thirty celebrations?" *What a stupid thing to talk about! Pull yourself together, man!*

"No. Can't say as I have. What's a centennial plus . . . what did you say?"

"Never mind. Not important. Are you looking forward to the Pumpkin Festival dance?"

"Should I be? I live in Hethrow, not Partonville. But maybe you didn't know that."

"I just thought if you were going to the festival dance that you would be looking forward to it."

"Festival dance." She said it as though she'd never heard of it either.

"Don't tell me you've never heard of . . ."

"Of course I have, you goofball. I'm just pulling your chain."

"So are you going?"

"Depends."

"Depends on what?"

"If anyone asks me. Anyone, that is, with whom I'd be interested in going."

Josh stopped walking, but it took Deb a few steps to notice. When she turned around and looked to see where he'd gone, she discovered him just standing in the middle of the hall staring at her, traffic oozing around him, opening and closing behind and in front of him. While she was walking back toward him, he'd decided he just needed to trip his trigger. He wasn't good at word games. "Are you interested in going with me?"

She sized him up for a good couple seconds, trying to decide if he was inviting her or just testing the waters — or now pulling *her* chain. "Are you inviting me?"

"Yes, Deb. Will you go to the dance with me?"

"Yes." The bell rang, and just like that, he had a date.

Now he had to talk to Kevin, whom he hadn't talked to since their uncomfortable encounter. Josh had managed to sit at the opposite end of their regular lunchroom table since their face-off, and to act as though he hadn't even seen Kevin a time or two in the halls. Kevin had done nothing to initiate contact, either. One more class and they'd be seated at the table next to each other, if the rest of his plan fell into place.

When Dorothy opened her front door, it was all she could do to keep from clutching Katie to herself. However, by virtue of having searched the faces of so many hurting people in her long life, she could see that Katie had her full emotional mental guard up in an attempt — a failing attempt — to hide her trepidation. She was, at this moment, physically unapproachable. Dorothy held back and welcomed Katie, but she could not keep her own eyes from welling up at this heartbreaking site: behind the outward appearance of this strong, self-sufficient, professional businesswoman was no more than a frightened child.

Katie seated herself at the table in the kitchen where Dorothy had led them. She rested her hands one on top of the other in front of her on the floral placemat with ruffled edges. She'd unconsciously done so in an attempt to anchor herself in the room to keep from fleeing what by now felt certain to be unwelcome news. Katie recognized the placemat as the same one that had been on the table when she'd first entered this house after Aunt Tess's death the past April. Everything was so different now that Dorothy had moved in and decorated. The place was so livened up that it was sometimes hard to recall the devastating mess in which she'd found it. But recall she did, since in the midst of all the mess of the rest of the house, the order of the kitchen and the aesthetic setting of the table had been a surprising mystery. While there were piles of clothing, papers and odds and ends everywhere else in the house, the kitchen table was set as though Aunt Tess had been expecting company: three ruffled placemats; a tall empty water glass at each setting (same as Dorothy had today, only now they contained water with a fresh lemon slice); a rose-scented candle; a vase with flowers, wilted since her death (a vase Katie now kept on her own kitchen table); a framed photograph of her mom and Aunt Tess next to the silo on Dorothy's farm, with a separate picture of her and a young Josh tucked into the corner of the frame, both of which Katie kept right next to the vase.

Dorothy sat in silence waiting for Katie to look at her. She could nearly read her mind as she watched Katie's eyes flick from the placemats to the water glasses. Dorothy, too, had been privy to the oddity of the table that left them all wondering who Aunt Tess had been cognizant enough to so carefully be expecting in the middle of her otherwise troubled mind — although Dorothy had always hoped . . .

Katie recollected the contents of that photograph and a zing raced through her. It had been quite a surprise during Aunt Tess's funeral dinner out at the farm to discover that the silo in the photo was Dorothy's. For the first time she wondered *exactly* how old her mother was in that photograph. *How long after it was taken did Mom move to Chicago? Since the timelines in those letters just do not add up, might Mom have* already *been pregnant with me?* Her heart was now pounding.

At last, Katie's eyes — eyes filled with questions and vulnerabilities — met with Dorothy's.

"It's time to begin," Dorothy said in a solemn proclamation. "But where . . . how . . . I have wrestled with God and angels about these decisions until I can wrestle no more. There's no point in dancing around it either. Lord, here we go. Be with us." She drew a deep breath, held it a second and then exhaled.

"Katie, your father is not who you've been told he was." She paused a moment, but clearly from the look on Katie's face, something in the letters must have already led her to at least suspect as much. And yet, the cold reality of hearing it needed time to settle in. "The man you've been told was your father has in fact never existed." Dorothy's voice dropped to a near whisper. "He was fabricated by your mother to hide a terrible truth." Katie's eyes welled with tears and her hands formed into fists as she fought to stay in control. *So it's true!* She swallowed numerous times and blinked back the tears.

"I wish I could tell you that what I have to say will get easier from here, child, but it will not. I wish to *God* I could have your earthly father standing in the next room, waiting to come to you at the end of what I'll unfold here today, but I cannot." Dorothy paused, making sure Katie was digesting each piece of information. Although Katie had weathered the news that her father wasn't whom she'd been told, Dorothy figured there could be no way for her to predict what she was about to say next. She reached across the table to take one of Katie's hands, but Katie withdrew them and put them protectively in her lap. Dorothy nodded, trying to send a signal to Katie that she understood . . . it was okay . . . whatever she needed to do. . . .

"Katie, honey, your birth father died more than ten years ago, around the same time as your mother."

Katie's emotions felt like they were in a pinball machine. It wasn't like learning about the surprise death of someone she'd known. Still, she realized that in the midst of her doubts and suspicions, she had subconsciously begun to cling to some vague hope that for the first time in her life, perhaps she might have a father she could meet.

A guttural moan rose from within Katie. With her eyes closed, she began to rock forward and backward in her chair. Dorothy prayed to know when to continue, what physical steps to take next, if any. Oh, how she wanted to reach out, and yet, she continued to feel prompted to sit still. Katie's brief rocking ceased and she bore her eyes into Dorothy, signaling her to proceed.

"I need to say this before anything else, because it is *truth,* and I pray you one day, no, *this* day, believe it: *You* are no mistake, Katie Durbin. You are loved by God and somehow, with His help, this can all work together for the good. I just know it."

During the brief silence something shifted in Katie. She swallowed, clenched her jaw and now glared at Dorothy, as though daring her to continue with this preposterous tale couched in God talk.

"Things were different back then, Katie. People did things differently when a baby was conceived out of wedlock. Clarice made a choice to move away and finally lead a life of her own apart from your aunt and the suspicious eyes of a small town. She made a choice she believed was not only best for her, but especially for *you*."

For the first time since she'd arrived, Katie spoke. "I'm listening, Dorothy." Her voice was ice. "I can hardly *wait* to hear the rest of this." Ice and cynicism. "Whoever my father is, was, he must have been a master of . . . well, of many things, including self-justification and abandonment."

"Your father, Katie, was a good man who loved deeply. A man who, for a brief moment, found himself succumbing to a temptation he never *imagined* could be his. But more importantly, Katie, he . . . never knew about *you*. Your mother never gave him a chance to find out." Katie's jaw clenched.

Help me to hear what you want me to say, Lord, and then have the courage and Your power and might to say it so it can be received! Shape my words, oh God! Speak to Katie.

"Your mother, Katie, was a warm, loving human being. She was raised by a sister who was no more than an orphaned and grieving girl of seventeen herself when she took on the full role of parenting her two-year-old sister, your mother. Clarice grew to be a strong, strong-willed, beautiful woman who had been brought up most of her life without the presence of a father — not unlike yourself." Dorothy paused to allow for that connection to be drawn. "Clarice and Tess only had each other, and although their relationship was a complicated one because of their circumstances and roles, God saw them . . ."

Katie jumped into Dorothy's heartfelt sentence, lashing out with biting disdain. "Spare me any more *God* talk, okay? I want to know if we're almost to the *good* part of the story now, Dorothy. The part where I get to learn who this *saint* of a man was? This saint who succumbed to a moment of temptation with my *saint* of a mother?"

Dorothy braced herself against the torrent of words that came at her like the biting winds of change that had blown into her home not long ago. The image of the tree branches bending — yet not breaking — flicked into her mind and steadied her. *Thank you, Jesus, for Your grace.* Dorothy also knew that anger masked fear and wound; ever so gently and softly, she spoke to the lost soul before her. "Do you *want* me to be to that part of the story, Katie? Do you really want to know who your real father is? Goodness knows, it won't be easy."

"Want? Do I WANT you to tell me?" Katie rose to her feet. "What I *want* is of no accord here, nor has it ever been. What I am left with is. . . ." She turned her back on Dorothy.

What *was* she left with? She had two choices: say yes and learn, or say no and leave. Learn and deal with it, never meeting the man who had sired her. Leave and never know, run . . . back to Chicago and forget this entire Pardon-Me-Ville sham of a town.

Chicago. What was there for her now? *Who* was there for her now?

And if she did run, how could she ever leave her questions behind?

Did she *want* to know?

She turned and stared at Dorothy, the question hanging between them.

Dorothy closed her eyes and began to pray aloud. "Lord, it needs to be said. Forgive me for breaking the covenant . . . *and* for being a part of it. Prepare Katie's heart, God, *now.* Prepare her heart and make strong my conviction to speak it."

Dorothy kept her eyes closed while Katie could only wonder, *Do I want to know? Do I*

WANT to know? Before she could account for it, Katie spat, "Do I want to know?" She bit her lip, first on one side, then the other. Her quieting voice and slumping posture indicated the resignation and brokenness in her next words as she sank back down in her chair. "How can I *not?*"

"Katie," Dorothy said in a firm voice, "your father is Delbert Carol. Pastor Delbert Carol, Senior."

16

"Eugene. Doc here. Seems you've been tracking me down like a beagle on a coon's trail. I got to the office and Ellie had your message waiting for me. She said she told you it might be this afternoon before I called you back, so I hope you haven't been sitting by your phone all day."

"You think that's all I've got to do?" Eugene chuckled — although Doc hadn't been far off the mark.

"I'm sure it's not. I stopped at Harry's to get a bite to eat before coming home; my refrigerator is nearly bare. When I got home, before I could even pick up the receiver, there you were on my answering machine. By *golly*, you are a relentless old dog. Along with your call, I also had four other messages from people who saw Sharon's article in the paper yesterday announcing the committees, including our names for history. Seems everybody thinks they're worthy of fame in our booklet."

"I got a few calls myself. Speaking of relentless old dogs, I bet if we compared our call lists, they'd nearly be one and the same. Cora Davis, right?"

"Right."

"Gladys, right? Although she said she was just calling to check in with our progress."

"Right. But we both know she better be on our lists, and at the top, too."

"Right. And then, let's see, Sam Vitner. Said, 'Who wouldn't want to read about how Swappin' Sam's came into being.' "

"Nope. I didn't hear from Sam. I did have a lengthy message on my machine from Maggie Malone, though. She said she probably has more living relatives and heirs in and around this town than anyone else. And you know, I believe she's right. Do you know anyone else who had nine kids who all had kids?"

"Nope. Rather than spending more time on our phone calls, though, let's get to our picks."

"I set it right here by the phone before I went to bed last night so I'd remember where it was when we talked. Hold on; let me get my reading glasses out of their case." The phone banged to the floor and Eugene heard Doc's voice from a distance. "Stay with me, Eugene! I dropped the phone!" There were a few clunking noises, then Doc was back. "All right. Ready. Who wants to go first?"

"Go right on ahead."

"I'll just read you my list, which is in no particular order. There's a couple you might not agree with, but then there's a couple that just seem obvious, aside from you and me, of course."

"Fire."

"Speaking of you and me, I'm assuming since Gladys put us on the history committee because of our birthin' and buryin' that she also wants our personal stories in the booklet, right?"

"You know, Doc, I hadn't really thought about it, but now that you mention it, I believe you're right about that. So should we make ourselves one of our five? Or put us on each other's lists?"

"Eugene," Doc said, then halted himself while he squeezed out a dose of patience. Like Ellie had learned this morning (and not for the first time), Eugene could occasionally become exasperating. "Read me *your* list first, just the way you got it, okay? You're gonna be burying *me* before we get the *easy* part of our task over with!"

"Okay. Here we go. First on my list of

important people who have had an impact on Partonville: Pastor Delbert Carol, Senior. What with he and his son pastoring the largest church in our town for nearly fifty years total — a landmark worth its own celebration — we'd be hard pressed to find a man who has had more of a far-reaching influence on as many lives as his, all the way into eternity. I'm sure Pastor Delbert (pause) *junior,* that is, would be glad to put together a piece about his dad and family."

"Excellent choice, Eugene! Excellent! Their family was at the top of my list too. I'll give Pastor a call as soon as we hang up."

Kevin was already sitting at the jocks' table by the time Josh made it to the service area in the lunchroom cafeteria line. Although Josh was making small talk with a couple of the guys in line in front of him, as well as being polite to Anita and Becky who were preening behind him and talking loudly about the upcoming dance — no doubt hinting at, and clearly vying for invitations (obviously Deb wasn't a tell-all) — he'd kept an eye on Kevin's every move, waiting to see if they might make eye contact so he could get a read on how welcome he'd be sitting next to him.

No eye contact. He'd been so intent on watching Kevin and fielding conversations that he'd mindlessly scooted his tray down the line, bypassing all the main-dish selections. By the time he woke up to the task at hand, all that was left were the vegetable choices, so he got two sides of mashed potatoes, a side corn and a turkey dressing. He plunked two cartons of milk on his tray and grabbed a banana from the fruit bowl near the registers. *Return to Doofusville.*

He mentally throttled down shades of anything that resembled evidence of what was beginning to feel like his new town of residence, shored himself up and approached the table with an air of bravado. "Hey!" he said to Kevin as he wedged his tray down to the table between Kevin's shoulders and the guy next to him, a guy who gave him a dirty look, but nevertheless scooted over enough for Josh to swing one leg over the seat bench, then the next, finally settling himself in.

"Hey yourself, Josh-o." Rather than look at Josh, Kevin looked at Josh's tray while he talked. "What's up with the vegetarian platter? You're not turning weird, are you?"

Skip asking him to never call you Josh-o again, and just seize the opening. "No weirder than I acted last week." *Atta boy!*

"Sorry about the attitude. I've gotten over myself. No hard feelings?" He held out his right hand toward Kevin, palm up.

Kevin stared at it for a second. "None, my man," he finally said with a half-grin. Kevin skidded his palm across Josh's in a familiar gesture of Hethrow High buddies.

"In fact, I'm so over myself, I wondered if you might wanna double to the dance."

Kevin held his fork in front of his mouth for a moment, then set it down on his plate and turned to face Josh square on. "Serious?"

"Serious."

"Who with, I mean besides you?"

"Deb."

"Deb?"

"Deborah Arnold."

"You joking?"

"Nope."

Kevin turned back to his plate and shoveled in a mouthful. After chewing, swallowing and loading up his fork again, he spoke, but again without looking at Josh. "You didn't ask her yet though, right?"

"Wrong. I already asked her."

"And she said yes?"

"It's a date!"

Kevin ate the bite that had been perched in front of his mouth, took a few gulps of milk and ate some more, his fork clanking into his plate with each reload as though he was trying to crack it open before scooping. "Double, huh?"

"Thought it might be fun. Think?"

"Does she know you wanna double, with *me?*"

"Not yet, but I can't imagine why she wouldn't think it was okay. You two know each other, right?"

"You could say that."

"So?"

Kevin drew up a corner of his mouth and wrinkled his brow in a look that said he wasn't sure. He seemed to be deliberating something with himself. "It could be . . . *interesting,* I suppose." After a few more bites, he shrugged his shoulders and said, "Why not!" After all, he'd decided, his own date was an impressive knockout who could make up for just about anything.

"You're kidding, right?" Deb sorted through her books to load in her backpack for the night's homework, then changed her mind about one of them and tossed it back in her locker. "I can handle that assignment in study hall tomorrow," she said to herself more than to Josh. "I mean you haven't

288

already set this up with Kevin without asking me, have you?"

Doomed. Dumb. Doofusville. Josh thought Deb would sound happier about the double date. It never occurred to him he'd made a breach of some kind of protocol he knew nothing about. *Just be straight about it.* "I'm sorry. I didn't think I'd need to . . . Oh, heck. I just didn't think. I'm sorry. I hope it's okay."

She donned her backpack. "It will be *interesting.*"

Exactly what Kevin said. What am I missing here? "So it's okay then?"

"Doesn't sound like I have much choice, unless I recant my acceptance to your initial invitation."

"Recant? You're a career shoe-in, Ms. Deborah Arnold, Attorney at Law. Sounds good enough to be a new television series." He held his hand up in front of his mouth, as though holding a microphone in it. Then he gave his best shot at an announcer's voice. "Deborah Arnold, Attorney at Law. Tonight! Prime Time Television at eight P.M.!"

Deb let loose with genuine and hearty laughter. "How can I resist this simple request from such a persuasive young man?"

"What woman can resist the charms of *any* good-looking young man?" he asked with a debonair tone in his voice right out of a fifties movie. *You are flying now, buddy!*

"Oh, but I can, and I *have,* good sir," she responded, mimicking a southern belle, having honed her skills in two school plays. "Between you and me and the barnyard," she said, swiftly waving her hand in front of her face as though she was demurely fanning herself whilst batting her eyes all the while, "I have, within the last week or so, declined an invitation to the very same dance you and I will be attending together, and the invitation came from none other than the dimpled and charming Mr. Kevin Mooney! That is why this double date should be so . . . interesting."

You might have been flying, Josh, but you have just crash-landed.

Kevin lived in Hethrow about a mile from the school and drove his own car. On the way to the parking lot, he caught up with Shelby just before she climbed the stairs to the bus. He wanted to tell her about the double date and ask her if she had any preference in corsages, like pin or wrist or . . . whatever else it is girls might ask for.

"No way!" she'd responded when he'd said they were double dating, before he could even *get* to the corsage part. She was clearly distraught. Angry seemed like a better description, Kevin decided. "You and I are double dating with Deborah Arnold and Josh Kinney?"

"I thought you and Josh were buddies! What's the big deal?"

"It would have been nice if you'd asked me first."

Kevin, who was as slick with the ladies as black ice, was apparently completely off his game. In fact, he wasn't even sure which sport he'd been playing since the lunch table. "Again I ask, why is this such a big deal?" He had an edge to his voice.

"If you haven't noticed, Josh Kinney has become a . . ." Shelby shut her mouth. It wouldn't do for her to carry on. First dance of her life and she didn't want to shoot herself in the foot; Kevin might uninvite her if he decided she was a cranky pill. She painted on a smile, then said in a gentler voice, "Let's just say he's gotten a tad heady lately, don't you think?"

"I think he's landed back in the realms of good guy. He went through a short spell, but he's turned around and come to his senses. This double date idea was his, you know."

The nerve of that . . . that . . . How could he be so. . . . Suddenly, visions of her wearing fabulous hair and makeup, a swell pair of Grannie M's earrings and a dress to die for raced in her head. There couldn't be a better opportunity to show that jerk just what he was missing.

Shelby smiled coyly at Kevin, which was this catcher's first attempt ever at coyness. She was more comfortable pounding her right fist into her catcher's mitt than she was acting like a girlie-girl. She thought it felt a bit unnatural, but she was no dummy: she could see it brought immediate visual results. *Wow, we are powerful when we turn on the charms! No wonder Grannie M keeps trying to coach me on these things.* With all the gusto she might use to slide into home plate, she quickly kissed him on the cheek. "You know, I think you're right. This *will* be fun!" Up the bus stairs she went.

Kevin stood watching the back of the bus disappear around the corner. "What in the world just happened?" he asked a squirrel scampering across the schoolyard.

17

Dorothy felt both stunned and relieved by her own naming of the name, sharing of the secret — the breaking of a forty-seven-year-old covenant.

Katie appeared to be returning from a trance. "Surely I've misunderstood. Surely you are not trying to tell me my father is, was, a *pastor?*"

"It is so." Dorothy knew it would be best to let Katie set her own pace now, rather than for her to start pouring out details.

Katie thought about the current Pastor Delbert Carol, *junior,* and a sudden wave of nausea enveloped her; she didn't speak until it passed. "My mother . . . with a married pastor of a church?" It was incomprehensible. Instantly, shades of recent news headlines about sins within the church raced in her mind. "Was she a victim of some type of clerical abuse, Dorothy?"

"No! No." Dorothy shook her head, refolded her hands and looked straight into Katie's eyes. "This was the doings of a man and a woman. A *man* and a *woman,* Katie. Your mother didn't even attend church. She had no faith whatsoever." Dorothy quickly labored to paint Katie a brief, yet careful account of the unusual circumstances in each of her parents' lives at the time of their transgression. Clarice was a twenty-three-year-old, headstrong woman, always older than her years, tired of being under the thumb of her overprotective sister. In a misguided attempt to at last experience her own autonomy, she struck out in search of the company of a man, whose presence she had so longed for in her life. Delbert had been a widow for a little over a year and was desperately lost, missing his wife, angry at God for allowing her to die, struggling to raise his young son alone, overwhelmed by all the emotional pulls of pastoring when he was so lost himself. "In one mistake, Katie, your mother and Delbert got caught up in each other's human wounds, needs and weaknesses as they sought to comfort each other."

"But my mother *was* a religious woman,

Dorothy. She attended church every week and tried relentlessly to get me to. . . ." Her voice faded. "It just doesn't add up."

"Neither your mother *nor* her sister attended church here in Partonville. No, your mother didn't find God until after she moved away. She didn't know a soul when she arrived in Chicago and was actually hoping to get lost in the crowd. She found herself lost in the crowd alright, but also isolated, lonesome, frightened . . . broken — which is often where we *can* finally hear the voice of God, who's been calling to us all along.

"One day, out of the blue, your mother phoned me. When she left town, I promised her I'd be praying for her every day. At the time, she'd just shrugged her shoulders and said, 'If that will make you feel better.' When she phoned me, she told me she had cried herself to sleep one night, worrying about how she could *ever* know how to raise a child alone. Here she was, she said, having been raised without a father herself, and now she was about to put the same fate on you. The next day, Sunday, out of desperation, she said she wandered into the back of a nearby church seeking . . . she wasn't even sure what. She didn't unfold all of the details; she just said God met her there, arms open. As sure as she was pregnant with you, she was, by the time she left that church, also pregnant with the new life she had found with her heavenly Father — one who had been there all along, just waiting for her to turn toward Him. The Father who would see her, and you, through."

Katie's heart faintly stirred. As much as she didn't really want to hear any God talk — for where had God been when she'd prayed for the mending of her marriage, for the sustained life of her mother, for the empty nights she'd cried herself to sleep? — she recalled with absolute clarity how strong her mother's faith in God had been.

Clarice had often called Katie her "blessed gift of grace." "Who's Grace?" Katie had once asked her mother when she was small. Her mom had laughed and hugged her. "Grace," her mother had said, "is a gift from God. And God is your loving Father in heaven, as sure as He is mine."

Katie tried to fight back tears, fearing if she allowed herself to cry . . . And yet she could not help but explode with tears, so powerful was the haunting image of her mother, sitting alone in the back of a church, pregnant with her, believing she had finally, at long last, found a father who would never leave her . . . a father Katie had always longed for herself. And here Katie had *had* an earthly father all along, but now it was too late to meet him — for him to learn about *her.* The mix of memories, loss, confusion about God and her immense pain was severe. From the depths of her, she cried. She hadn't cried like this since she'd broken down in the church basement shortly after she'd moved here and Pastor Delbert had asked her personal questions about her aunt . . . and she'd had no answers.

What was it about . . . church? God?

Dorothy stood up and retrieved a napkin from the counter, then she scooted her chair to Katie's side, handed her the hanky and put her arm around her shoulder. After Katie blew her nose, she said, "How did you get involved, Dorothy? Why do *you* know these things when Delbert didn't? And *why* didn't she tell him?"

"Your mother was quite determined, Katie, that even if she hadn't gotten pregnant, even if they'd started dating, it was too early after his wife died. He was obviously still so in love with her . . . had spent the better part of their evening talking about it, which is what so touched your mother's heart to move closer. . . . And he was overcome — over*wrought* — with guilt and grief immediately after their union. He begged her forgiveness. It was agreed they'd *both* made a terrible mistake for she, too, felt the shame of what they'd done, what she'd . . . *encouraged.* God forgive our human nature, but she used that exact word, Katie." Katie stared at Dorothy, tears continuing to spill.

"After your mom found out she was pregnant, she was certainly not about to give her child away, nor was she willing to stay in this small town and endure the speculations, the whispers, and, God help us all, the judgment and endless suspicions that would surely follow her . . . and moreover, one day be shrouded around *you.* Clarice also believed she was not cut out to be a pastor's wife, even if they had one day been able to grow a relationship. She said she'd been under enough scrutiny all of her life. . . ."

"But why *you?* Why do *you* know about all of this?"

"As you can well imagine, when Clarice told Tess she was pregnant, she was crushed.

When she told her she was leaving, Tess went to pieces, announcing she was pulling up stakes and going with her. She said she had no life apart from Clarice — which was one of the reasons Clarice wanted to flee. I think she actually hoped if she were gone, Tess might finally find *her* own place in the world, too.

"Clarice needed help convincing Tess she *was* going alone. Tess wanted someone to beg Clarice to change her mind. Since they had no relatives, and I guess I knew them about as well as anyone, in an act of trust, they reached out to me, each hoping I could be persuasive. Tess begged Clarice not to tell even me who the father was, such was her humiliation at the thought of it — thereby cementing Clarice's resolve to leave this small town, where whispers and rumors can so easily breed. If her own sister responded this way. . . . But Clarice believed *somebody* else had to know, just in case something happened to her while her child was still young. But I was *sworn* to secrecy, Katie. I had been trusted, I gave my word and we signed a covenant. Clarice said if Tess or I ever told Delbert and she found out about it, or if, worse yet, he tracked her down, she would disappear and none of us would ever hear from her again, and that included Tess.

"When your mother packed up her car and left, that was the day your aunt began to turn in on herself, Katie. Not long after your mom was gone, word was spread that she'd met someone in Chicago, fallen head over heels in love and a child was on the way. Of course, then I heard talk about the sorrowful loss of her husband, and . . ." Dorothy rang her hands. "And I knew the lies, but what could I do?" Dorothy dabbed at her eyes with a napkin. "Before long, Tess refused to talk to me. I think because it was too painful knowing I knew . . . everything. I am so sorry, Katie. I am so terribly sorry for everything."

"*Carol!* Katie Mabel *Carol* Durbin. When I asked Mom why I had two middle names, she always told me Mabel was a strong name and that my father had come up with the name Carol. Delbert Carol. *That* explains it. But where . . . how did my mother get the last name of Durbin?"

"As soon as she moved away, she had her last name legally changed to Durbin, knowing it was such a common name in the state that neither would people question it nor easily be able to trace it to someone specific."

The table before Katie blurred as she allowed images of her mother to flood her. Katie had always felt that even in the midst of her mother's loving care, there was also something deeply sad within her mother, but she'd credited it to her mother having lost her husband so early on in their marriage. Now she knew. She knew it all.

"Katie, God is here for you, too. God, *your* heavenly Father, can meet all of your needs for healing, just like He did with your mother. I know this is awful for you, but the unveiling of Truth ultimately releases light into our *cavernous* desperations. I've lived long enough to know how many people have lived with secrets all of their lives. Their secrets. Those of their families. Taking darkness to the grave. Lightness never having a chance to bathe and cleanse their sorrows.

"God," Dorothy said, closing her eyes and lifting her face as she entered into spontaneous prayer, "Father who walks with us, may we receive Your loving light."

Whether Katie closed her eyes because of Dorothy's prayer or because she was too broken and weary to hold them open, her body too tired to do anything but lean back, she did not know. But she, too, lifted her face.

"Lord," Dorothy continued, unaware of anything other than her gratefulness for the God who hears our cries and never stops loving us, "we have feet of clay because you gave them to us. We make our choices — right or wrong we make our choices because you let us. We make our mistakes, and then we move on. And You move right along with us, no matter what. Waiting for us as surely as You waited for Clarice, unmarried, child in her womb and all, to look Your way. Waiting to forgive us — and OH!, THANK YOU, God, for forgiving Clarice, and Delbert, a man whose heart, even in the midst of his grief, pain and terrible mistake, clearly understood both remorse and redemption. Lord, that man went on to inspire so many lives with his sermons about our human failings, God's mercy and unconditional love for us . . . and especially His forgiveness. He surely knew firsthand, didn't he? No wonder he spoke with such passion.

"Thank you, for forgiving *me*. . . ." Dorothy's voice faded off as she wept tears of gratefulness at the loosing of her guilt and the influx of God's grace, the touch of

God's arms — as soft as satin — enveloping her with assurance. For a minute, she did nothing but sit in silence receiving God's love and light, healing and hope.

Katie Mabel Carol Durbin briefly opened her eyes. While chaotic winds of emotion blew through her, Dorothy's face radiated serenity. Katie closed her eyes again and this time bowed her head. With timid yet desperate words she prayed, *God, please help me. I am lost. This is all too much to hear. To take in. To know.* She wondered if this is how her mother had felt when she was pregnant and alone, wandering into a church. She longed to once again feel the arms of her mom around her, to hear her gentle laugh . . . to feel whole. "Grace is a gift from God. And God is your loving Father in heaven, as sure as He is mine." Clarice's words began to loop in Katie's consciousness — like a lullaby. "And God is your loving Father in heaven, as sure as He is mine. And God is your loving Father . . . And God is . . ."

God, I cannot handle this on my own. I need You. And then she wept.

"Amen!" Dorothy said aloud with gusto.

Neither woman was sure how much time had elapsed since they'd settled into their prayerful silence. Katie continued to be assaulted by a wild range of thoughts and emotions, but she was also acutely aware that something had shifted — and settled — deep within her.

After she and Dorothy exchanged a few quiet good-byes, Katie headed home to Crooked Creek Farm. While driving down the gravel road, she noticed Challie Carter's tractor in the distance. He was turning the soil after the harvest, exposing the black earth, preparing it for next year's seed. Something about the dark soil being turned up toward the light rekindled Dorothy's statements about light bathing the darkness. *Yes.* Katie realized that like her mom, she had now possibly discovered Whose child *she* could, might — she even dared to whisper *Already* — had become. And in the end, *that* was the most shocking discovery of her day!

18

Nellie Ruth had lived in the second story of Bernice Norris's stately home for thirty-five years. It was only her second dwelling since she'd arrived in Partonville as a parentless teenager, not counting her brief healing stay at Dorothy's after Dorothy had rescued her from the parking lot at United Methodist Church, where Nellie Ruth's car had run out of gas. Even though Nellie Ruth didn't own the place — she was a renter who always paid her rent exactly one week before it was due — both she and Bernice felt like the entire floor belonged to her in every sense of the word, aside from that of "taxpayer." In fact, more than a half dozen times over the years, Bernice had tried to sell the house to Nellie Ruth for under market value, saying that *she* would gladly become the boarder. "I just cannot imagine my life without hearing your beautiful saxophone music wafting its way to my ears! It's like getting to tune in *live* to my favorite musician every day of my life." Although a few times Nellie Ruth had actually considered buying the house, she realized the offer usually came when the roof needed repairs, the porch needed shoring up or the plumbing was having a spell. Nellie Ruth also realized, in one of her countless moments of self-examination, that she liked her ordered and independent life just the way it was: rooted in Partonville, sans financial anchors.

She'd been practicing her saxophone for nearly an hour now. Although she had already memorized several of the band's performance numbers for the Pumpkin Festival and the Centennial Plus 30 doings — memorization being one of her gifts, which is why she was so good at quoting bible passages — she still disciplined herself to keep her eyes on each note while practicing. When she was playing for her own pleasure, however, it was a different story. As soon as she was done with official practices, she'd fold up the music, file it in the appropriate notebooks (even the spices in her spice rack were alphabetized), stow her music stand, take off her shoes, sink her toes into her deep-piled hand-hooked rug and just play away. So as usual, that's just what she did. She'd never understood why she was able to play faster when barefoot — although curling her toes around a few strands, clamping onto them and pulling upwards did seem to help her reach those high notes — but it was just one of those oddities she'd come to accept and enjoy. (Little did she know Gertrude most enjoyed playing keyboard barefoot too, especially when she sat at the Hammond organ, where her toes could dance across the foot pedals.)

It had been a busy day at work, what with Your Store's usual mid-week, one-day sales and double coupons. Both the official practice and her barefoot playing had helped her to unwind. She finally felt relaxed enough to move on to her next task. Although she loved her God, her job, music, Partonville, the band and her Hooker friends, she'd been going through a spell — "We all have little periods of adjustment," Dorothy had told her — wherein she longed for change. This ebb-and-tide of discontent had lasted about two years. Not until she'd arrived home from bunco at Dorothy's house had she figured out what, exactly, needed to change: her decorating! Compared to Dorothy's red ceiling and sunshiny bathroom, Nellie Ruth's apartment was drab. (She would never, not for the *life* of her, understand why sometimes the obvious just wasn't.)

With tender care, she packed up her saxophone and retrieved the paint chips she'd splayed on her kitchen table time and again since picking them up at Menard's in Hethrow. Although she'd tried to shop locally at Wal-Mart, they just didn't have anything that seemed, well, "pizzazzy enough" is how she'd described it to Jessica when running into her in the checkout line, paint chips and new plunger in hand. ("I cannot *believe* we're both here in Hethrow, in the very same *store,* in the same LINE!" *She is* so *easily excited,* Nellie Ruth had thought to herself.) While they'd moved toward the cash register, Nellie Ruth expressed that she might need Jessica's creative eye to help her pull a few things together. After seeing the delicate flower border and beautiful mailbox Jessica had painted for Dorothy, and listening to the continued praise from Katie about how Jessica had helped her decorate her living room with no less expertise than her Chicago interior designer, word had spread that Jessica was the local decorating genius.

"You know, Jessica," Nellie Ruth had said, walking backward in the line, "maybe you should get out of the motel business and launch your own cable decorating show. You know, just like on HGTV." Since Jessica and Paul didn't have cable television, she couldn't picture exactly what Nellie Ruth was talking about, although she'd certainly heard about the channel. But regardless, she was highly flattered and completely intimidated by the mere thought of talking to a camera. She'd blushed just thinking about it, and continued to do so until she'd paid the cashier and walked to her car, afraid the clerk had been wondering just who she thought *she* was to even consider a career in television.

Nellie Ruth lined up the paint chips in a perfectly straight and even line, then began the process of elimination, pushing them up and out of the line one at a time, closing the gap after each dismissal. At last, there was only one chip left. "Splendid Rose!" Nellie Ruth exclaimed to the paint chip. "That does it!" It was the same color she'd ended up liking every time, even though she tried not to be prejudiced, giving every color more than one chance. She retrieved her handbag from the back of the kitchen chair next to her, where she always hung it, and tucked the chip into her wallet. Next time she went to Hethrow, her selection would be readied.

Once she'd experienced her decorating epiphany and selected the paint color, it was nearly unimaginable to her she'd never once noticed that the only cheery colors in her dwelling were those in the multitudes of items she'd hooked. At sixty-two, she was the only Happy Hooker who still hooked rugs, toilet seat covers, wall hangings, tissue-box covers, throw pillows, coasters. . . . She surveyed the living room, kitchen, both bedrooms — one she used as her music and craft room — and the bathroom. She counted fourteen hooked items! *What is WRONG with me!* The rest of the hookers had, decades ago, tired of the craft and its look, although they had each continued to accept her occasional fluffy gift with graciousness. *Nellie Ruth McGregor, how can you be so full of music and yet such a one-note person in other areas of your life!*

Splendid Rose would be a good complement to her playing rug, the only hooked item she was going to allow herself to keep on display. The rest were going to get packed in a box and stored . . . in the music room, at least for a while — just in case.

Gladys had spent the entire morning with

one salesperson after another, comparing the benefits of digital clocks versus analog, small versus big, multipurposes versus plain-and-simple. But then *he* had arrived with the super-duper of all choices. Something for everyone. Something with an excellent *WOW!* factor. Something to equal Gladys's "superb vision to steer Partonville into the future," he'd said.

Like any good salesperson with intuitive skills — especially those that led to closing the deal — he not only listened to Gladys's every word, but said he'd often read about her in the papers. He knew just how to reel her in.

Much to her surprise, he'd started his pitch by convincing her that she could probably get the old one fixed, something no other presenter had even mentioned. Of course, odds were ("if I was a betting man, which, of course, I am not") it would cost more than a new one by the time any electrician or clock repairman would undoubtedly have to not only disassemble the old one but rewire its connections to bring it up to code. "And who *knows* if they'd for *sure* be able to find parts for it — and if so, *how* long might that take, and when, exactly, was the celebration again?" And he just *knew* what a good "stalwart steward" of the town's money she had been since taking over for her dearly departed husband, the esteemed former mayor, and he was *sure* she wouldn't want to squander any of her "prudent budget."

Hustling right along . . .

The first small catalog he'd pushed across her desk showed clocks that looked exactly like the one that had been hanging off the corner of the building for as long as she could remember. Of course, who would be able to appreciate her fine taste if it appeared to be just like anyone else's? he wondered aloud. "But what about keeping the integrity of the old building?" she'd ask. "Integrity, madam, is sticking with your vision of stepping into the future, moving forward in time." It was a direct quote from her own mouth and she could hardly *believe* he remembered it!

Sounds of cha-chink.

Two more brochures came and went, each falling short of her expectations, he was sure. And then, then he pulled out the prestigious mother of all brands, presentation binders — and prices. He presented her with the first phase of the digital *ensemble,* which would not only display the time, but the temperature.

"But wait, there's more!" When he had used *that* phrase while flipping to the grandest portion of the *ensemble,* acting like he was the first person ever to utter it, Gladys pursed her lips. *Does he think I'm that gullible?* She knew for a fact they used that phrase on nearly every infomercial created, and she'd seen her fair share of them late at night when she couldn't sleep, after having been awakened by a strange sound — or then again, was it usually her bladder? Didn't matter which; she was awake and on high alert for intruders, a bathroom run or . . . and then . . . television to help her stop thinking about either of them. What's more, she'd actually ordered a few things from those crazy programs (admittedly, sometimes because of the "more" that followed the "But wait"), although when they'd arrived, she couldn't think for the life of her why.

The day she opened the box containing the contents of something she'd seen after midnight on one of the shopping networks was the day she swore off turning on the television in the middle of the night. She'd ordered a set of hair accessories to create all kinds of up-do's. The ladies had looked so glamorous and happy with them that Gladys was sure they'd give her a lift, too. Trouble was, Gladys all but forgot *her* hair was only about two inches long, for goodness sake. "There ought to be a law against taking advantage of tired people," she said, putting them back in the box in which they'd arrived. She stuffed the "stupefied and deranged decision" under her arm and stomped straight to the post office with it.

"And heeeeere's the MORE!" the clock salesperson said as he turned the page in his slick binder while simultaneously handing her a four-color brochure. She had been just on the verge of dismissing him (*This man thinks he can cornswaggle me!*), when . . . "Along with the time and temperature, there is a streaming light banner that can be programmed to announce *anything* you believe important for the worthy citizens of Partonville, and all visitors, of course, to know, Mayor McKern."

Cha-chink, cha-CHINK!

"Where do I sign and how soon can you deliver it? And I'm assuming expert installation is included in this outrageous price!"

"Actually, Miss Mayor, . . ."

"That is Mrs. Mayor. Acting Mayor

Gladys McKern."

"Actually, I believe, since you are officiating as the mayor, you are not acting at all." His smile was so affirming. At least *somebody* understood all the work she did! "Mayor McKern, installation is not included. How could we *possibly* include installation fees with our products — which are, might I say, very *fairly* priced for the market — when we have no idea what we'd be dealing with in terms of code or even electrical availability to the point of service, for that matter? Our prices are strictly for the merchandise, although they do include delivery."

Gladys glared at him, but no amount of her best evil eye was going to get him to include hooking the thing up. Nonetheless, she figured she could get Edward Showalter to handle any electrical work and installation for a song. She'd heard Dorothy bragging on and on about the "wonderful job Edward Showalter has done" and the "wonderful way he knows just what you want" and the "wonderful way . . ." Although Gladys knew nobody could be *that* wonderful — and she wondered if Dorothy wasn't sweet on the man, the way she carried on — she figured he must at least be staying sober.

As soon as Gladys got off the phone, making what she had termed an emergency appointment with Edward Showalter (and why *did* everybody always refer to him using both of his names?) to come by and give her an estimate, she began fretting about the committees — which she hadn't had a lot of time to do for the last several hours since she'd been so busy holding court with clock salespersons, not to mention ordering street signs. She decided she'd best collect a few reports. She made her first call to the office of the *Partonville Press.*

"Sharon, have you talked to Harold about the printing of our Centennial Plus Thirty booklet?"

"Yes, I have. Harold said he'd be glad to donate the printing of the booklet itself, but that somebody would have to pay for the paper and supply any artwork or photographs, as well as hopefully pay for his pressman's overtime, in case we were running close to deadline with our submission." Although Harold had for many years been able to handle the entire printing operations of the newspaper alone, using his circa 1969, Harris V15A web press, it had been several years since he'd been strong enough to handle the heavy rolls of paper and mechanical apparatus by himself. Besides, it had been a long while since OSHA would allow anyone to be running the equipment alone, just in case someone got caught up in the whizzing machinery and found themselves appearing in — as in *in* — the morning headlines. "He also liked the idea of running a 'Meet Your Town' column for the two weeks before the festivities, which as you well know will be four issues since we publish twice a week."

"Splendid work, Sharon."

"Actually, I'm just doing my job, both for the committee and for Harold, who pays me. But to be honest with you, it's more fun than I might have suspected. I really think the whole weekend is going to be very special."

"Uh-huh. That's nice," Gladys said, already having tuned out Sharon since she was busy looking up Eugene's number. "And what did you say Arthur's doing?"

"I haven't assigned him anything just yet, but I think I'll have him start going through our archives in search of tidbits for the column and images from the past."

"Great. I'll see you Tuesday then."

"Tuesday?"

"Of course! We can't possibly get everything done meeting only once a week, especially since you and Harold are already worried things might be running late. Mark your calendar for every Tuesday and Thursday evening until the festival. You said you didn't have anything else on your calendar anyway, right?"

Although that might have been true, Sharon was always hopeful. It rankled her hide that Gladys assumed Mr. Debonair would not be waiting right around the corner! Before Sharon could protest either Gladys's presumptions or mention that Tuesday was tomorrow, Gladys had hung up and started dialing Eugene.

"Eugene. Mayor McKern here. How's it going with the interviews?"

"Doc and I are getting along right nicely, thank you. We finally did touch bases earlier today. We've made our lists and have already started contacting a few folks. Pastor Delbert was quite excited about the opportunity since he said not only would it be a chance to honor his father, but to put in a good plug for God. Maggie and Ben Malone's family makes up for such a large portion of our current population that . . ."

"Well, I haven't received a call from either of you."

"Oh, you're on both of our lists alright. You can believe we have talked *plenty* about you." Eugene's whole face broke out in a wry smile. "We haven't called because we assumed you would be wanting to put your own story together since you know you better than we do. You also knew the past mayor better than either one of us, too. We figured we could never tell it as . . . *well* as you can." Of course, what he and Doc had decided was that nothing they'd say would be good enough for her, so why not let her just write the dang thing herself!

"In fact, I've already started writing a little something, Eugene. I'll turn it straight in to Sharon, if you don't mind. Just make sure you leave me plenty of column inches."

Even though she'd said "if you don't mind," Eugene knew it wouldn't make a bit of difference, even if they — and perhaps God Almighty Himself — did. "We're leaving layout to whoever is doing layout. Will that be Sharon?"

"I'm sure Harold will ultimately do the layout. I've got a few things to report about all of that at our meeting Tuesday. I'm having Harold attend, too." Although she hadn't talked to him yet, she made a mental note to make sure he was there since it was becoming obvious he needed to be.

"Did you say Tuesday? I thought our meetings were on Thursdays, like it said in the newspaper. That's what I've got written down here on my calendar."

"That was only for our *first* meeting, Eugene. There is no way we can possibly get everything done meeting once a week. Goodness! That would mean we'd only have three meetings left! We'll be meeting as an entire committee on Tuesdays and Thursdays, but of course you subcommittee people have to be dogging your tasks every day, if we're to do things right. We'll be lucky to make it, even at that.

"But I don't have time to keep explaining myself, Eugene. Like I said, I have other calls to make. I'll see you. . . ." Gladys flipped her calendar and was stunned to discover that Tuesday was tomorrow. "I'll see you tomorrow night at seven sharp!" She hung up the phone and dialed the Lamp Post Motel. She was nearly beside herself with the reality of the racing of time itself, no matter which way anyone was driving.

"Lamp Post Motel! Would you like to

book a room for Partonville's Pumpkin Festival and Centennial Plus Thirty?"

Gladys sat with her mouth open, trying to decide if she was annoyed at having to wait so long to talk, or excited — yet completely surprised — that Jessica Joy had become a one-woman advertisement. She decided she would do nothing to discourage such a good promotion for her event. "I do not need a room, Jessica, since as the mayor I live right here in town; but what a grand way to give our event attention! I applaud your ingenuity!"

"Well, thank you, Gladys. I . . ."

"I'd love to chat," Gladys said, interrupting Jessica, "but I'm just phoning to see how your plans for the dedication ceremony are coming along."

Jessica looked at the small stack of bookmarks in the plastic bin in front of her. She'd gotten so tired of dragging everything out and putting it away, she'd gathered her supplies all in a container so she could take advantage of surprise pockets of time. "Um, I, well . . . To tell the truth, not exactly. I've had my mind on other things the last couple days."

"I realize you and Paul don't have a whole heap of things to prepare, but it's not something that can be put off until the last minute. You two put your heads together this evening so you can present a plan at tomorrow night's meeting."

"Tomorrow night? Our meetings are on Thursdays, right?"

"We're meeting twice a week now since time is so short. I'll see you, or you and Paul, or . . . I'll see *somebody* from your committee at seven sharp. Good-bye."

Jessica sighed and put her plastic bin back in the closet. It was time to remove her imaginary bookmark production-line hat and put on her committee face. There was a sketch to be made.

But wait! There's more! A car pulled in with a new set of this evening's motel guests. She had to let that committee face fly right on by. It was time to don her Welcome-to-the-Lamp-Post smile.

"May Belle, it's Gladys. We're going to need refreshments for tomorrow night's Centennial Plus Thirty meeting."

"But tomorrow is Tuesday."

"That's right." Silence. More silence. Gladys uttered a loud sigh. She was getting tired of having to explain the same thing over and over. "We're meeting twice a week now, May Belle. Tuesdays and Thursdays. I trust you can lay out refreshments for us then?"

Before Gladys said good-bye, May Belle turned the dial on her oven to 350 degrees. Whatever she was going to bake, that would at least be close.

Edward Showalter's van was a sight. It was painted multicolors of green and beige, creating a camouflage pattern. At first glance, one might have thought he was a hunting zealot, especially since it was bow season for deer and more than a few men wore combinations of camouflage and blaze orange. On second glance, you knew he *was* indeed hunting, but not for deer. Big, black lettering declared "Edward Showalter, Electrician. Affordable. Dependable. Sober. Jesus Loves You. Even if you don't SEE him coming again, HE IS!"

"Mayor McKern!" he said, bounding out of his van and extending his hand before he even closed his door. Gladys shook heartily, readied to butter him up, maybe even get him to donate his time for the sake of the Centennial Plus 30. See that he got a nice mention in the booklet.

Cora Davis sat in the window at Harry's drinking an afternoon cup of coffee, watching the curious duo. She hadn't seen Gladys smile like that for months. *What on earth?* She watched Gladys walk Edward Showalter to near the corner of the building where she pointed up, Edward Showalter's gaze following her pointing finger. They were looking at the clock. Gladys's mouth was flying two-forty and her arms seemed to be indicating the size of something. Edward Showalter was nodding his head, rubbing his chin, nodding some more. They took turns studying a paper Gladys held in her hands.

Edward Showalter went back to his van and retrieved a clipboard. It had a long string hanging from it, a string as long as the chain that looped down Edward Showalter's backside connecting his belt to his long wallet, which was protruding out of the top of his painter's pants' pocket. Cora thought that if he wasn't wearing painter's pants, he might have been mistaken for a biker, or a hippie — or worse yet, a vagabond, gypsy or con artist! *What a sight! Even painter's pants can't legitimize that pitiful vision.*

Edward Showalter looked at the paper Gladys now unfolded in front of him. He plucked the pencil from under a clip and

Cora realized the string was attaching the pencil to the clipboard. *Does the man lose things that easily, or does he have some kind of a phobia?* Cora looked back to his van, wondering if it, too, was somehow attached to the ground. Like maybe he'd tossed out an anchor after he stopped, although she saw no such evidence. He was glancing from the paper to the clock, then scribbling on the paper on his clipboard. After a few minutes of this behavior, he and Gladys talked their way into the building.

"Lester," Cora said, leaving her table and walking over to the counter. "Heard anything about clock repairs over on the square building?" which is how many referred to the one-story structure.

Lester bent down in order to give himself a view of the clock in question. "Nope. Can't say as I have. One-fourteen and all is still well, same as yesterday and year before."

"Seems Edward Showalter and Gladys are making a good study of it. They must be finally going to fix that thing."

"Maybe. Maybe not," Lester said as he rinsed the final plate in the pile of dishes he'd been doing up.

"What do you know about Edward Showalter?" Cora asked as she gathered her purse to check out.

"That he pays his bill and leaves a better tip than most when he eats here," and clearly, he'd thrown a direct barb, "which isn't very often."

"Well, if you ask me, he looks shifty."

"Good thing I didn't ask you then, isn't it." Lester snapped the dishtowel, then flipped it over his shoulder.

Cora handed over her money and received her change, intending to plunk the coins into a collection jar Lester always kept on his counter promoting donations for one needy family or another. She suspected it would be for the Bedfords, whose great-grandmother had just passed last night. She'd overheard somebody talking about it at the counter this morning. Before she let go of her contribution, she read the big sign wrapped around the jar, taped to the back with duct tape. It was written in Magic Marker as bold as you please. "HELP SUPPORT THE CENTENNIAL + 30." Rather than drop in her coins, she decided to do one step better. "You know when that Centennial committee is meeting, Lester?"

"I think yesterday's paper said the meeting had been on Thursday."

Cora dropped the coins in her handbag

and headed straight home to mark her calendar.

19

Katie sat in her living room on her mud-colored, kit-leather couch, legs curled up under her, sipping a double-strong latte, wondering how she was ever going to tell Josh. And Delbert. How on *earth* could she tell Pastor Delbert Carol, Jr. What would it be like to learn your father . . . and then, there *she* would be, standing before him.

She was glad Dorothy encouraged her to just sit with this news herself for as long as it took to decide what, if *anything,* who, if *anyone,* to tell or do next. "Just pray for God to lead you," Dorothy had said. "But I don't know *how* to pray, Dorothy." Dorothy had smiled and patted her cheek. "Just say, 'Help me.' That works as swell as anything!" *Help me.*

It was bad enough she might spend a lifetime coming to grips with it all, and yet, she realized she felt vaguely relieved. Oddly grateful for finally putting a suspicion to rest. To be able to look at photos, which she hoped to do soon, and see the eyes of the man who was her father. But especially, it felt good to at long-last feel at peace about God. *With* God. Ever since she'd met Dorothy, her ongoing prayers and affirmations about God loving us, no matter what, had quietly helped her to lose what she at last realized had been a "not good enough for God" fear that had followed her all of her life. Why she'd always felt that way, she wasn't sure. Maybe not having a father . . . being divorced. . . . Like Dorothy often said, *whatever.* At the moment, those things didn't seem to matter that much anymore. It was the next steps that caused her to fret.

Help me.

As much as she dreaded tackling a thing like this or tried to talk herself out of ever revealing the truth to anyone else, she felt fairly certain they both had to know. Her mind began to imagine how many other people might ultimately find out. What if it became public knowledge?

Did anyone else *really* need to know? Might there be *another* Core Four Covenant between she and Dorothy, Josh and Pastor Delbert? Now that light had finally entered her soul, she was not anxious to step into more uproar and receive the possible judgments of the town.

Help me.

For the first time, she clearly understood the temptation, no, the *choice,* to bury the truth.

Help me.

She wanted to see Pastor Delbert — Delbert — and study his face. Not talk to him. Not yet, anyway. Just see his face. She recalled how when she'd first met him, something seemed familiar about him. *No wonder!*

20

For the next several days, Partonville was a whir and blur of preparations. Raymond Ringwald had been thrown into a complete tizzy when Gladys requested he supply a special song before her pronouncements — like the band didn't have enough to pull together for the whole shebang: chili dinner entertainment, talent show backup, and about one-third of the music for the dance. Same as for the last five years, it had been advertised there would be "live" music by "Partonville's own Community Band" as well as "modern tunes spun by a popular and well-known DJ," which had been the Pumpkin Festival committee's attempt — and a hugely successful one at that — to lure back the younger crowd. Raymond wondered why they billed the Partonville Community Band as "live" music. Wasn't that obvious? What would the alternative be for the band? Music from the beyond?

(Never mind they sometimes sounded like it.)

When Raymond inquired of Gladys what song she had in mind, she answered, "You know, that song that talks about accenting the positive and eliminating the negative. I don't know what the title is; you're the music man!" He knew no amount of rehearsals would help his rag-tag group of musicians be able to do that melody justice, not with only a handful of rehearsals left. It would serve her right if he had Arthur Landers play it solo on his harmonica, which is just what he decided to do. Upon Raymond's request, Arthur said, "Raymond, there probly twern't a harder song wrote to play on the harmonica," but Raymond assured him if anyone was up to the task, it was Arthur. "And no need to mention this to Gladys; we'll surprise her with your solo! Won't that be grand?" After all, Raymond decided, she'd only requested he "supply a special song." She hadn't said how, exactly, it was to be presented. If technicalities counted on Court TV (and they did), they could do for Gladys. But nonetheless, he'd stepped up rehearsals to twice a week and he didn't care how many people groaned, which was all of them.

"Didn't ya know the dern Centennial Plus

Thirty committee is meetin' twice a week too?" Arthur had reprimanded more than asked. Between two band practices, two committee meetings and Sharon having him prowl through newspaper archives for old photographs and Partonville "tidbits," "whatever the gol-fool whatchamajiggy those were supposed ta be," he was barely ever home. "I'm beginnin' to worry my La-Z-Boy might forgit how ta hug my butt!" he lamented to Jessie. She just smiled. She smiled like a cat with a mouse dangling from its mouth, he thought.

He did have to admit, although not to Jessie, that he enjoyed spending time at the *Partonville Press* offices, digging through the old papers in the archive room in the basement. It was quite a trip down memory lane for him. Just seeing the old Buick advertisements made him want to pick up a wrench again. He didn't even need to look at newspaper dates to figure the era; he could tell the year by the model of the car. He had to keep prying his eyes away from those beauties, though, or he'd never get done in time for the next meeting. "Tidbits is the task," he reminded himself aloud. "Think I just wrote me a poem!" He laughed, enjoying the sound of his voice bouncing around

333

in the cellar amidst the old stones and mortar.

More than one headline ushered him down memory lane. *PARTONVILLE HOSTS FIRST FROG JUMP CONTEST.* What a day that had been! When he'd pulled his frog out of the bucket, more than a few gasps were heard, including one from Jessie, who'd given a wolf whistle to rival any man's. "No creek like a Crooked Creek to find the biguns!" he'd said.

"What's his name, Arthur?" Harold, notepad in hand, had wanted to know.

"Jessie Too."

Harold looked up, pencil poised over his notebook. "Is that t-o-o or t-w-o, Arthur?"

Arthur glared at Harold as though he must be daft. "Forgit it," Arthur said, shaking his head, gently setting his big bug-eyed frog back in its bucket and covering her with a damp shop rag. "I jist renamed her Dolores."

Arthur smiled remembering the exchange. Old stories were pure gold. He felt warm inside thinking about how attached he was to this quirky town. Couldn't even imagine having lived anywhere else. "Aw, now don't go gittin mushy, Arthur," he chided himself aloud.

He took the stenographer's pad Sharon had given him, flipped to the first page and printed "TID BITTS" across the top. "1) First frog jumpin contest in (he flipped through the paper until he found a Buick ad) 1953." He checked the paper's date, though, just to make sure since he didn't want their booklet to be incorrect. "Dead on!" The photo that ran with the headline was a close-up of three frogs crossing the finish line. Too bad one of them wasn't Dolores. His only consolation was a winning ribbon for the Biggest Frog. It had taken him three more years to come up with the best jumper. Sadly, that was the year the contest was canceled due to lack of participants. He guessed the novelty had worn off, at least in Partonville.

Although Shelby's mom was delighted by Shelby's enthusiasm for the dance, she truly despised shopping and was relieved when Shelby had asked her if she'd be *too* hurt if she went to Hethrow with her Grannie M. A reasonable budget was determined and the cash handed over. Shelby gave her mom a kiss on the cheek, stuffed the wad of bills in her tiny handbag she draped over her shoulder, said she didn't know what time they'd be back and ran out the door to Maggie's car. Maggie had already tooted her horn twice. As soon as she jumped in the car, they were all a-twitter.

"I'm wearing my power-shopping shoes and have my elbows all sharpened for the crowds," Maggie told her. "We've got to get going, Shelby! Not a minute to spare; the stores close at nine!" They chatted a mile a minute, discussing the pros and cons of wearing different colors (the latest trends lifted straight out of a recent glamour magazine Maggie subscribed to), designs (scoop neck, boat neck, sleeveless — "just nothing too *too*"), the height of heels ("NO! Don't make me wear *heels!*") and fragrance. "Stop by the shop before dance day, Shelby, and we'll give a test drive to some of my aromatherapy fragrances. They smell different on different women, you know, what with body chemistry and all. And since I only carry *essential* oils, it will only take the teensiest drop. We want something . . . mysterious. Might have to blend a couple." She was so excited by all the possibilities that she had to force herself to concentrate on driving.

When they entered the first store, Maggie insisted they put together a game plan.

"Let's see: dress, shoes, nice new petticoat, since I doubt you own one. . . ." Shelby confirmed her Grannie M's suspicions with a head nod. "That's what your budget has to cover. How much have you got?" Shelby retrieved her funds and they counted it out together. "Of course, you'll need accessories too, but I've got an entire dresser *full* of those, yours for the hunt-and-peck. Let's start with the dress. First things first. It'll probably take up most of your budget anyway. We'll just do the best we can with what's left." Although Maggie would have been happy to subsidize, she knew Shelby's mother wouldn't approve.

By mall number two and store number . . . Shelby had lost count by now. All she knew was that she was exhausted and her great-grandmother seemed to acquire more energy by the moment.

"The store will be closing in ten minutes," the automated voice said over the loud-speakers. "Please take your purchases to the check-out counter." Shelby was glad to hear the announcement, having slipped, stepped and struggled her way into and out of countless dresses. As soon as she'd be done with one stack, Maggie would show up with another. Wouldn't you know the final one she tried on — *Halleluiah!* — was *the* dress. "Absolutely *perfect!*" Maggie said, clapping her hands as Shelby turned in front of the mirror.

"What size shoe do you wear?" Maggie asked through the dressing room door while Shelby was putting her jeans and sweater back on.

"Eight."

"I'm going to run your dress over to the shoe department and see if I can find something on the sale rack. I'll meet you there."

"Grannie M, I've got homework to do. How about we look for shoes another day?"

Silence. Before Shelby was to the end of her sentence, Maggie was already holding the fabric up to the row of shoes on the "Size 8–9" rack.

Crafters' fingers were flying; keyboards clicked away as family histories were recollected and set to paper — whether into a computer or hand-scrawled; Edward Showalter worked up endless schematics and calculations for the square's new clock; in-home rehearsals for the talent show had folks excited, frustrated, arguing, preening and making costumes; gentlemen ordered corsages; and pumpkins, bales of straw, gourds and cornstalks were being hauled by wagonloads to the park district building where the dance would be held. Gladys's constant dogging of *everyone* had some folks fearing nobody would last the two-and-a-half weeks until the big weekend.

The only person who truly seemed to have *nothing* to do for any of the festivities was Cora, who, when she showed up for Thursday's Centennial Plus Thirty meeting, was informed by Gladys that she had already missed too many meetings to jump in now, thank you very much. Cora looked so deflated that Jessica offered her a job helping to decorate the platform for Gladys's pronouncements, but Cora declined, saying, "I believe my talents could be better used elsewhere." Arthur said he was happy to learn she *had* such good talents, then asked her if she'd signed them up for the talent show yet. Sharon kicked him under the table. "I was jist askin!"

Feeling stung from all sides, Cora spun on her heels to leave. Then she turned and dropped a momentary bomb. "What's going on between you and Edward Showalter, Gladys?" You could almost hear the snap of heads turning toward the mayor.

"What*ever* are you talking about, Cora Davis?"

"You know very well. I saw the two of you carrying on, right out there on the square, right out there across from Harry's. I mean it's not like I was spying. I just looked up, and there you both were. Then you disappeared into your office talking a mile a minute. I just think you should tell us all what your intentions are."

Gladys was so angry that Cora (who had been inquiring about nothing more than the clock, which she assumed Gladys understood) had given away her second-best announcement for the evening (at least Gladys assumed Cora had already blabbed about the clock to everyone — which she hadn't) that her face turned beet red. Of course, everyone else thought it was because Gladys's new beau had been disclosed. The miscue was thankfully short-lived, coming to a halt right after Gladys clarified her comments about finally replacing that "old dead ticker with a new one." (*Gasp! Surely* you're not referring to your deceased *husband?* OF COURSE NOT!)

Kevin was surprised Josh didn't want to drive his mom's showy SUV to the dance, but Josh insisted they take Kevin's beater car. Josh wanted to be seated *behind* Kevin and Shelby. Should Kevin decide to park or try any funny business, it wouldn't go unnoticed.

The guys had shared how surprised they'd been at their dates' responses to the doubling news, but were happy it seemed like the dust had settled. Kevin said Shelby had even stated she was stoked about the chance to get to know Deb better, and Josh said that it had played out vice versa in his camp. Kevin chalked up their initial odd behaviors to "an obvious hormone flare-up."

Josh never let on to Kevin that he knew Deb had turned him down. It just didn't seem necessary or prudent, but nonetheless, he felt clever just knowing it — not to mention a tad triumphant *he'd* gotten a *yes* from her. *But no more big head!* The truth was, he'd decided that he did enjoy Kevin most of the time, so he didn't want to put another wedge in the way of their friendship either. Besides, since learning about Deb's turndown and Kevin's silence about it, Josh was beginning to wonder if Kevin was really as advanced as he let on. Maybe underneath it all, he was just as insecure about dating as every other guy.

One thing he knew for sure, though, was that he needed Kevin to stop calling him Josh-o. He'd been reminded of that on Wednesday when he'd finally — and thankfully — received an e-mail from Alex. Among other things, Alex admitted to having his nose out of joint enough to have intentionally blown him off when he was in Chicago. Josh was in the middle of e-mailing Alex back when the phone rang, and it was Alex!

"Josh, if you haven't read my e-mail yet, just delete it first."

"Too late. I was already e-mailing you back. Why didn't you want me to read it?"

"Because I figured you'd razz me for being a sap, since I said I missed you."

"Sap."

"I knew it."

"That's okay. I've missed you too. If there's anything worse than reading it from a guy, it's probably having to hear it. So there, I've said it, and now you're a less sap than me, okay? But neither of us will ever admit this to anybody."

Their conversation lasted forty-five minutes. Alex talked about his upcoming date for the homecoming dance, which was the same night as the Pumpkin Festival dance (*drats!*), and Josh shared the whole story about Kevin and Shelby, Dorothy's advice, and, of course, Deb, the dance and Doofus-ville. Alex couldn't stop laughing.

"It's not *that* funny, dude."

"You don't see the humor in Josh Kinney, former Latin School attendee now going on a double date in the back of a beater car to a Pumpkin Festival dance? It's *hysterical!* I feel like I'm hearing the Cinderella story in reverse!"

"Welcome to life in Pardon-Me-Ville."

"The Lamp Post Motel."

"Jessica!" Katie was thrilled to hear her friend's voice.

"Your call is important to us and we're sorry we missed it. Please leave your phone number — slowly — and we'll call you back as soon as we can. If you're calling to inquire about reservations for the Pumpkin Festival and Centennial Plus Thirty, I'm sorry but we're sold out for both Friday and Saturday that weekend. Please try us again."
BEEP.

This was the first time Katie had received a machine at the Lamp Post. In fact, she didn't know they even had one. Either Jessica was gone, or waiting on a customer and not answering, or . . . she had Caller ID

343

and wasn't interested in speaking to the woman who had not only left her standing in the middle of the road waving for a ride after bunco, but who hadn't returned *her* messages.

"Jessica," she said into her mouthpiece, "it's Katie. I didn't know you had a machine. But then it's been so long since you've heard from me, there are probably many things I don't know. I miss you. I'm sorry I haven't been in touch. I was in Chicago for a couple days, but mostly, I've been going through some . . . stuff. I really can't talk about it because . . ." *BEEEEP!* The machine cut her off. *What are you thinking, spilling your guts on a business machine!* She dialed again, but this time she was brief. "It's Katie. I miss you. Call me."

"Thank you, Dorothy," Katie said into the receiver. "I'll pick you up around three then. Josh has been taking the early bus home this week and we'll be sure to beat him back. Worst-case scenario, he calls and says he's taking the late bus, which will just give us more time to visit. If I wait until I feel like I'm totally ready to tell him about my father, it will *never* happen."

She'd made up her mind about one thing:

344

she would not raise her son with the secret. He had a right to know.

Jessica hated answering machines, but after last Tuesday's Centennial Plus 30 meeting, they'd arrived back to the motel to find a hand-scrawled note stuck under their front door. "A friend of ours gave us your listing. Phoned this afternoon to make a reservation before we left our house, but no answer; your machine must be broken. Dropped by on the way through town hoping for a room. Maybe next trip. Looks nice."

"Oh, Paul! Sarah Sue and I ran to Yorkville this afternoon to get some more yarn. I couldn't have been gone more than thirty minutes! They must have phoned then. I hate we missed business!"

"Me, too. Especially if you were out *spending* money." Her face flushed with embarrassment. "Honey," he said, giving her a quick hug, "I'm just kidding! You deserve a break now and again, same as *we* did tonight. Let's don't worry about it, but let's do get an answering machine. If we're going to stay in business, we need one. I don't know what we were thinking by not having one before. I guess we were thinking we'd just never have a life. I'll run to Hethrow after work tomorrow and go to Best Buy or Office Depot. I'm sure they can steer me to just what we need."

Jessica was glad Paul had done the shopping for such a contraption. He'd made her record the announcement, though (of course, he pushed all the buttons), saying her voice was so pretty that surely everyone would want to stay once they'd heard it. But now, now she had to listen to her *friend's* messages ("This is why I don't like these dumb things!"), and for the life of her, she couldn't figure out how to make the machine stop beeping when she was done. In spite of the annoying, hiccupping device, she phoned Katie, only to get *her* machine again.

"Katie, (*beep*) it's Jessica. (*beep*) Darn it! How on (*beep*) earth do I (*beep*) stop this dumb thing! (*beep*) I got your message. (*beep*) I can't wait to (*beep*) talk to you. (*beep*) Try me again." (*beep*)

Although Katie was sorry to have missed Jessica's call, it gave both her and Dorothy a good laugh when they listened to it after they arrived at the farm. It was just what they needed to help them relax before Josh's arrival.

Fridays always made Josh happy. He was looking forward to an evening with no homework and a chance tomorrow to just hang out by the creek. Forecasts sounded pretty good, but it was funny how weather could change so swiftly in the fall. The last few days the area had been enjoying warmer temperatures than even longtime residents were used to this time of year, so it was especially welcome to a couple of City Slickers from up north. He was, in fact, surprised how much of a difference in temperatures a mere five hours could make.

As he was walking up the lane, Sheba came running lickety-split right at him. "SHEBA!" he said, bending down to swoop her into his arms. "Are we baby-sitting, or is your mom here?" Josh had his answer when he recognized the sound of Dorothy's voice before he was even up the back porch steps. He bounded through the door and into the kitchen.

"DOROTHY! I knew I loved Fridays, and this makes it all the better!" He set Sheba down and they both scurried right over to give her a hug.

After some easy conversations about the

upcoming dance and the double date — during which time Josh and Dorothy exchanged a few thumbs' up signals — Katie sighed, collected herself, and began. "Josh, there is something I must tell you. Something I have recently learned myself. Dorothy's here to help me. She knew the whole story before I did. In fact, she is a part of that story. It's a story about our family."

"Family? You mean like Aunt Tess and Grandma Durbin family?"

"Yes. That family . . . and more. It's about my father, Josh. Your grandfather." And then, piece by piece, they unfolded the truth. Katie did most of the talking, but she often deferred to Dorothy, either for clarity, reminder or backup.

It was something for Josh to take in all right, but surprisingly, he seemed not a smidgen as disturbed as Katie had been, or as she thought he would be. He'd occasionally look puzzled or shocked, but he barely ever interrupted with questions, although they both kept asking him if he had any. When they got to the end of the story — all the way past the part where they'd told him that Pastor Delbert, Jr. still didn't know — of all things, he smiled.

"Josh, do you understand what all of this

348

means?" Katie asked, somewhat incredulous.

"I certainly do!" Rather than sounding ashamed about the fact his own mother was illegitimate (a word none of them had used, and Katie fought to avoid thinking about), or riled about secrets, his voice indicated he was . . . happy.

Katie studied him with astonishment. "Joshua, are you *sure* you understand?"

"Yes, I do, Mom. This must have been a bummer for you. But to tell you the truth, for me, it's the *good* news! My Friday just keeps getting better!"

"What on earth are you talking about?"

"I've got family! Right here in Partonville! I've got an . . . well . . . I guess I've got a *half* of an uncle, and sort of cousins — Pastor's children — and . . . I have a grandfather I can learn something about! See pictures of! And the best part of it is, Dorothy knows my family already, and so do I, at least a little. You know, from the funeral and all."

Dorothy was giving silent prayers of thanks to God, who had so miraculously used what *they'd* seen as the *bad* news to be received as the good.

"I mean it's not like I don't know *my* dad;

I do. I know this is a big bummer for you, Mom. But . . ." He stopped talking when he saw his mom rear her head back, as though his words had knocked her a good one.

"I'm sorry, Mom. I guess I can't possibly know what this feels like for Katie Mabel Carol Durbin. I got that whole mouthful of a name right, right?"

Katie shook her head in the affirmative, obviously chagrined.

"You know, Alex was right!" Josh let out a laugh.

"Alex! He couldn't possibly have known a thing about any of this!"

"I'm not talking about our family secrets, Mom. But Alex said to me just this past Wednesday that I was like a backwards Cinderella story. First I give up my spendy private school for Hethrow High. And I'm going to the dance in a beater car rather than the SUV. And rather than the dance being a homecoming, it's a pumpkin festival. And now . . . now I've got a mom with a middle name of Mabel!" He laughed like a lunatic, knee-slapping and hopping around the kitchen. Katie, who up until that moment had seen no humor in her middle names, could do nothing but chuckle herself. Dorothy laughed too, noticing that

Josh's bright enthusiasm was helping Katie to catch a few light rays. *Thank You, Lord. THANK YOU!*

21

Nellie Ruth was not only surrounded by a sea of Splendid Rose, she was wearing it. With heightened enthusiasm, she'd stepped onto the child's stool she'd purchased from Now and Again Resale just for this purpose (much more economical than those metal ones in the store, she'd proudly told herself), bucket of paint in one hand and paintbrush in the other. When the leg to the little stool buckled, before she even had time to realize what was happening, down she went. Her backside and the bucket had hit the floor at about the same time, ribbons of paint sailing high into the air, then landing on everything like a splatting hailstorm, including the top of her head, her arms, the wall and the lower pane of the living room window.

She sat, paintbrush lifted in the air as though she were about to take a stroke, trying to catch her breath. Rivulets of Splendid

Rose oozed their way across the unleveled floor toward the legs of her prized end table and she was momentarily helpless to do anything but watch. When she finally activated, her feet took to slipping this way and that, and for a few futile moments she wrestled around on the floor like she was in a bowl full of jelly. The more she moved, the bigger the mess became. "Horse feathers!" she exclaimed after she stopped thrashing about. Never in her life had she uttered such a profanity — at least for Nellie Ruth.

Helplessly, she watched the paint ooze around the table legs. Although she hated to move, realizing that every gesture broadened the scope of the mess, she finally had no choice but to scoot backwards, remove her shoes and tiptoe to the kitchen where she grabbed two rolls of paper towels, toe prints dotting the dark wood. She didn't know whether to laugh or cry, but within a few short moments, it didn't matter because she became so hysterical she didn't know *which* was the truth. Never in her life had she experienced such a mess.

"You mean you didn't have a drop cloth?" "You mean to tell me you've never painted before?" "You are *not* telling us you were intending to paint that entire room with a paint brush?" The band members at practice had a grand time ribbing her about her "rosy freckles." After she'd told the story for the third time, it had become one of the highlights of her life, no matter if it did cost her her pride, the price of a gallon of paint, a pint of paint remover and hours of work repolishing patches of the old wooden floor. She'd also decided that the first thing the next morning, she would phone Edward Showalter. She'd been assured by everyone that he was the man to handle her painting task. "Leave the painting to Edward Showalter while you do the playing, Nellie Ruth. We each have our own gifts," Raymond had reminded her. "Amen!" Loretta Forester had said, then pounded out a *ta-bam-bam boom* on her drums.

Lord, Nellie Ruth prayed when retiring for the evening after band practice, her aching backside and paint in her cuticles reminding her of the day's events, *thank you for helping me laugh at myself today. It's probably time I learned to loosen up a little anyway!* As for the rest of the band, even though they didn't pray about it, they continued to be grateful for the laughter during what had otherwise been another head-banging rehearsal.

Between the unveiling of the Core Four, band practices (one Dorothy'd had to miss, she was feeling so weary — and wouldn't you just *know* it was the one everybody was talking about after Nellie Ruth's Great Adventure!) and fielding phone calls about the talent show, not to mention Gladys' Centennial Plus 30 meetings, which seemed to come and go as quickly as her oven door opened and closed, May Belle and Dorothy had barely had time to touch bases. Dorothy called May Belle's house; she needed the company and comfort of her longtime friends. Before May Belle could engage her in conversation, though, Dorothy asked to speak to her groundskeeper. She invited Earl to come right on over and take care of things around her yard. "And please invite your mother too, Earl."

Within ten minutes, they'd arrived at Dorothy's door and Earl had gone straight to work. He was gathering twigs that had blown down into Dorothy's yard during the last week's on-and-off-again winds. He was breaking the larger branches into little pieces and putting them in a yard waste bag for garbage pickup, which was a whole new world to Dorothy, since on the farm, she'd just piled up yard debris and used it for bonfires. Earl was well acquainted with the procedure. "Just like at home," he'd said, showing Dorothy how it needed to be done.

Dorothy and May Belle stood next to each other in front of the kitchen window, heads nearly touching as they watched Earl work out in the yard.

"You smell like chocolate chip cookies," Dorothy said.

"Is that good or bad?"

"Depends on if you brought me a few."

"Now what do you think?"

"Cough 'em up!"

May Belle retrieved the worn-and-patched canvas bag she toted around when she was either running quick errands in town or making a trip to Your Store, which was only a few blocks away. If she was doing a "right good shopping," she pulled her collapsible metal cart with the big wheels. "Here you go. There's a couple snickerdoodles thrown in for good measure. I was going to warn you to not eat the whole bag at once, but you look like you could use a good sugar rush. Are you sleeping well?"

"I've done better in my life."

"How's your . . . whatever you can't talk about going?"

"It's going. God is good, even when we're not."

Earl came bounding through the back door, letting Dorothy's screen door bang behind him. "Close the big door too, Earl. It's kinda blustery out there. What do you need, sir?"

"What do you want me to do next, Dearest Dorothy?"

"You are a fast worker, Earl. Let me think now." She untied the curly ribbon from the bag of cookies and offered one to Earl. He declined by shaking his head. He still had his hand on the doorknob since closing it, waiting to be sent out again. Dorothy grabbed a cookie and polished the whole thing off. She selected another one — the one she noticed had the most chocolate chips in it — then used it to point at Earl. "How about you get my big clippers out of the little shed and cut down my peony bushes back near the alley. Do you know what peonies are?"

Earl's eyes darted to his mother. "They're the pink and white ones by our sidewalk, right?" May Belle nodded. "Yes. I know," he assured Dorothy.

"Then I reckon you're on your next assignment!" In a flash he was gone, screen door banging behind him. Dorothy walked over and closed the big door. "Wish he could handle the assignment *I* have later today."

"Oh? What's that?"

"Can't talk about it. Just keep praying."

Dorothy had phoned Pastor Delbert just before she'd invited Earl and May Belle over. She'd asked if he might be available for a meeting after lunch. "Yes. I have some errands to run; how about I drop by for a few minutes around one-thirty."

"This is something that will definitely take longer than a few minutes," she'd said. "Maybe a couple hours. Might you have more time later in the day?"

"What's this regarding, Dorothy? Can we wait until after church tomorrow?"

"Let's just say it's related to my favorite topic lately: forgiveness. And let's say I could wait until tomorrow, but I've already waited forty-seven years, which is plenty long enough."

"I must say I'm intrigued. How about two-thirty?"

"We'll be here."

"We?"

"It's a surprise." *Boy, is it going to be a surprise.*

■ ■ ■ ■

When Pastor Delbert pulled onto Vine Street, he saw Dorothy was right: Katie Durbin was the last person he expected, and everybody in town recognized her cashmere beige Lexus 430 SUV that was parked out front.

"Howdy do, Pastor Delbert," Dorothy said, greeting him at the front door and quickly ushering him in to close the door behind them, keeping the blustering winds outside. They weren't cold winds — and her heart was racing plenty fast enough to keep her warm, even if they had been — but whatever winds they were, they needed to be kept at bay, just in case they were of the winds-of-*change* variety. There'd been quite enough of that going around.

"Howdy do to you too!" His eyes scanned the living room, but he saw nobody else. "Isn't that Katie Durbin's SUV outside?"

"It is! It is. Come right on in; she and her son are waiting in the kitchen for us. I thought the kitchen table would be a nice cozy place for us to chat. What all have you been up to today?" she asked over her shoulder as they moved toward the kitchen.

"I had to stop by Wal-Mart, then Richardson's Drugs, then Doc's."

"Doc's? Everything okay with you?" She'd stopped just short of the kitchen to ask.

"Fine and dandy. I was just dropping off our family history for the Centennial Plus Thirty booklet. I've been working on it for several days."

Dorothy's breath caught in her throat, as did Katie's and Josh's. Here they were about to introduce him to an entire family history he knew nothing about.

When Pastor entered the kitchen, Josh stood and shook his hand, as did his mother. As soon as they were seated, Dorothy jumped back up, retrieved another placemat from a drawer and set it before him; she usually only kept three on the table. "What can I get you to drink, Pastor Delbert?"

He looked at the three iced teas already served and thought they looked pretty good. While Dorothy was getting his drink, Josh and Katie were intently staring at him: his nose, his eyes, chin, ears, the top of his head. Katie's face looked half puzzled, half frightened; her son's expression was more one of wonder. Pastor decided he must look a sight from the wind. He raked his hands through his hair and straightened his glasses, then gave his mouth and chin a swipe with his hand, making sure he didn't have crumbs stuck on them — something his wife was always having to point out.

"Pastor Delbert, would you mind if I open with prayer?" Dorothy asked as she seated herself. He looked puzzled; he was usually the one being asked to pray, but he was never one to decline an offer of prayer.

"Lord, here we are, but I reckon you already know that since you see us plain as day. You already know *everything,* and have *forgiven* not only us, but those who are not at this table with us. You have forgiven us and loved us, right up until this moment, and I know You're not going to stop showing us the way now. God, may what we have to say be shared not by our might or power, but by Your Spirit. Amen."

"Amen," Josh said, then Pastor, who was now a little unnerved.

"Katie, I've known Delbert here since he was a mischievous little squirt of a boy. Would you mind if I start?"

"No," Katie said, continuing to study his face. Pastor hadn't heard Dorothy refer to him without the pastor part of his name since he'd become the pastor. It flashed through his mind that it felt good to be reminded that he, too, was still a child of

God, while at the same time being a shepherd.

"Delbert . . . Do you mind if I just call you Delbert for this meeting? I think it will be better for all of us — for *you* — to remember that you are first a child of God, then a pastor."

It was as though she had read his mind! "Of course not, Dorothy!"

"Delbert, we have something to tell you today that is going to be hard to believe, but it is true. Living witnesses are sitting at this table to prove it." And so for the third time, Dorothy told the story. Not until she was solidly into it did she realize it was a little less painful this go-around, now that it had been exposed to the light for a while. She had already repeated it twice, which helped, and Katie and Josh now flanked her, lending strength in numbers. Although it was by no means easy, she hadn't been quite as emotionally batted around by the telling. *Where two or more are gathered . . . ,* she thought.

Katie jumped in and out to talk about her mother, *her* life with her mother, a mother who had raised her with dignity and care, but especially with faith — even though that topic still felt awkward to her. Since Katie had lived with the story for the past several days — turned it over in her mind, reread the letters, even somewhat self-consciously prayed about it — she felt calmer than she might have imagined.

Same as he'd done at the farm when first learning the news, Josh enthusiastically stepped into the telling now and again, which at worst felt momentarily out of place to everyone at the table, especially Delbert. He'd had no time to process things yet. But at best, Josh's youthful and wholehearted acceptance almost felt to Delbert like a life-rope, thrown by God to keep him from drowning in this truth that was piercing his soul like a thunderous calamity of deceit. *How could this be, Dad? How could you have let this happen? And me, only a child myself when you did this!*

When they'd all come to the end of their words and emotional reserves, Dorothy closed by imploring Delbert to remember what she herself had clung to in the midst of her storm. "Delbert, now is the time to remember what you know. Do not rely on your emotions; rely on God. A very wise pastor told me just last Sunday that if we cannot forgive on our own, we need to trust the Almighty to work that work in us.

Somehow I just know that wise pastor saw that pure-gold act of faith modeled by his own father, who knew what it meant to not only extend forgiveness, but to *receive* it, and from none other than that same God Almighty."

"Doc, Pastor Delbert. I apologize for the late hour of this call. You haven't turned my family's history in for the centennial booklet yet, have you?"

"No. We don't have another meeting until Tuesday."

"Good. I'll be right by to pick it up."

"I can bring it to church tomorrow. No need to go out of your way."

"Yes, there is." But he didn't explain. For now, he just needed to hold all the pieces.

Delbert was awake nearly all night, replaying the whole afternoon's conversation in his mind, trying to remember his own young experiences with his father back when all of this had taken place. He remembered his father's terrible crying after his mother died. *Fast-forward.* He remembered his father's impassioned sermons about extending and receiving forgiveness, impassioned to the point of his father's own tears. *Fast-forward.*

He remembered . . . his father used to call on Tess Walker about once a month, up until his death! Obviously, Dorothy knew nothing of this. Once he began studying for the pastorate himself, he figured that since Tessa Martha Walker was not a church attendee, his dad was simply bringing God's love straight to the house of a self-isolated woman most in town just chalked up as crazy.

What transpired, Dad? Did you talk to her about Clarice? Learn about your daughter? Did you speak to her of God, maybe even help her mend her fences with Him?

Oh, God, only You will ever know now, and that will have to be enough for me. Please, make it enough for me.

And then he remembered that he now had a . . . half-sister, and, as Josh had called it, one-half of a full-blooded nephew.

He ushered Sunday morning's dawn into the world with a rain shower of tears that spilled onto the desk in his home study, onto the pages of the family history he'd so proudly written. Would his tears water those words until they grew a new chapter, or would they simply evaporate, along with all else he had known to be true?

■ ■ ■ ■

MEET YOUR TOWN: Partonville, settled 130 years ago by the Walter Parton family, including Walter and his wife, Beatrice, and Walter's brother Seth.

QUESTION: Why did they decide to settle here?

ANSWER: Recorded in ink, in a bound, leather journal bearing his initials, and in beautiful cursive handwriting, Walter wrote, "When I saw the rich black earth, I knew we could raise plenty of staples to sustain us. When I asked Beatrice, my newly betrothed, what she thought, she said, 'Walter, my heart tells me we're home.' "

TIDBIT: Beatrice died giving birth to her stillborn twins, but to this day, we give thanks for Beatrice Parton's perceptive heart that ultimately paved the way to help us *all* find our homes here in Partonville.

The last time Katie had set foot in a church after her mother died was when Delbert had conducted her Aunt Tess's funeral services. Now, though, for the first time since, she had the desire to worship. She had a longing, almost a felt *need,* to be with other faith-filled people. She'd also never heard Delbert preach, and she wanted to study him, watch him, *know* him. He was the closest link to her father, and she didn't want to lose another opportunity, like she had with Aunt Tess, to stay connected to her roots. When she arose, she knocked on Josh's door and told him to start dressing. "It's Sunday and we're going to church."

Dorothy, May Belle, Earl, Katie and Josh were lined up in a pew next to one another, right behind Gladys. Pastor Delbert, however, was not only absent from church; he was not even in town. When a layperson from Yorkville made the announcements, they included that Pastor Delbert was taking a little time off and that he'd be back in his office on Tuesday.

When they came to the last *Amen,* although Katie had somewhat enjoyed the service, she was, of course, disappointed Delbert hadn't preached. But moreover, she felt wounded, wondering if he might have been shunning her. Shades of Dorothy's comments about a town's judgments danced in her head. On the way out, she spent several focused minutes in front of Delbert Senior's portrait, grieving her loss at having never met him, and fretting that her closest link to him might be trying to shut her out. *Dad. Dad* . . . She stared into his eyes, wishing she could press her face against his portrait and try to imagine the warmth of his skin, what his scent might have been. . . .

Dorothy was worried. What was going on in Pastor's head? His heart? His spirit? To where had he run? *And just look at Katie's face. Lord, just* do *something!*

Delbert, child of God and son of Delbert Senior, sat at a desk in a small, stark room — twin bed, chair, desk, sink and no decorations aside from a small wooden cross above the bed — at a Catholic retreat center in Hethrow. When he'd gathered his notes to preach this morning, he realized there was just no way he could overcome his own emotional mess and stand before anybody, so he made his first phone call to a layman, his second to a retreat center, and then he gathered his family's history — clinging to it as Katie had to her letters — a notebook and his Bible.

Throughout his years of friendship with Father O'Sullivan (they met once a month, just to spend time with somebody else who "got" what they did), they'd often talked about finding more time for their own personal reflection. On several occasions, Father O'Sullivan had encouraged him to consider a trip to the center. "Always does me a world of good!" he'd say, plump red cheeks bulging up near his eyes as he'd smile. "When I make it a priority on my calendar, I go. Twenty-four hours with just God and me and the Word and I feel like a new man! And you don't have to be Catholic to use the facilities, you know. They even let in the most unlikely candidates," he'd say. "I've heard tell they even allow *Methodists!*" Then he'd throw his head back and laugh, as though he'd never said that exact same thing a half dozen times before. "Really," he'd add with a sobered voice, "you ought to try it some time."

Little had Delbert ever imagined he'd actually find himself here one day. But where was he to go? Like the story of Jacob and the angel in Genesis, he was determined to wrestle with his new truths until they blessed him — and he hoped that was before Tuesday at noon when he had to be back in his office.

22

It was a fiasco of epic proportions. On a Richter scale of one-to-ten, this was nothing short of a seven-point-nine for early-morning Partonville travelers whose lives had come to a complete halt. Shock and dismay, confusion and mayhem ruled. Not since The Tank had bitten the back of a garbage truck and caused a commotion had the square been tied in such a knot. Some thought trickster aliens had possessed their town in the middle of the night; others who were more sensible remembered having read about their mayor's ridiculous idea to change the direction of traffic. They all assumed someone had stopped her or that she had finally come to her senses.

Wrong!

No amount of nay-saying or absolute refusal to go along with her idea — not even by dedicated and outspoken committee members who *assumed* they had dissuaded her — had knocked sense into that determined woman's head. Acting Mayor Gladys McKern had, in the pre-dawn hours of this Monday morning, changed the direction of the one-way arrows leading onto the square. (Everybody knew she couldn't have literally done it herself. For years folks would speculate as to who might have been daft enough to conspire with her, but nobody ever admitted to it.)

Early on in the day, most longtime residents hadn't even noticed the new signs, so used to traveling in their own set ways were they. They had proceeded onto the square, turned right, parked in front of Harry's for breakfast or journeyed on around the square to peel off in the direction of their destination. Those who *did* notice, and who always played by the rules, first slammed on their brakes, shook their heads in confusion, and, if nobody was in front of them to suggest otherwise, shrugged their shoulders and turned to the left. By a miracle, some of them never met a single other car while passing through. But more often than not, they would see a car coming straight toward them, its driver wildly honking and trying to signal them that they were going the wrong way on a one-way, causing them to wonder if they had hallucinated the arrow change. And just *forget* about it if they had followed the new rules and were trying to park on the square, since all diagonal parking lines slanted the opposite direction from which Gladys was trying to route traffic, something their dear mayor hadn't thought about. Cars were parked every which way.

By rush hour (kind of an oxymoron in Partonville), traffic had come to a halt. Drivers yelled at themselves and out their windows, and the cacophony of blowing horns was all but deafening.

The worst part for Gladys was that she had, as usual, arrived at Harry's the minute Lester opened (6:00 A.M.) to witness, firsthand, Partonville's glorious surprise step into the future. By 6:45, nobody was being served since Lester, Harold and Arthur were all outside trying to help Mac undo what was quickly becoming not only the *Partonville Press*'s next headline, but that of the *Daily Courier* as well. The fact the *Courier*'s photographer couldn't reach the square was the only thing that kept the humiliation from being even worse than it was.

"Where in tar-nation *is* that woman!"

Arthur yelped to anyone who would listen as he exited her office. It seemed she had plumb disappeared. "Maybe those folks thinkin' aliens done messed with us in the middle of the night were right, and hopefully they took Gladys with 'em when they left afore I find her!"

The only consolation, Gladys thought as she headed out of town — at least until she had the courage to return after dark that night — was that she'd been so excited about this vision-gone-bad for so long, she hadn't waited until the grand weekend to unleash it.

Katie was upstairs moving the last few things around in the Chaos Room, which was at long last almost completely organized. In fact, she'd taken to calling it the spare room, resolving to leave chaos behind. It had become clear the treadmill wasn't going to fit, so she'd decided to instead purchase a little television and DVD player, stock up on a few new and varied DVD exercise routines, bring up her hand weights, roll out her Pilates mat and call it a day. While she'd been in Hethrow making her purchases, she'd also checked out a couple of health clubs, deciding to wait and see how accommodating her tiny spare-room-home-gym felt after a couple of weeks before making any decisions.

Her cordless phone rang just as she was surveying the fruits of her labors. "Katie?"

"Yes."

"This is Pastor Delbert. I mean Delbert. This is Delbert. I'd like to talk to you, privately." He looked at the clock on the church wall; it was 1:00 P.M. "I just got back in my office, but I have a quick check-in meeting every Tuesday at one-thirty. So since it's Tuesday . . . how about right after that, say a few minutes after two, maybe a little earlier if there aren't any unexpected hot-button issues? And would it be okay if I came out to the farm?"

"I'll see you when you arrive. Should I call Dorothy, or do you want to?"

"I'd rather it was just the two of us, okay?"

She hung up and went to work tidying up the kitchen. She wondered, heart racing as she wiped down the table, if, when Delbert was young, he'd ever longed for a sibling, too. She forced herself to dismiss such thoughts, after having been blindsided by them to begin with. She couldn't decide if the idea of cultivating a blood relationship with a relative stranger was romanticized, wishful, corny, dreadful or impossible. For now, hearing what he had to say would be enough.

"Katie," Delbert said, resting his forearms on the kitchen table and leaning across toward her, "I have been off at a retreat center for a couple of days, trying to make sense out of . . . I mean, I don't know if you can imagine what this is like for me. My whole life as I know it feels turned upside down."

"Yes. I imagine I *do* know what it feels like," she said with a little more edge in her voice than she'd intended.

Delbert swiped at his nose, adjusted his glasses and cleared his throat. When Katie looked in the mirror-of-her-eyes sitting across from her, they both realized they were clearly struggling with a vast range of emotions. "I am so sorry," he said with gentleness. "Of course you do. Please forgive such a careless and self-centered statement."

"I've had a few more days with it," she said, her voice now softening, identifying with his topsy-turvy state of mind. "Time helps a little. But the whole thing can still throw me for a terrible loop."

"Time. The great healer, so they say. 'Time, prayer and God's sovereign hand in our lives,' my dad used to say."

"Delbert, if *your* dad used to say that, then so did *mine*." Her eyes veered off toward the kitchen counter, landing in a faraway land. "Time, prayer and God's sovereign hand in my life . . . ," she repeated in a whispered voice.

He could see by the look on her face that she was filing the words away, perhaps grasping for pieces of the man whom she had never known. For a moment, she was transparent enough to allow him a peek into the depths of her pain and he felt a remarkable tug on his heart to tell her the things he knew to be true about his dad, things that would help paint a picture of the man who had raised him with such love.

It was then he knew he was done wrestling.

By the time Delbert left the farm, they had entered into their own new covenant: there would be no more secrets. They could each, including Dorothy (Delbert would call her about this), feel free to tell whomever they felt they most trusted and with whom they shared the greatest intimacies. This included Delbert telling his wife, which he was embarrassed to admit he had not yet done.

"No wonder this all got buried," he'd said to Katie, who completely understood his sentiment. They would give themselves two days for this private sharing as they gathered the support and prayers of their best friends. It would also give them at least some idea of what initial reactions would be.

Then they would stand strong for each other when he broke the news to Partonville. Sunday. During church. Sunday during church when Pastor Delbert Carol, Jr. would preach what he would refer to as the second and most personal revelation of his two-part message on God's awesome grace and forgiveness. Of course, he didn't know it then, but he would go on to preach a sermon impassioned to the point of his own tears, just like his father before him.

Tuesday night's Centennial Plus 30 meeting was . . . unusual. Gladys arrived ten minutes tardy, a first. Where she got the gumption to finally enter that room, she and many others would never know. Then again, she *was* Gladys.

Sharon had threatened to stuff her entire handbag down Arthur's throat if he verbally jumped on Gladys, when, and *if,* she ever arrived. He'd done nothing but rant on about somebody having to keep a closer eye on that woman "lest she turn the dern celebration into a three-ring circus clown."

"I'm sure she's embarrassed enough, Arthur."

"You wish."

May Belle greeted Gladys with a warm hello and a hot mug of coffee she'd kept on standby. "We're all ready for you," she'd said, immediately wishing she'd just kept quiet since it made them sound like a firing squad. After May Belle scooted back behind the partition, Gladys was left standing alone before the uncomfortably silent and seated group. She cleared her throat and sat down, then just stared at her hands for a few moments. She looked at her watch, nodded her head, stood again and said, "Well, now, we're late getting started. As you know, it is my goal to keep these meetings running on time. So let's just get to it. I believe my traffic idea was . . . an excellent one. Still is. Admittedly, it wasn't executed very well, but if I would have had more support and . . ."

"Gladys," Doc said, jumping in before Arthur did, "that is behind us now, and I think it's best we *leave it there* and just move on to our reports. Eugene and I will begin. Go ahead, Eugene." Gladys, sensing a possible mutiny, slammed her mouth closed and sat down.

Eugene had obviously been thrown an unexpected curveball, but he reached out and bunted just the same. "Right. Here's who we've already collected stories from," he said, unfolding his paper and reading the list he and Doc had put together while they were waiting for Gladys, "and here's who's still working on them."

"Although Harold couldn't make the meeting this evening," Doc said, "he assured us that what's getting turned in is just dandy. Said he'll only need a couple days lead-time to roll it out."

The rest of the meeting was pretty perfunctory and Gladys remained low-key. The only real downside was the unanimous reporting that advertisers and patron donations, which they had all been trying to gather, were sorely lacking. They decided they could defer some of the chili proceeds to cover expenses if they ultimately fell short, and Gladys — verging on Gladys the Gladiator, but overtly stifling herself — encouraged rather than demanded them to keep vigilant records so bookkeeping matters could never come under fire.

Katie stopped by the Lamp Post at eight-thirty Wednesday night, which was the first chance Jessica said she would have time to visit, hopefully without interruptions, if everyone got checked in early and Sarah Sue went down on time. At eight-twenty-five, Jessica flipped on the NO Vacancy sign, which would also indicate to Katie she should come right to their home entrance, which was a modest three rooms attached to the motel. Wouldn't you know Sarah Sue had cranked around half of the afternoon, and Jessica was just settling in to nurse her when Katie knocked on their door. Paul greeted Katie, then settled down in his chair in the living room and went back to reading his paper.

"Katie!" Jessica tried to exclaim in a quiet voice to express her joy yet not startle her baby, who she wanted to nurse and go down. "I need to hug you, but it'll have to wait." Katie didn't want to chase Paul out of his own living room, so she quietly said to Jessica, "Would you mind if we go sit in your office lobby? I have something personal to share."

"Oh, *Katie!*" Jessica stood from her chair, the office lobby lit only by the pale blue glow from the new neon Lamp Post sign outside the office door. "Stand up here,

Katie, so I can hug you! Now I've *got* to hug you!" With one arm, Jessica, who was still nursing since her daughter had kept craning her neck to watch Katie rather than nursing, hugged Katie, who had poured out her whole story. Jessica backed off and looked at Katie's tear-laden face, then hugged her again. After standing in silence for a minute, during which time Jessica, without words, unquestionably affirmed Katie *and* their friendship, the women sat back down again.

Jessica looked down at Sarah Sue's face and stroked her cheek. "*All* children are children of God! How sad Pastor Delbert Senior never had a chance to hold his beautiful daughter. I can't help but believe he knows about you in heaven, Katie, and is just so *proud* of you." Such simple statements. Such gifts of continued healing for Katie's mending heart.

"Thank you, *dearest* friend," Dorothy said to May Belle as they sat at May Belle's kitchen table, Dorothy having wound down from what was now her fourth recital about the Core Four Covenant. "Bless you, bless you, *bless* you for your prayers. No doubt they made a world of difference. I can't imagine what I would ever do without you!"

"Like they say, Dorothy — whoever *they* are, and sometimes I think they wouldn't recognize a hill of beans if they saw it in front of them, but in this case they're right when they say it" — May Belle briefly chuckled at her own silly self, "With God, all things are possible, so I reckon you'd still get along just fine."

Dorothy looked around May Belle to the pie tin on her counter. "But like they also say — and I'm talking about the same *they* as you are — with May Belle, all things are baked. How about a nice big slice of pumpkin pie and a hot cup of cinnamon tea to celebrate the end of the secret? I don't know what's going to happen after church on Sunday, but that'll give us both something else to pray about while we're eating it!"

Alex,
When's a good time to call you? Be home tonight? Have I got a story to tell YOU! (It's on the QT for now, though.) Talk about Cinderella in reverse! You have no idea, man!
Josh

■ ■ ■ ■

"Delbert, when I married you, it was for better or for worse. You are exactly the same man to me as you were before you learned all of this.

"I agree with you, Dorothy's role in this does not need to be revealed; she was just caught up in it, really, as a go-between. All that really matters is that a man and a woman each willingly made a mistake, a child was conceived, a secret was kept, and in the end, God loved everyone through it — including you and Katie now. And I can't help but believe that your, *our,* new relationship with her and her son isn't going to bless us all in a very special way.

"But, Delbert, if Dorothy continues to *insist* she 'fess up to the public,' as you said she put it, and you think it will help her to fully heal . . . and she's *determined* to own her part . . . what else are you to do but let her?" Delbert sighed.

"Something I *am* kind of sorry about, though, is that you didn't feel you could come right to me rather than running off to a retreat center, but one of the reasons I love you is because you first love God. I'm happy being the pastor's wife, Delbert, even now when it means our private lives will be paraded in front of an entire congregation. But I stand beside you. And if you should ever feel a need to step down, or somebody forces you to do that, know I will still be a very proud Delbert Junior's wife."

If only everyone in town would respond with the same grace and love. But, of course, they wouldn't.

23

For maybe the first time ever, Gladys Mc-
Kern and Cora Davis found themselves on
the same side. Their behavior was shame-
less, Doc decided, several times trying to
divert their conversations. The two jabber-
ing women were all but working the early
Monday-morning crowd at Harry's in an
attempt to rally support to have the Carols'
family name omitted from the centennial
booklet, and to stir up trouble about Dorothy.

"I tell you," Gladys said to anyone who
would listen, and a few who wished not to,
"after what that man told us about his
father at church on Sunday," and she
prattled on with the short version for those
who didn't attend the United Methodist
Church, "standing up there as big as you
please, talking about grace and forgiveness
as though there was nothing more to all of
this than a nice story, when proof of his own

father's failure was sitting right there in *church* with us. . . . Why I have never seen or heard anything *like* it!

"And *Dorothy Jean Wetstra* standing up and giving what she called a testimony! I'd call it nothing short of disgrace! I mean here we are trying to let folks know what Partonvillers are made of, and we sure do *not* want them to think *that's* the kind of people we are!

"And that Katie Durbin, or Katie Carol, or what*ever* we're supposed to call her now, owning Crooked Creek Farm, the very land that our new park is going to be named after! And her sitting right there in church, an illegitimate . . ."

"That is ENOUGH!" Arthur's voice thundered throughout the small restaurant as he banged both fists on the counter and stood. He walked over to Gladys and got right up in her face, stretching himself to his fullest stature.

"*Now you listen to me, woman!* I don't care if you ARE the mayor! You are plumb out of line and that is ENOUGH! You are trying to create a soap opera nothin' short of historical — and hys-*terical* — potions here, and I tell you I will not STAND for it!" Gladys's eyeballs were pasted to the back of her head, he yelped so loudly right in her face. Cora walked up behind Arthur, looking like she might be intending to bean him, but Eugene stepped in front of her, facing her square on. He'd been on the verge of intervening right before Arthur stepped in anyway.

"I'll admit," Arthur said, facing Gladys, then scanning the rest of the folks at Harry's, "when I first heard Pastor tellin' the story, I thought, 'Now *this* is a disturbin' new sitchiation.' But dad *gum* it!" He turned to have his next words drill right into Gladys again. "Here you are blatherin' on about what we're made of, when the fact is, no doubt most of us right here at Harry's have lived long enough to collect a few of our *own* rascally stories." Many folks looked away from Arthur, as though hiding from the sear of his conviction.

"What *are* we really made of?" he asked. "It BETTER (he reached his fist past Gladys and banged it on the counter again) be stuff that holds us together, and tearin' folks down AIN'T (pause) HOW (pause) THAT (pause) WORKS!"

Eugene looked straight at Cora and began to clap. Within a few seconds, so was everyone else in the restaurant, aside from Cora, who stormed out, and Gladys, who suddenly felt ashamed of herself.

Gladys nearly whispered into the phone. "Father O'Sullivan?" she asked, never revealing who she was and speaking a few notes higher than her usual voice so as not to be recognized. "I am not a Catholic, but I'm wondering if you would listen to me . . . well . . . I have to . . . Can I just phone my own . . . Do Catholics still do confessions?"

"Yes. Would you like to . . ."

"Well, I confess," she said, then she hung up.

Thursday night's run-through of the opening events went pretty much without a hitch, but definitely it was crunch day. At least traffic thankfully circled the square the way it had been circling ever since there'd been a square, which was not too many years after the Parton family — who received liberal coverage in the official Centennial Plus 30 booklet — first settled there.

Of course, the chili makers, who consisted mostly of guild members from all the Partonville churches, plus both genders of scouts, their parents, the 4-H club and

Lester, had been chopping and dicing up a storm since Wednesday. Nearly every Tupperware bowl in town was filled and readied for action at Friday's 5:30 A.M. "sizzling, stirring and stewing kickoff" (Sharon had just *adored* inventing that phrase in her recent *Meet Your Town* festivities recap column) which would be under May Belle's able direction in the park district building's kitchen. May Belle was the only one who knew the secret formulas for multiplying recipes, which was trickier than one might think. Wilbur would, as usual, arrive with the ground chuck. The chili makers' brief Thursday meeting consisted of a check-off list of ingredients, condiments (including several degrees of hot sauce and two kinds of jalapenos) and paper goods. All seemed to be in order, including two large bottles of antacids donated by Richardson's Rexall Drugs, dollar-off coupons attached. "Just make sure we get a mention under donations *along* with the advertisement we paid for in the booklet."

The new digital clock and temperature were right on the money; Edward Showalter had outdone himself working nearly around the clock (literally and figuratively) on installations, although not for free, and Gladys was actually receiving congratulations for the long-overdue update.

Jessica, who was on the verge of a nervous breakdown after getting a combined seven hours of sleep the last two nights, had managed to please the fine mayor with her special archway with "We Proclaim" written across the top in vibrant red letters (paint left over from Dorothy's ceiling), then splattered with multicolors to look like confetti. Although Gladys wished the archway could be more mobile so it could be moved center stage for her proclamations and pronouncements, she acquiesced when it was pointed out to her that the band would be taking up a portion of the stage once they set up, and that the archway, which was constructed out of chicken wire and baler twine, might not hold up too well if it was shuffled around. Once Jessica showed Gladys her sketch, complete with streamers and balloons that would hide the framework, Gladys was satisfied — although a little worried about the balloons all being blown up and in place on time. "Oh, that *can't* be done today," Jessica said, brushing her bangs off of her eyebrows. "We don't want to risk possible deflation before your big moment!"

With much gratitude, several days ago Dorothy had made the decision to turn over most of the talent show responsibilities to

Sheila, one of Maggie Malone's grand-daughters, saying she just didn't have it in her this year. "It's time someone brought more youthful ideas and energy to the annual event anyway. Yes, things have gone alrighty and some say don't fix what isn't broken, but Sheila, I know things can be improved and you're just the woman to do it!"

There was something about Dorothy's genuine trust and praise that helped folks rise to new levels. Her vote of confidence gave Sheila the ammunition she needed to try a few new things, like having an adorable set of twins run onto the stage — one from each side — with sparkling streamers, then meet in the middle to announce each new act, rather than to march her own self up there time after time, just to make introductions. Dorothy applauded the idea and came to the Thursday rehearsal to cheer Sheila's creativity and to pass on a few insights she'd gleaned after all these years: "Make sure you keep yourself off of the judges' panel; do not allow an intermission or folks both in the audience *and* in the acts will disappear; try not to cringe when T.J. Winslow plays sour notes during his Lady of Spain clarinet solo. He takes enough guff from the band."

By 3:00 P.M. Friday, both inside and out, the park district building was a wondrous site to behold. All in all, most thought it resembled the most bountiful and inviting horn-of-plenty they'd ever seen. A giant banner framed the entrance to the park and a special box ran on page one of the *Partonville Press* with the same announcements.

Friday:
5:00 P.M. Acting Mayor Gladys McKern: Pumpkin Festival *and* Centennial Plus 30 Proclamations and Pronouncements
5:00 P.M. to ? Chili Galore! (Bring your appetite!)
7:00 P.M. to ? (dependent upon the number of registrants): Talent Show

Saturday:
9:00 A.M. to 1:00 P.M. Craft Fair: More than twenty exhibitors!
1:00 P.M. to 7:00 P.M. Building closed to public

Friday night's proclamations, which most thought were a little too long, but nonetheless did Partonville proud, chili dinner and talent show — and no, Cora never did sign up — ran like clockwork. Sheila had done a marvelous job of directing the talent show; the twins never missed a cue; and much to the disgruntlement of the audience, the judges declared a singing trio from "unincorporated Hethrow" the winners. Next year, Gladys huffed under her breath, they might make contestants show certificates of residency.

The Centennial Plus 30 booklet was selling like hotcakes, some families buying multiple copies, including the Carols . . . and Katie. Their family history was just as Pastor Delbert Junior had written it the first time, unfolding a beautiful story about the legacy of the church, and how a father and son had ministered at the same facility for nearly fifty years. There was one addition, however, to his original copy. On the page where he spoke of his father's passing, to the list of survivors he had added ". . . and his daughter, Katie Mabel Carol Durbin, who lived in Chicago at the time of his death, but who is a new Partonville resident." It was all that needed to be said.

There were three anonymous platinum-level patron donors whose monies alone covered the entire costs of the booklets. A brief note had come with each cash donation. The first to arrive said "THANK YOU, JESUS!" The second read "Families are forever, on earth as it is in heaven. Amen." And the last: "From Cinderella."

Josh was a nervous wreck. He relentlessly fiddled with his tie and paced to the front window to see if Kevin was on his way up the lane. The plan was Kevin would pick up Shelby first, then Josh, then the three of them would journey to Hethrow to pick up Deb. From a geographical point of view, this routing didn't make sense, since Kevin and Deb actually lived closer together than anyone else; but from a strictly social standpoint, nothing *else* made sense.

Katie stared at her son, fighting back tears. She was blindsided by her own emotions. He looked so much like his father, and yet . . . she'd studied family pictures in the Centennial Plus 30 booklet of Delbert Senior, and there were *her* father's unmistakable ears, pinned back on the top. Same cleft in his chin. Same shape of his eyebrows.

"What's wrong?" Josh asked as he paced back toward her.

"Absolutely nothing. You look very handsome, Joshua. Very handsome."

"Thanks, Mom. I hope I don't sweat through my jacket before they get here, though, or all I'll look is gross." Just then headlights flashed in the front window. They were here. Josh immediately started out the door.

"Josh! The corsage! I'll get it." Katie scurried to the refrigerator.

"Just a sec!" he hollered out the door.

Katie handed him the box and gave him a peck on the cheek, but not before he ducked back into the house so nobody would see it. "Have a good time. And don't forget your curfew!"

"Got it!"

He loped to the car and opened the back door, seating himself behind Shelby. "Hey!"

"Hey!" Kevin said back.

"Hey, Shelby!"

"Hello, Josh," she said with a hint of reserve. This was harder than she thought it would be, *the bozo.*

Idle, somewhat stiff, conversation occupied them all the way to Deb's house. "So how was your day?" "Hope the DJ is good." "I heard the park district building is really something." Josh kept trying to figure out what Shelby had done to her hair whenever another car's headlights briefly lit up the back of her head. It looked all . . . fluffy, piled up or something and . . . *Are those highlights? Nice.* And those earrings . . . dangling, swinging, brushing her beautiful long neck that he'd never noticed before. He had yet to see her face; she'd never turned her head remotely around. He received occasional wafts of an enticing fragrance he surely did like.

At last they pulled up in front of Deb's. Josh sat there, staring at her house.

"Earth to Josh-o! Dude, you gotta get out of the car if you're going to pick her up!"

"How about you just call me Josh, okay?" he said as he exited the car. His heart was beating a mile a minute as he walked to the front door. His first date — and what a complicated one! The doorbell played the longest song he'd ever heard. When the door opened, there stood her dad. "Hello. You must be Josh. I'm Deb's father. It's nice to meet you." He held out his hand and Josh dropped the corsage box while fumbling to shake hands. He picked up the box as carefully as a piece of broken glass, hoping he hadn't managed to knock the flowers apart.

Deb made a grand entrance down the open staircase; she lived in one of the new upscale subdivisions, her family having upsized about a year ago. She looked beautiful. "Hi, Josh. I see you already met my dad."

"Yes, I have."

She walked up to him, eyes on the corsage box. "Is that for me?" she finally asked, since Josh wasn't making any attempts to hand it to her.

"Oh! Yes. Here," he said, jutting it out toward her. He watched her open the lid, then with relief saw her smile.

"It's beautiful," she said, holding exactly what she had asked for, which was a wrist corsage with a purple orchid. "Can you help me put it on, please?"

"Sure." He fumbled with it, suddenly realizing with horror that the main stem was indeed broken. The flower dangled by a thread when he tried to slip it over her wrist.

"Deb, I am so sorry. I . . . dropped the box and then . . ."

Deb laughed. "We seem to have a thing going like this, don't we?" She handed everything, box and broken corsage, to her dad. "Don't worry. I'll live without a corsage. It's a beautiful flower. I'll float it in some water or something. Let's just go have a good time."

They said their goodnights, which were followed by curfew mentions, making Josh feel more relaxed since hers was the same as his, which was eleven, a half hour after the dance was to end.

Shelby watched the two of them walk to the car, Josh holding Deb's elbow. Her dress was stunning. *Dregs!* Shelby noticed Kevin was doing his share of mouth-open oogling, too. *Double dregs!*

So far, the evening had gone fairly well, Josh thought, aside from the fact that the top of Deb's shoes were covered with scuff marks from him stepping on her toes. A dancer he wasn't. Of course, Kevin could dance as well as he did everything else, which was to perfection. Josh just wished he wouldn't be holding Shelby quite so closely, which, unbeknownst to Josh, Shelby was wishing too. Deb had caught Josh on several occasions craning his neck to watch Kevin and Shelby, same as Shelby had caught Kevin staring at Deb, even though he was about to squeeze her lungs out, not to mention smashing her first-ever corsage to bits.

Shelby was a sight to behold, Josh thought as they all stood near the refreshment table during a music break. Deb was beautiful, but Shelby. . . . He'd never seen her with lipstick before. It wasn't much, but it brought out the rose in her cheeks and . . .

"Mind if I ask your date for the next dance when they start back up again?" Kevin quietly asked Josh.

"Not as long as you don't mind if I ask yours."

"Deal."

Four songs later, Kevin and Deb were still dancing, laughing . . . flirting, if Shelby wasn't mistaken. The good news was, she and Josh were doing the same. While Josh stepped on Shelby's toes — which were numb anyway from her stupid heels, which she hated and vowed never to wear again — Shelby looked over Josh's strong shoulder (*Nice! When did he grow these?*) at Maggie Malone, her beautiful Grannie M, and Great-Grandpa Ben. They were gliding and twirling, swaying and . . . kissing. In their seventies and still *kissing!* It was just dreamy. Almost as dreamy as the guy who held her:

not too close and not too far away, but just right.

Katie was curled up in a blanket watching an old Tracy and Hepburn movie. Even though Dorothy had convinced her many people went stag to the dance, she'd decided to stay at home and just let Josh have his night. Now if Jacob, Dorothy's single attorney son who lived in Philadelphia, had come in for the weekend festivities, she might have changed her mind. Although they'd butted heads, Jacob at first having trouble trusting that Katie's offer to buy the farm wasn't simply an attempt to take advantage of his mom (and truth be told, she *did* have mixed motives back then — and sometimes even now), by the time they'd worked side-by-side during Dorothy's farm auction and spent some collective hours with everyone afterward, she and Jacob had settled into a truce — of sorts. She'd even found herself curiously . . . *intrigued* by him, especially after getting a stolen glimpse of his tender heart for his mom and, she did have to admit, surveying his fit body in cutoffs and a T-shirt.

After learning from Jessica how many family members traveled "back home" to Partonville each year for the Pumpkin Festival, and especially how many more had come this year because of the Centennial Plus 30, Katie had been surprised — and admittedly disappointed — that neither of Dorothy's sons returned for the festivities. At the very least, Josh had been hoping Steven and Bradley, Dorothy's teen grandsons, might arrive from Denver with their dad, Vincent, who was divorced. Josh had had a great time with them when last they were in town, and he knew enough girls now that he could have fixed them up with dates for the dance. Although a few encouraging e-mails had flown back and forth between them, in the end, it wasn't to be. Katie noticed Dorothy had clearly sounded disappointed when she'd inquired, but like always, Dorothy said she understood and that she had high hopes they might all be home for Thanksgiving, or Christmas for *sure.*

Last Katie knew, Dorothy was going to the dance, though. She'd told Katie she was going to "stand by the sidelines with the rest of the old hens," then she'd thrown her head back and laughed until Katie began to laugh too, both of them commenting on how good it felt to do so again. "You know, Katie, it just does an old ticker good to see those young ones out there having a swell

time. Brings back such memories . . . ,"
she'd said with a momentary faraway yet
happy look in her eyes as she gave silent
thanks to her smile, which didn't even need
an ounce of coaxing.

What Katie didn't know, however, was
that while she was home alone feeling sorry
for Dorothy, Dorothy was slow-dancing
with first Doc Streator, who bowed before
her when he invited her to "twirl a whirl"
with him, then Lester K. Biggs, who had no
sense of rhythm but looked incredibly dap-
per in his new haircut, and Arthur, who
wore his coveralls but who hummed sweetly
to one of his old favorites, "Tenderly."
("Wish we'd a played that tune rather than
that darned doo-dah-daying one!") The
next tap on her shoulder had come from
none other than the Joshmeister, who she
believed was possibly the most handsome
boy at the dance.

Dorothy couldn't help but look over Josh's
shoulder at Nellie Ruth, who was sure talking up a storm with Edward Showalter
while they swayed to the music, dancing
from one side of the floor to the other. If
Dorothy was right, those two had been
dancing together every dance since the Partonville Community Band's "live music"
had come to an end for the evening. And

there'd been quite a buzz about their playing, too. People weren't sure if it was the acoustics of the building, the beautiful harvest-moon night, the breathtaking decorations, the fizz in the fruit punch, reflections of the mirror ball, the Centennial Plus 30's excitement or *what,* but the band had sounded pretty darn good! Jessica certainly agreed, but she was too tired to even utter the words. She danced with Paul, Sarah Sue held between them. It was all she could do to stay awake. "I have to (yawn) go home, honey, as (yawn) soon as this song is over." Yawn.

The double-dates dropped Shelby off first and Kevin walked her to the door. Josh craned his neck to see what was as clear as day under Shelby's front porch light: he did nothing more than to give her a polite peck on the cheek. When Kevin got back in the car, he turned on the interior light and looked at his wristwatch. "You know, looks like we're running toward curfew. How about I drop you off first, Josh-o, and then take Deb home so she doesn't get in trouble? She lives in my neck of the woods anyway."

"That would be perfect," Deb said, flashing Kevin a broad smile.

"Aside from you calling me Josh-o again, yes, that would be perfect."

"Sorry. I'm *trying* to remember," Kevin said apologetically, but he was looking directly at Deb when he said it.

"Thank you for a lovely evening, Deb," Josh said when he closed the door for Deb, who had moved into the front seat. "See you at the lockers!" End of date.

All that worry for nothing.

24

All Saints' Day fell the day after the dance. A long-standing tradition for parishioners at United Methodist Church, Partonville, was, of course, to remember the saints, including departed friends and relatives who had touched their lives. For a couple weeks beforehand, parishioners turned in special cards bearing the names of those they held dear; homebound folks could just call the office with their requests. After Pastor's sermon, which helped them to reflect on the saints and their roles in their lives, a few parishioners, who had practiced pronunciations, would then read the names. This year, however, the worship committee had decided to add a new element. The little notice had been printed in the bulletin for the past several weeks, and a special collection basket to cover expenditures had been set up near the coffee pot during the meet-and-greet time.

When members entered the church on All Saints' Day, they were, of course, greeted by the morning's greeters and handed a bulletin. But they were also directed to a special table that had been set up in the narthex upon which several vases of long-stemmed flowers were arranged. They were told that if they would like to participate, they should select a flower (up to three) for each person they would like remembered. When the time came, they would be instructed to walk, one at a time, to the front of the church, face the congregation, and say the name of the person for whom they put their flower in the vase set up in front of the pulpit. There would be a response by the congregation, thanking God for them.

When the time came, Gladys, sitting in the front row, went first. "Jake McKern," she said facing the congregation, her voice cracking. She turned and put the very first flower in the vase. "His memory is a blessing forever," came the congregational response. His flower looked so lonesome in that big vase, she thought as she sat down. *Oh, Jake! You should have seen our Centennial Plus 30, the clock in your name. . . . You would have loved this whole weekend, dumpling.* Dumpling had been her private nickname for her beloved Jake.

One by one, men and women, young and old, came forward with their flowers, naming names. "His memory . . . Her memory . . . Their memory is a blessing forever." There were older people like Dorothy giving thanks for *their* parents, and Dorothy's third flower was, of course, for her beautiful Caroline Ann. A young parent gave thanks for a child he had lost in a car accident. A young girl gave thanks for her dog. With each flower, the bouquet grew. "For my Homer," May Belle said. Earl was right behind. Although he did not speak or face the congregation, his flower for his father was placed with gentle care next to the one his mother had added.

Josh held two flowers in his hand. He had no intentions of going forward, but somehow watching Earl stirred something within him. Suddenly he could do nothing *but* stand and walk up the aisle. He placed his flowers one at a time in the nearly overflowing vase. "For *all* my grandparents," he said in a quiet voice, making eye contact with Pastor Delbert. Although he didn't speak their names, he was understood. Pastor Delbert swallowed hard, then placed his flowers next to Josh's. "For my mother and my father," he said. "Their memory is a blessing forever," Dorothy repeated with the rest of the congregants, dabbing at her eyes.

While Josh was sitting down next to his mother, Katie Mabel Carol Durbin stared at the flowers in her hand. It still felt too early and awkward, and a bit too uncertain, for her to publicly participate in a religious ceremony, especially this one. But silently she thanked God for her mother . . . and her father.

After Pastor had collected himself, he pointed to the colorful bouquet. "May this bounty of beauty serve as a symbol of the cloud of witnesses who surround us."

"Their memory is a blessing forever. Amen."

Harold Crab's editorial in the Sunday paper was all about "the weekend that ran like a well-greased wheel." He'd even gone so far as to thank Acting Mayor Gladys McKern "who dedicated herself above and beyond the call of her duty" to see that Partonville got its due. (He didn't mention the square fiasco, figuring it had already received *more* than enough ado.) Harold had been at Harry's the morning Arthur had railed on Gladys; he was glad somebody had silenced her, at least for a spell. But he also truly did appreciate so many things she had single-handedly set in motion, like the booklet, the celebration and the streaming light banner on the new digital ensemble that was put into operation during her proclamations: "WELCOME TO PARTONVILLE: PROUD TO BE 130 YEARS YOUNG!"

Of course, if you were driving by, you might have to circle the square twice before you could read it all, but nonetheless, it did them all proud.

A NOTE FROM THE AUTHOR

I write to you from Partonville. It's cloudy here today in the northern part of southern Illinois, but just the same, I'm happy to be here circling the square with my friends. Is there *anything* more delicious than seeing the faces of those we love (whether they're related to us or not) grinning back at us — even when we're lost, even when we're crabby, even when we're crying, even when we're just plain old living in *Duh*-land for a spell? I think not.

As you can tell, my Partonville characters (and they certainly are characters, aren't they?) have become a part of my Real Life. Just the other day I said something truly crabby. (I know that's probably shocking to you, but it is true, right dear?) "Yikes!" I shouted after spewing the cantankerous words. "I think Arthur Landers just woke up!" It made me want to run to my keyboard and stare off into that mysterious "creative space" to see what he was up to!

Of course, I wished I could more often catch myself cooking like May Belle, playing the saxophone as passionately as Nellie Ruth (okay, know how to play it at all) and being as sweet as Jessica Joy rather than cranking around like Arthur; but the reality is, I never stop desiring to grow up to be my Dearest Dorothy.

Most importantly, however, I continue to hang out with my Partonville friends because they model to us what matters most in life: faith, family and friends.

— Charlene Ann Baumbich
www.welcometopartonville.com

ABOUT THE AUTHOR

Charlene Ann Baumbich is a popular speaker, journalist, and author. Her stories, essays, and columns have appeared in numerous magazines and newspapers, including the *Chicago Tribune,* the *Chicago Sun-Times,* and *Today's Christian Woman.* She is also the author of the first two books in the Partonville series, *Dearest Dorothy, Are We There Yet?,* and *Dearest Dorothy, Slow Down, You're Wearing Us Out!,* and six books of nonfiction. She lives in Glen Ellyn, Illinois. Learn more about Charlene at www. welcometopartonville.com.

The employees of Thorndike Press hope you have enjoyed this Large Print book. All our Thorndike and Wheeler Large Print titles are designed for easy reading, and all our books are made to last. Other Thorndike Press Large Print books are available at your library, through selected bookstores, or directly from us.

For information about titles, please call:
  (800) 223-1244

or visit our Web site at:
  www.gale.com/thorndike
  www.gale.com/wheeler

To share your comments, please write:
  Publisher
  Thorndike Press
  295 Kennedy Memorial Drive
  Waterville, ME 04901

NE

2/07